ELEGY IN SCARLET

Books by BV Lawson

Scott Drayco Series

Novels:

Played to Death
Requiem for Innocence
Dies Irae
Elegy in Scarlet

Short Story Collections

False Shadows
Hear No Evil
Vengeance is Blind
Ill-Gotten Games

Other Short Story Collections

Best Served Cold
Deadly Decisions
Death on Holiday
Grave Madness

Elegy in Scarlet

A Scott Drayco Mystery

BV Lawson

Crimetime Press

Elegy in Scarlet is a work of fiction. All of the names, characters, places, organizations and events portrayed in this novel are either products of the author's imagination or are used fictitiously. Any resemblance to actual events, locales, or persons, living or dead, is entirely coincidental.

Published in the United States of America.

For information, contact:

Crimetime Press
6312 Seven Corners Center, Box 257
Falls Church, VA 22044

Trade Paperback ISBN 978-0-9975347-0-2
Hardcover ISBN 978-0-9975347-1-9
eBook ISBN 978-0-9904582-9-6

Acknowledgments

Many thanks to the lovely folks on the Eastern Shore of Virginia who helped inspire some of the sights and scenes in this book and in the entire Drayco series. Both Cape Unity and Prince of Wales County are purely fictional and an amalgam of various towns and counties on the Delmarva Peninsula.

Special thanks to C.E., Sylvia, and Ben for their amazing editing expertise and assistance.

Most of all, I give my undying gratitude—to infinity plus ten—to my amazing family for their encouragement, especially my astoundingly patient husband Charles, who is, as always, my Supporter-in-Chief.

GAVOTTE

Memories long in music sleeping,
No more sleeping,
No more dumb;
Delicate phantoms softly creeping
Softly back from the old-world come.

Faintest odours around them straying,
Suddenly straying
In chambers dim;
Whispering silks in order swaying,
Glimmering gems on shoulders slim:

Courage advancing strong and tender,
Grace untender
Fanning desire;
Suppliant conquest, proud surrender,
Courtesy cold of hearts on fire—

Willowy billowy now they're bending,
Low they're bending
Down-dropt eyes;
Stately measure and stately ending,
Music sobbing, and a dream that dies.

poem by Sir Henry Newbolt (1919), music by Herbert Howells

1

If the hearing was a farce, it was nicely choreographed. The members of the Board of Appeals and Review looked down on Scott Drayco from behind their table on the elevated platform, two men wearing glasses bookending a woman in the middle. All three sported black suits as if attending a funeral, and in a way it was—the potential death of Drayco's career.

The man standing next to Drayco, Benny Baskin, Esquire, wasn't wearing his usual platform shoes, making him closer to four-six than his usual four-nine. Benny had opted against a black suit, his olive green number reminiscent of a military general dressing for battle.

Drayco tried his best to look neutral and professional, despite his own charcoal tweed getup that made him itch in the hot, windowless room. He'd be wearing a white flag of surrender, if D.C. Mayor Gavin Kozell had his way—the same mayor who'd been good friends with Andrew Gilbow, now lying in his grave thanks in part to Drayco.

As if the images of the dying Gilbow enveloped in a wall of flames weren't enough to hijack Drayco's thoughts, he was distracted by the odor of the room, like someone had mopped up vomit with a saccharine-sweet cleaning solution. It was a fitting accompaniment to the maroon razor blades that squeals from the heating vents were flinging into his eardrums. He silently cursed his synesthesia and tried to block out the assault on his senses and focus instead on the tribunal trio.

Board member Saul Bobeck peered at Drayco. "You understand this conference is to refine the issues before your evidentiary hearing?

Stipulations, pending motions, approval of prospective witnesses. An assessment of your case's settlement potential?"

Drayco nodded. He almost looked around, but there was no audience to see. Benny had gotten his way with that one—no gawkers, no media, just empty seats.

Bobeck droned on, "Mayor Kozell requested this action due to D.C. Code section 2010.1, pertaining to the licensure of private investigators. And violations of the code, including any offense involving fraudulent conduct in the judgment of the mayor."

Baskin spoke up. "May I remind the board my client was not charged with any crimes by the Metropolitan Police Department? And absolved of any foul play in the death of Professor Andrew Gilbow? In fact, they found it was self-defense on my client's part and decided not to press charges. I can only conclude the mayor is mistaken in his assertion of any alleged 'fraudulent' conduct."

Bobeck doubled down. "The MPD agreed the bullet in Professor Gilbow's skull was from your gun, Mr. Drayco, is that correct?"

Baskin had warned Drayco not to speak unless he gave a quick flip of his left wrist. Baskin's hand stayed by his side, so Drayco let the attorney answer. "Yes, but the primary cause of death was from the fire. And for the record, it's Dr. Drayco."

"Well then, *Dr.* Drayco, you admit Gilbow was still alive when shot?"

Baskin shifted his feet but not his hands. Again, Drayco stayed silent. "The Medical Examiner determined that to be the case, yes. But only barely alive. He would have died within moments, regardless."

The woman in the middle, Carlotta Peggs, asked, "This gun was fully registered with the MPD as required by law, is that correct?"

Baskin flicked his wrist, and Drayco finally replied, "That's correct."

She shuffled through some papers on the desk. "I don't see any witnesses listed for the evidentiary hearing." She stopped on one piece of paper. "Ah, here we are. Two names. Detective William Gonzalez of the MPD and FBI Special Agent Mark Sargosian. They were both present at the scene, it says here."

Peggs glanced at the other two board members. "I have no objections to these witnesses, do you?"

The two men shook their heads, and the third member, Douglass Scarpato, finally spoke. "I think we know why we're here. Professor Andrew Gilbow was an esteemed member of the academic community. A nationally known consultant in high-profile court cases and on television." Was there a hint of sarcasm in his voice? Drayco couldn't tell by looking at the man's blank face. Best not to read anything into it.

Baskin added cheerfully, "You forgot the part about being a serial killer. Whose horrific actions my client," Baskin nodded at Drayco, "unmasked, thereby preventing any additional murders. In my opinion, this board should be convening to offer him a medal, not grilling him on baseless charges."

Scarpato coughed and hid his mouth behind his hand, making it hard to tell if he were frowning or trying to stifle a laugh. Perhaps Scarpato *was* on Team Drayco. Just, as it seemed, was everyone except the mayor. Benny had hit the ceiling upon learning about the mayor's "bee-up-his-butt vendetta" and fought to get the mayor's case dismissed. No dice.

Benny had also told Drayco earlier he thought he could count on Scarpato and Peggs. He wasn't as sure where Bobeck stood since Bobeck and the mayor were a lot closer than the other two board members. That suspicion was borne out when Bobeck continued the questioning, "It's the preferred procedure to capture a suspect alive, is it not? To give his side of the story, perhaps prove his innocence?"

Drayco almost jumped into that one, but Baskin beat him to it. "And if law officers are killed first, *their* side of the story will be silenced. In the heat of battle, they hardly have the luxury for a meeting like this before taking action to protect themselves."

Benny grabbed a stack of documents and waved them at the board. "The evidence against Gilbow is overwhelming and verifiable beyond any shadow of a doubt. Had he lived, he'd be warming a jail cell right now and facing life in prison. His survival would not have changed that cold, hard fact."

Peggs leaned forward in her chair. "My colleague makes a valid point. However, I disagree with its intent or relevance. Do you have any motions to present on behalf of your client at this time, Mr. Baskin?" The frown on her face at the mention of her colleague was interesting and made Drayco sit up straighter. Maybe Team Drayco just added another member?

Baskin tossed the papers back into his briefcase. "I'm requesting a dismissal of the case on the grounds it is fundamentally baseless and unfair."

Not surprisingly, Bobeck was the one to reply. "There must be complete agreement on that count. And since I do not agree, your request is denied. The evidentiary hearing will go forward." He looked at his watch and jumped up.

Drayco joined him in standing as did Peggs and Scarpato. But before his exit stage left, Bobeck added, "The hearing will be held on February the twenty-first. I expect to see you there."

The man didn't glance at any papers or digital calendars before making his pronouncement. Which could only mean one thing—he'd decided before the hearing started that Drayco should be forced to endure a protracted legal battle. The mayor wanted a scapegoat, Drayco was the target, and Bobeck the facilitator.

Drayco waited for the remaining two board members to depart, leaving him and Benny alone. The air vent whistled and started blowing out hot air again, making the sweet-vomit smell grow stronger. Either that or Drayco was having a stroke. He flicked his wrist at Benny and rocketed past the rows of deserted khaki chairs toward the exit and much-needed fresh air.

2

Once out in the hallway, Drayco leaned against a wall and waited for the cooler air to evaporate the sweat at the back of his neck. A glance at an old-fashioned wall clock made him laugh at the little hand pointing to three—merrily ticking its way toward technological obsolescence above the people absorbed in their sophisticated cellphones.

Baskin stopped bouncing on his feet to gaze up at his client. "I thought it went okay, but not *that* well, boy-o."

Drayco shook his head, not bothering to explain about the clock. Maybe he was just in the mood for absurdities.

Benny continued his bouncing. "This whole pre-hearing conference thing is a sham, anyway."

"That's not what the board thinks, is it? Or I wouldn't be here."

"You did shoot an important man. Albeit an almost-dead one who tried to kill you. Still, self-defense, yada yada."

The face of that almost-dead man, the only part of him not engulfed by fire at the time, kept rising up from the mental lockbox in Drayco's subconscious where he tried to keep it buried. It was the man's eyes—those eyes trapped in a living hell—that would haunt him forever. But Drayco wasn't sorry for what he'd done and damn the consequences.

Benny stopped bouncing to cross his arms over his chest. "The mayor had to look like he was doing something. I'll bet my third-born grandchild the board won't suspend your P.I. license. Or gun carry privileges. Besides, even if they do suspend you, we'll appeal. And you can still do consulting—that doesn't require a license. It would just be a teensy bit of a black mark on your record."

"Who would hire me?"

"Plenty, with your background and brainiac reputation. You're a damned fine crime consultant. Hell, I'd hire you, you know that. I'd find a way to make it all nice and legal. Natch."

A delivery man from a flower shop bumped into Drayco, and the vase of yellow and pink roses the man carried slipped out of his hands. The man caught it in the nick of time, but some of the water from the vase splashed onto Drayco's sleeve. The man mumbled an apology and moved on.

Drayco had forgotten it was Valentine's Day. One thing he didn't have to worry about. Then he winced when he thought of Darcie and made a mental note to wire her flowers as soon as he got a free moment. Velvety red roses to match her velvety red voice. He stifled a sigh. Darcie deserved better, in more ways than one. With his record of failed relationships, maybe every woman deserved better.

Behind Drayco, a different feminine voice tinged with a familiar coppery shimmer said, "Here are the files you asked for, Benny."

As Drayco spun around, Benny nodded from him to the woman. "I believe you know Deputy Nelia Tyler? She's doing some work for me while she gets her J.D."

Drayco's feet turned to concrete as Benny's words registered. The concrete moved up his legs and through his spine, turning him into a statue.

He hadn't seen Nelia since the incident with Gilbow and the warehouse fire. Her look of shock and disapproval that day over his actions still hung like a cumulonimbus over him. Since then, not one word from her. Not that it was all her fault. He hadn't sought her out in her stomping grounds in Cape Unity when he'd visited Darcie or other friends there. Why should he be surprised at bombshell news like this?

He willed away the concrete. "You resigned from the Sheriff's Department?"

She shifted the files to one hand, using the other to finger her blond, braided hair. "Sheriff Sailor is being generous with a staggered work schedule. And I've heard you going on about Benny Baskin for so long, I thought I could earn extra money doing legwork for him."

"You didn't tell me you'd decided to get your law degree." He didn't mean for it to come out like an accusation, but the defiant glint in her eyes told him it had.

"I wasn't aware I needed to inform you first."

Benny looked from Nelia to Drayco and raised an eyebrow. "Now, now, children. If we're going to be one big happy family, we need to get along."

Drayco didn't want to give Benny the satisfaction of knowing he'd struck right at the heart of the problem with his "getting along" comment. Besides, Drayco had used up his absurdity quota for the day. "Tell you what, Uncle Benny. Buy us some balloons and ice cream, and we'll have a nice sing-along to seal the deal."

Nelia gritted her teeth and thrust the folders into Benny's hands. "'Happy families' isn't something I'm very good at right now."

Drayco couldn't help himself. "And why is that?"

"For starters, I notice I wasn't added to the witness list for your hearing."

A sideways glance at Benny showed the attorney's one good eye had grown as wide as the black eyepatch over his other. Drayco replied, "Maybe it's because we didn't know whether to list you in the defense or prosecution column."

She gave Drayco a frosty glare as she said, "Benny, is that all you needed for the moment?"

Benny didn't answer either one of them. He was looking beyond Drayco with his face formed into a mask of wrinkles, all pointing downward. "Thought you said your father wasn't coming today."

"He's not. A crucial deposition with the McDonald case he's working on."

"Then that must be his doppelgänger heading our way."

Brock Drayco strode up to them, dressed in his usual elegant, tailored clothes with a silver tie that matched his hair. And as usual, the smell of his favorite musk cologne preceded him.

Drayco couldn't contain the groan that escaped his lips. "The meeting's over, and—"

"I'm not here about that."

Drayco took in details of his father's appearance he'd missed at first, a twitching eyelid, hands clenched into fists, and a posture so rigid, it resembled rigor. Well, more rigor than usual.

Brock was never partial to polite niceties. "It's about your mother. And murder."

Drayco rubbed his temples. The day's absurd-o-meter had just pegged the top of the scale and zoomed off into the Twilight Zone. "Her body was found after all these years, I take it. How did they make a positive ID?"

"It's pretty easy to make a positive ID when someone is very much alive."

Drayco stared at him. He must have heard his father wrong. Alive? His mother couldn't be alive. "You told me she was dead. Years ago."

"I believed she was. All signs pointed in that direction." Brock held out his hands to his sides. "But there's no question in my mind it's her. Guess we'll know for certain after the DNA tests come back."

"Then what did you mean about that murder bit?"

"She's the one who's charged with murder."

The hands on the wall clock seemed to stop as if somebody opened a rift in spacetime, trapping Drayco in an alternate universe where nothing was what it seemed. He caught a glimpse of the concerned faces of Benny and Nelia out of the edge of his suddenly burred vision.

Brock said, "Let's go grab some coffee."

Drayco followed, surprised his feet actually seemed to work. No matter what Brock told him, the orderly arrangement of everything in his little corner of the universe would never be the same.

3

After buying the coffee, Drayco and his father sat at a mahogany-and-steel table so small, it was like a child's toy. They'd chosen a remote corner of the Tex-Mex cafe next to the courthouse to avoid any eavesdroppers, but it didn't matter. It was later in the day, and they had the place to themselves.

Drayco inhaled the dark-roasted aroma from the java before sprinkling salt into his Styrofoam cup. Most people wrinkled their noses when he did that, but it really did cut the bitterness of the coffee. Brock stared at him, even though he'd seen him perform this ritual many times. He never asked his son about it. One item in a long list of things they didn't discuss.

Drayco's mother was another. At least, they hadn't discussed her in a long, long time. Vague remembrances and snippets from those conversations bubbled up to the surface. "You told me she was declared legally dead."

"After seven years, the court granted a presumption of death." Brock took a sip of coffee and winced. "We've been through all that."

Drayco was twelve when they finally had the conversation. He'd wondered how they could do that without a body, a grave, or any kind of proof. Part of him wanted to prove his father and "them" wrong, but the part that hated his mother won. He never pursued it afterward.

Drayco tasted the coffee. Still bitter. He stirred in more salt. "How'd you get the news of her being alive and the murder charge?"

"Not from her. In fact, she refused her phone call privilege. Instead, I got a call from Detective John Halabi of the Arlington County homicide unit. Maura didn't have many possessions on her, but my name was in her wallet."

"You've talked to her?"

Brock picked at the rim of his cup, creating a mini Styrofoam snowstorm. "I identified her from her mugshot. I have no interest in talking to her. What can she possibly say that would set everything right? To make up for all the pain and suffering she caused?"

That was one item they agreed on, it seemed. "The evidence. Is it conclusive?"

"She was caught standing over the body of the victim, a former TSA agent by the name of Jerold Zamorra, holding the knife that killed him. Her prints are all over the thing. The man was stabbed in the abdomen and the groin."

"Did she admit her guilt? Or say why she did it?"

"She told the police she stabbed him. But only once. And he was already dead." Brock gave a small laugh. "Would have expected a better excuse from her."

"What did the autopsy show?"

"Body's with the Medical Examiner now."

Drayco had only seen a few pictures of his mother, ones he rescued from the trash after his father threw them away. They now lay hidden in a photograph album buried under other unused items in his attic, probably as faded as his mental snapshots of her. She was always smiling in those photos, the real ones and the ones in his head.

"Any chance of bail?"

"The arraignment hasn't been held yet. She's being kept as a pretrial detainee because she's considered a flight risk. Imagine." The plastic spoon Brock grasped in his hands broke in two with a loud crack that startled both men.

"Where has she been all this time?"

"I have no idea. Mars, Atlantis, Timbuktu, what's the difference?"

"Are you telling me you aren't the slightest bit curious about any of this? To find out why she left? Why she never tried to contact us?"

"I'm saying she's as dead to me now as she was then."

Brock tossed the broken pieces of spoon on the middle of the table. "Do what you want, son. I've told Detective Halabi everything I know about Maura before I married her and after, which isn't much.

I'm washing my hands of the whole thing, and I'd advise you to do the same."

His father jumped up from his chair, the no-nonsense mask his former FBI colleagues knew so well firmly in place. "After you talk to Halabi, that is. I told him you haven't seen her since you were five, but he insists. Said to stop by tomorrow morning. The earlier, the better."

As he turned to leave, Drayco remained planted in his seat, staring at the spoon shards. Brock started to say something, paused, then mumbled, "I'm sorry."

He left before Drayco could ask what he was sorry about.

Moments after Brock disappeared, Benny and Nelia joined him at the tiny table. Nelia sat across from him while Benny grabbed a nearby chair after snagging a couple of extra cups of coffee. "We're your new stalkers. We followed you here. You okay, boy-o? You look a little pale."

"Ghosts will do that to you, or so I'm told."

"Ghosts, shmosts. You got a real-live woman claiming to be your long-lost mother, but we don't know it's her. Could be some ploy."

Nelia swept the broken spoon and Styrofoam flakes into a napkin that she folded into a neat square. "Stolen identity rings are big business. And they particularly target identities of the deceased."

Benny nodded. "Nelia's right. Another scam. What did Brock say? Did he talk to this imposter?"

"He refuses to talk to her. Says he doesn't care if it's her or not."

"He may not have the luxury, he should know that. The police'll push him to do it, at any rate."

Drayco nudged the sugar container over to Benny, who dumped half of it into his coffee. Coffee-candy, as Drayco called it. Drayco said, "You know Brock. Stubborn as a mule. No, that's too ordinary and clichéd for him. More like as stubborn as the Ebola virus."

Nelia tentatively reached out and placed a feather touch on his arm. A simple gesture, yet it felt like a shot of pure adrenaline. "What are you going to do? Will you go and see her?"

"I suppose it depends on what the DNA tests show. If this woman is not my mother," his tongue tripped over the word, "then the police don't need me. And if it is her ... I don't know. Guess I'll do whatever is required to assist the police on this. And maybe that's all."

Benny squinted his right eye, making the eyepatch on the other rise an inch. "I hate to remind you bad things come in threes, what with this news and your case hearing. You should hit the hay early. Safe and sound at home."

Drayco didn't look at Nelia and bit his tongue to retort that Benny wasn't good at counting. No, seeing Nelia wasn't so much a bad thing as a ... what? Confusing thing? Painful thing? Awkward thing? Then it hit him—if he ignored the hair-color difference, Nelia bore a slight resemblance to the woman from those fading photos in his attic.

4

For once, Drayco thought Benny had an excellent idea. Hay-hitting never sounded so good. It was strange enough being on the wrong side of the bench during the hearing, but the whole recounting of the warehouse fire and Gilbow's death was far worse. As if his subconscious hadn't already punished him the past few months with a series of violent dreams—dreams of being trapped in a fire that made him wake up sweating.

He wasn't sweating now as he made his way to his car in the twenty-degree weather. Fortunately, the forecast for snow had been downgraded, and he was able to make a stop by a florist on the way back to his Capitol Hill townhome.

Would Darcie like the roses? Or was that too flashy? He popped himself on the side of the head. This was Darcie he was talking about, definitely roses. The more expensive, the better.

Flowers ordered—with a very high same-day delivery fee added—he headed home under the dark, moonless sky for time alone with his piano and a glass or two or three of Riesling before bed. Just as he stepped across the threshold, he got a whiff of coffee. And was that garlic bread he smelled?

He dropped his coat on the wingback chair near the door, grabbed a baseball bat from the umbrella stand, and strode into the kitchen. Darcie Squier greeted him with a glass of red wine and a kiss. "You're early. No problem. The food won't take long."

Drayco lowered the bat. After eying the smoke detector and not seeing any signs of Darcie's usual burned cuisine, he said, "How did you get in?"

"Your lovely neighbor, Mrs. Chapman. She's seen me here enough I was able to con her into letting me in. You told me you gave her a key in case of emergencies. And this was an emergency. Well, a Valentine's Day emergency. And I've seen you punch in your code."

Drayco made a mental note to change his security codes. And ask for his key back. "You didn't tell me you were coming. I wired some flowers to Cape Unity."

Darcie opened the oven and pulled out an aluminum-foil container, kicking the door shut behind her. "I knew you couldn't come to me with your board hearing and all. So, I came to you, instead."

He pinched the bridge of his nose. So much for being alone with his piano and his thoughts. "It was sweet of you. Truly. But I've had a horrible day. Not sure I'll be great company."

"Nonsense. What could possibly be so bad it would ruin the most romantic day of the year?"

"Finding out your mother has risen from the dead and was arrested for murder."

Darcie almost dropped the pan in her hands, but Drayco rescued it in time. "She's still alive? That's awful." She stood there a moment, then grabbed a couple of plates and served up the lasagna. Drayco spied a takeout bag from Luigi's Primo Pasta on the counter.

"Not quite the response I expected from you."

"Not awful she's alive, I suppose. But after turning her back on her family decades ago. I mean, why now? Unless she's dying and trying to make amends."

"People don't usually try to make amends by killing a government employee."

"She murdered somebody? Oh, God, that *is* awful. Too bad she didn't stay missing." Darcie balanced the plates of lasagna in her hands. "Ever wonder if your mother abandoning you makes it harder for you to trust women? Because I've wondered that."

He glared at her. "Are you my shrink now?"

After putting the lasagna on the table she'd set with red placements and candles, she grabbed his hand and pulled him after her. "Eat. You'll feel better on a full stomach."

He wasn't hungry but didn't want to offend her after all the trouble she'd gone to. Luigi's had the best Italian around, and it wasn't as difficult a task to wolf down the meal as it would have been otherwise.

She hopped up from the table to grab something out of the refrigerator and put it on the table. "For the *pièce de résistance*," she opened the lid. "Tiramisu. They say it's an aphrodisiac."

She winked at him, then put her hands on the zipper of the dress she wore. It wasn't her usual getup, hardly form-fitting and more like a tent. The reason became clear when she pulled down the zipper and let the dress fall to the floor. "And if the tiramisu doesn't do it, maybe this will."

She wore what resembled a red ribbon, with thin straps over the shoulders, bows that barely covered her breasts, and a strap hanging down just below her navel. And that was all. "Aren't you going to unwrap your present?" She winked at him.

Maybe it was the pent-up anger from long-simmering emotional fires, maybe it was the stress of the hearing, maybe a little of it was seeing Nelia unexpectedly. But he did more than unwrap Darcie. He picked her up and carried her to the bedroom, removed his clothing in seconds flat, and proceeded to engage in some of the most torrid and rough sex of his life. Not thinking, not feeling, not caring, just primal and raw.

Afterward, Darcie rolled on top of him and nibbled on his neck. "If this is what having your mother return from the dead does to you, I take it back. It's not awful at all."

He lay there, staring at the ceiling, barely feeling Darcie's presence. The sex hadn't helped his frustrations one bit. He should grab a block of C4 and go blow up something instead.

She poked his shoulder. "Tell me what you're thinking, darling."

"Your flowers are going to be pretty sorry looking when you return home."

"We'll get more. Nothing lasts forever." She slid out of bed, and he heard her going downstairs. When she returned, she had the tiramisu in hand. "And this won't last much longer if we don't eat it now."

"Not sure I have the appetite for it."

"Well, I sure do." She dipped into the creamy cake with her finger and smeared some on his body in various sensitive places. He relaxed and gave in to his fate of becoming her dessert, banishing thoughts of the photos in his attic and of their subject, now locked firmly away in an Arlington detention facility.

ॐ ॐ ॐ

The observer put down the infrared binoculars on the passenger seat, then grabbed some seeds from a plastic bag and popped them in his mouth. As he chewed, he watched the townhome across the street, but there was no new activity inside or out. The light in the upper window switched off, making him smile.

He picked up his cellphone. After thumbing the screen over to the phone list, he pressed the first entry and then said to the voice on the other end, "Scott Drayco is at his townhome with a brunette."

He listened for a moment then repeated back what he heard. "Darcie Squier? Is she a problem? No? Okay, then. One less person to follow. What about Drayco? I think he's settled in for the night."

After more instructions, he replied, "A sound plan. I'm getting too old to use a car headrest as a pillow all night, anyway—get a crick you wouldn't believe. I'll keep an eye on Drayco when he meets with that Arlington cop tomorrow. And good night to you, too, boss."

He rang off and flipped through the photos on his sim card. Lots of Draycos—both of them—also Benny Baskin, the brunette, of course, then Drayco's neighbor, and Nelia Tyler. He stopped on that one. The brunette was a looker, all right, but if he were Drayco, he'd be banging Tyler. He'd always been a sucker for the whole beauty-and-brains combo.

With one last look at Drayco's window, he started up the car and pulled out of his parking spot. He flipped the radio to a station playing folk music. Sounded like the Wemyss Weavers playing a Scottish ballad. A good omen.

He hummed along as he cranked up the heater and drove down the street with regular glances in his rearview mirror. You could never be too careful, even with the night on your side.

5

A young female sergeant chewing cinnamon gum nonstop ushered Drayco into a small office half-way between neat and cluttered. The papers on the tan-speckled laminate desk formed perfect rectangular monuments. But books on a corner shelf teetered at skewed angles, with more crammed into charcoal plastic bins on the floor. A bipolar office.

It looked like every diploma, degree, or award Detective John Halabi ever received hung on the walls in matching gold frames. Drayco missed his friend Sheriff Sailor's wall-mounted fish with the piranha teeth. Hell, he missed Sailor.

A man with short-cropped black hair who sported a purple paisley tie breezed into the room and parked in the black leather chair behind the desk. He motioned for Drayco to take a seat in the only other chair in the cramped space then stared at him for several moments before speaking. "Glad you could come so early this morning. Looks like you survived your board hearing yesterday. Those things can be brutal, can't they?"

And the gloves were off. Halabi knew, and he wanted Drayco to know—*you're under suspicion and I don't trust you.* Drayco replied, "Not any more than that Markson abduction case you worked last year."

The detective's appraising scan of Drayco morphed into a full-fledged study. Now he knew Drayco had researched him, too, learning about the controversial outcome of the Markson baby's kidnapping and the resulting lawsuit, eventually thrown out.

Halabi opened a desk drawer and whipped out a file. "Both you and your father are former FBI agents turned crime consultants. Work on cases together?"

"Rarely." Halabi either didn't notice or didn't acknowledge the edge in Drayco's tone. Time to focus on something calming, like a Chopin nocturne. Or puppies and kittens.

"Your mother disappeared a little over thirty years ago when you were five, is that correct?"

"She abandoned us, yes."

Halabi opened the file. "You had a twin sister."

"Casey died of leukemia when she was twelve."

Halabi nodded. "And your mother didn't contact you in all this time?"

"No, she didn't. I thought she was dead."

Drayco tried to read the upside-down text in the file. "Did you find out where she's been? An arrest record, perhaps?"

"We haven't learned anything. It's as if she dropped off the grid thirty years ago."

"Brock said you found a paper in her possession with his name inscribed. Was there anything else?"

"A fake driver's license using the alias of Maura McKewen. Not too far off from her maiden name, McCune. Also some Tic Tacs, fifty dollars, and possibly a house key. And there was another piece of paper that spells BRISBANE in all caps. Your father didn't know what that means. Do you?"

"Other than the city in Australia, no."

"We're contacting Australian law enforcement. Guess this means we can count on the FBI to get involved. Seeing as how she's the ex-wife of an ex-higher-up FBI agent, the mother of another, and this may involve international ties."

Drayco drummed his fingers on the armrest of his chair and took pleasure in the clacking sound. "The victim, Jerold Zamorra, was a former TSA agent. Any ties between them?"

"I doubt it was random. We'll find out, sooner or later."

"Brock told me the victim was stabbed in the groin and upper body—was it the chest or back?"

Halabi frowned. "The front, meaning—"

"He was facing his killer. Any defensive wounds?"

"No, so he likely knew the murderer. It appears the first knife blow made him trip and fall backward, and he hit his head. Or so it appears from bits of tissue and skull we found on the kitchen cabinets. We don't have full autopsy results." Halabi closed the file when he saw Drayco looking at it.

"Was there much blood spatter?"

"By falling away from his killer—and the deep wounds—it minimized the blood spatter. Which could explain why she didn't have any on her clothing." Halabi grunted. "I'm the one who's supposed to be questioning you."

Drayco ignored the jab. "What was she wearing? A raincoat, boots? It was raining hard that night."

"Neither, but maybe she changed her clothes."

"Did you find any bloody clothing?"

Halabi didn't answer, but his silence said it for him. Drayco said, "You *didn't* find bloody clothing. And why was she still holding the knife? Doesn't this lend credence to her story?"

"Okay, she killed him, had time to get rid of the clothes, and then stabbed him one more time."

Drayco drummed his fingers some more. "Again, why?"

"To make it look like she did just the one stabbing wound after he was dead. How else do you explain that crazy story of hers?"

"So, there weren't any other prints on the knife?"

"Look, I've been patient with you so far—"

"If just her prints were on the knife, it could have been washed clean."

Halabi narrowed his eyes. "You saw that in the file. Yeah, we found minute traces of blood in the sink, but that could've been her washing blood off her clothes. And the only prints in the place were Jerold Zamorra's and Maura McCune's."

"Yet you said she was found standing over the body. Why go to the sink, wash her hands and clothes, then go back to the body to stab him? Seems kind of elaborate and time-consuming to wash the knife and then use it again to stab the victim—just to make it appear he was already dead. Why not simply leave and take the knife with her?"

"You know as well as I do criminals aren't always in the sanest frame of mind."

"Motives?"

"She left a heated message on his cellphone. Didn't say what she was angry about."

"You didn't say she had a phone on her. Did you track the number?"

Halabi grimaced. "We didn't find a phone. And we can't trace back her phone number, probably a burner. A warrant will fix that."

The detective's grimace and clenched teeth made Drayco speed up his staccato questioning. He didn't have much time before Halabi threw him out on his ass. "Was Jerold alone? What about a wife or girlfriend?"

"Jerold's wife, Ophelia, died a year ago. She was murdered, too. Before you make anything out of it, Jerold and his wife had already been divorced for a year. And the Falls Church police arrested two young toughs. Random robbery at a bank ATM. Poor woman was in the wrong place at the wrong time."

Halabi returned the file to the drawer. "Look, I know this is difficult for you. But your mother admits she stabbed him, she didn't feel threatened, and she isn't insane. It doesn't look good for her."

Drayco sat studying Halabi's framed documents on the wall. They were in a nice, orderly progression, from high school through college, to the academy, and then the commendations. An unbroken timeline of experience with no gaps, no signs he'd considered any other life or career. Some would say that was enviable. "Who called you, detective?"

Halabi furrowed his brow. "What?"

"Someone had to alert the police there was a murder in progress for them to get there so soon. Did the victim scream? Was there a witness?"

"We got an anonymous tip."

"Anonymous?"

"The voice on the dispatch records sounded disguised."

"Disguised? What, like an actor? Or mechanical?"

"We're analyzing it further. Probably just one of the illegals who live nearby who doesn't want to get involved further. Look, I know I'm dealing with two big-shot FBI agents—well, former agents—with lots of important connections."

The detective's jaw was clenched so tightly, it was a miracle he could open it to speak. "One of my superiors worked with you before and said to cut you a little slack. I know I should tread lightly. But I've got a job to do. This is my investigation, and I'm not going to let any Draycos get in my way. Let us handle it."

Halabi stood up and walked to the door, which he held open. "We'll keep you posted on any major developments. Until then, you might take a page from your father's book. He seems completely uninterested in this case." He frowned at the still-seated Drayco as he added, "Not that he'd be objective."

"You're probably right." Drayco thrust himself out of his chair and headed down the corridor toward the front lobby. He neglected to mention the meeting Benny Baskin had arranged for Drayco starting in an hour—a visit to the Arlington Detention Center next door to talk to one Maura McCune.

6

The woman sitting across from him beyond the glass barrier was like a phantom image from a dream that fades when you awaken, then returns as pieces of fractured memories. As he stared at her, he tried to match her appearance to his attic photos.

She didn't look all that different, except for the orange jumpsuit. No laugh lines, no frown lines on the fifty-seven-year-old woman. Did she not feel any emotions that would be expressed on her face? No heart, no soul, no empathy?

There were few identifying marks of any kind, save for a scar on the side of her neck. Had she always had it? He couldn't remember. It was hard to tell if this really was her or an imposter as Benny had suggested.

"Hello, Scotty." Her voice, with the same auburn-flecked sparklers that matched her hair, brought the reality of her presence to his conscious mind at last. He might forget a face, but he never forgot a voice. He didn't need DNA results. This was really her.

She leaned on the edge of the wooden table bolted to the floor. "I almost forgot how blue your eyes are. Even when you were a wee bairn, they were so bright and intense. You got those from my kin."

Her accent was hybridized, mostly "American," but her Scottish upbringing peeked through, at times. "Not your dark hair. You can thank your father's Navajo grandma for that." She tilted her head. "Dark hair, violet-blue eyes. Bet you're a hit with the ladies. I imagined you'd be hitched by now."

"Engaged, once. She wanted a pianist for a husband, not an FBI agent."

Maura McCune clasped her hands in front of her and picked at her thumbnails. Like Drayco, she couldn't seem to keep her fingers still. "The carjacking injury, when you were twenty. I ... I heard about it at the time."

She'd kept tabs on him? Not that it mattered since she hadn't bothered to contact him. "It's ancient history."

She looked at his hands. "Can you still play the piano? With your arm crippled and all. I mean—"

"I play. For myself and occasionally friends. The arm works, it just cramps up when I use it too much."

She kept staring at his hands as if afraid to look at him in the face for too long. "You took to Bach right away. Bach's always been my favorite. You said his fugues were rainbow-colored circles within circles."

"It's how I experience them. It's called synesthesia, feeling sounds as colors, shapes, textures."

"You got that from my father, who played the fiddle beautifully. The way he described it, it was a world of intense sensations in his head. I imagined it as a rainbow of counterpoint."

Images from Drayco's childhood flipped across his mind, at the piano with his mother next to him on the bench, a musical cheerleader who encouraged him from the sidelines. She was the one who'd set him up with piano lessons against Brock's wishes.

"You probably shouldn't expect a visit from Brock."

"You call him Brock? Not Dad or Father?"

He bit his tongue. She would have known that had she been around. Or maybe if she'd been around, he wouldn't call his father Brock nor have such a distant relationship.

He wasn't ready for this, wasn't ready to pick at the old scabs, to listen to her excuses or lies. He reminded himself he was in the presence of an accused murderer and sat up straighter. "What was your relationship to the victim?"

She'd unclasped her hands, and they were now in constant motion—rubbing her fingers together, fiddling with her sleeve. "We were good friends."

"Lovers?"

She jutted out her chin. "Like I told the detectives, that's all I'm going to say on the subject."

"Did you know he was a TSA agent?"

"Ex-agent. And Jerold was the one who called me, wanting me to come see him the night he was killed. He didn't sound angry, maybe a little strained."

"What were his exact words?"

"I didn't understand them, then or now. He said, 'I need you to come over right away. It's about that trip we're going to take to Nevada. It's important.'"

Drayco frowned at that. "What trip to Nevada?"

"That's just it, I don't know of any such trip. I think I once said I'd always wanted to go to Reno—that's where they shot *Melvin and Howard*, isn't it? That's my favorite movie. Or maybe Jerold had a craving for some slot machines. It's as good an explanation as any."

"Let me get the timeline straight. You went to his condo, you were angry, and you admitted to the police you stabbed him. But you said he was already dead?"

She took a deep breath. "When I got there, he was lying on the floor. I could tell he was dead—his eyes were open, staring."

"And then you just decided to stab him?"

"It sounds crazy, and maybe it is, a little. I'd been so upset with him, but here he was robbing me of my chance to tell him off. I wasn't thinking straight, Scotty, I admit it. I would have wiped my prints and just left, but the police arrived first. How did they know to come?"

"An anonymous tip to the police."

"But it was raining and dark. No one would have seen me." Her eyes grew thoughtful, calculating. "The killer was watching. I was set up, don't you see? I didn't kill Jerold but whoever did wants you to think so."

Drayco leaned back in his seat. If she were lying, she was good. Then again, she'd somehow managed to disappear off the grid for thirty years, so she was likely a practiced evader and manipulator. On the other hand, a convenient witness who disguised his voice when calling the police—what were the chances of that?

Her eyes were hazel, not true blue, and the way the fluorescent lights hit them right now, they looked more greenish-gold. There were hints of pleading in those eyes, but also traces of something he'd seen in other suspects. An almost-imperceptible shifting. He made a leap of intuition and asked, "Who are you protecting?"

She hesitated just a few seconds too long. "Why would you think that, Scotty?"

The way she called him by the long-ago nickname, the lying, the anger bubbling up inside—he needed to get away from her, to catch his breath. He also knew, as the warden came to signal that his twenty minutes were up, he was going to disappoint both Detective Halabi and Brock.

There was no way in hell he could walk away from this case. It was truth time. And just like with his board hearing, any and all consequences be damned.

7

Benny Baskin might be the "world's most diminutive attorney," as one prosecutor labeled him, but he seemed to delight in making everything in his office tall. The bookshelves went all the way up the fifteen-foot ceilings, the lowest rung on a corner coat rack was at Drayco's eye level, and even the table and chairs were two inches higher than standard-issue.

Benny was heading for a bookshelf when Drayco walked in but stopped as soon as he saw his visitor. "Oh goody. My human ladder is here. Get that green book on the third shelf for me, would you?" Baskin's voice was twice as deep as his stature, sounding a bit like a bull terrier. Or to Drayco's ears, a salmon-colored tumbleweed.

Drayco didn't have to stretch, his six-four frame reaching the book easily. As he handed it over, Benny said, "After I got your call an hour ago, I made some calls of my own. I'm deeply disturbed your mother talked to the police sans attorney. But she waived her rights, God knows why."

"The full autopsy might help. If it shows a knife wound after the victim was dead, verifying her claims, that is."

"Her kooky behavior is helping an insanity defense, for sure."

"And we've got the oh-so-coincidental anonymous witness."

"About that. I got a friend at the Arlington PD. I called him up and asked him what he knew. Told me the report says Mr. Anonymous heard a scream, yet none of his condo neighbors heard a thing." Benny lifted his eyepatch and rubbed the scar underneath, grunting as he did. "You really looking into this?"

Drayco nodded and plopped down on the Sangria-colored leather chair next to Benny's desk. He loved that chair. It was suspiciously present whenever Benny knew Drayco was coming, and mysteriously absent when he made a surprise appearance.

"Well, boy-o, if you're hoping to prove her innocence, you'll be alone on this one. The police are confident she's guilty. I think your dad is secretly rooting to see her executed. And I anticipate only half-hearted attempts at a defense from her court-appointed attorney."

"What if I can prove she's innocent of the murder charge? Legally speaking."

Benny crossed his arms. "She's still not out of the woods. Could be charged with desecration of a corpse. Or not. Insanity and all."

"Did you get any additional information about Jerold Zamorra?"

"More your bailiwick than mine. You said on the phone your mother refuses to say what their relationship was other than 'good friends'?"

"And that worries me. A lot. Maybe they were lovers, or maybe they were partners in crime. I know as little about him as I do about her."

Benny perched on the edge of his desk next to Drayco, the only way he could gaze down at him. "You're taking this remarkably well. Mother showing up after all these years. After taking off without so much as a how d'ya do. Or whatever." He kicked one leg against the desk, rhythmically. "You never talk about her."

"Why should I?"

Benny stopped kicking. "You going to ask her? Why she left?"

Drayco gazed out the plate glass window as a nearby church bell chimed twelve times. In the distance, the silhouette of the Capitol rose like a domed magnet drawing power, greed and corruption toward it.

They sat in silence for a few moments, until Benny piped up, "If there's anything I can do—"

"There is. Represent her. You know I'm good for it."

Benny knew as well as Drayco that Benny's fees would drain a lot of people's bank accounts, let alone Drayco's. And he certainly couldn't count on any financial help from Brock.

Benny cleared his throat. "It's not the kinda case I'd ordinarily—"

"It might ruin your perfect record. I know. I'll do everything I can to keep it from going to trial."

"By proving her innocent." Benny's bluntness was always something Drayco could count on, one reason they worked so well together. "Ordinarily, I'd take your instincts and bet 'em all on the sixty-to-one nag. But this time, you're from that horse's stable. Your objectivity is manure."

Drayco relaxed into the chair. "You'll take the case?"

Benny glared at him. "Of course I'll take the case. Goddamn you. I'll have to make like The Flash if the arraignment is this afternoon." Benny grabbed the phone on his desk, but paused to add, "Look, you're a big boy," and as Drayco stood, Benny added, "a very big boy. But this thing could get ugly. The kinda ugly that wounds worse than bullets."

Drayco grabbed his coat from the coat rack. "Shall I use the usual update method?"

"None of that texting crap. And put the evidentiary hearing on your calendar. Don't forget I'm already defending one Drayco. Better tell your father I said he can't run any red lights."

After Drayco closed the door, he briefly considered opening it again to see if the comfy chair was still there, then thought better of it. That was one mystery best left unsolved. Outside the building, he took the stairs one at a time instead of the usual two. It was nice to know he had at least one person in his camp.

He pulled out a keychain from his pocket and rubbed a thumb over it. Large capital letters spelled out RANGER, with smaller text beside that read BROTHER. The giver of the keychain came to him for help a few months ago when his daughter was in danger. Perhaps it was time to return the favor.

Their relationship was on better footing these days, if not quite terra firma, but he wasn't sure what reaction he'd get. He stuffed the keychain back in his pocket. He hated asking for favors. Oh, well ... One down, one to go.

8

After checking his cellphone for the fourth time for new messages, Drayco was beginning to believe he'd been stood up. The hushed voices and clicking of women's high heels in the hotel lobby reflected off the gold panels and marble floors, bouncing up to the vaulted ceilings. The sound created a stormy echo chamber of teal hailstones raining down on Drayco. It was giving him a headache.

He eyed the restaurant and strode inside to order coffee, savoring each sip as he kept checking his watch. Five minutes passed, then ten, fifteen. Just as he was going to signal the waiter to pay for his coffee, a familiar figure in standard FBI attire walked in—although Drayco's former partner Mark "Sarg" Sargosian didn't so much walk as stalk into a room. Once an Army Ranger, always a Ranger.

Sarg slid into a chair at Drayco's table. Unlike the lobby noise, the gold-green sine waves of Sarg's baritone massaged Drayco into relaxation. "Thought you might like to meet here, since I had to be at HQ today. Walked the mile from there to here, but there was some kinda protest thingie on Pennsylvania. The usual daily D.C. parade. Boom-de-ya-da."

"And here I suspected you'd fallen into one of the District's manholes and that's why you didn't send a text."

Sarg pulled out his cellphone from his pocket and held it up. "Tried. Got a bunch of gobbledegook error messages."

"All that Washington hot air blocking the signal. Either that or the NSA or CIA. Or FBI."

Drayco's companion winced and replied, "Yeah," as he surveyed the room, likely noting as Drayco had that its brick and artsy-techno stylings didn't match the historic hotel.

"You and Elaine ever stay here at the Mayflower?"

"Nah, we get the heck out of Dodge whenever we need an escape. Even this is too close to Freddyburg. You ordered yet?"

Drayco flipped open the menu. "Not yet. Think I should get the J. Edgar Hoover special?"

Sarg tugged on his ear. "Can't believe the man ate here at the same table for twenty years and all he got was chicken soup, toast, cottage cheese, and grapefruit."

"Technically, he ate at the old Rib Room, long gone."

"Semantics." Sarg scanned the menu and closed it after only a few seconds. The waiter took that as his cue, reappearing at their table as Sarg handed back the menu. "I'll have the Beet Carpaccio salad."

Drayco read the description. "What's black lava salt?"

Sarg explained, "Solar evaporated Pacific sea salt combined with activated charcoal. It complements the delicate flavors of the golden and red beets. Lightly accents the gorgonzola."

"I'm not hungry." Drayco handed over his menu to the patient waiter. "I'll just have a burger. Without the fries."

Sarg-the-gourmet's eyes widened in mock horror. "What will you put on the burger this time—candy corn? Or maybe Nutella? And no truffled fries? Blasphemy I say."

"I doubt they're half as good as that truffle dish you served me at your place. Better than anything I've had at the Ritz."

"Idle flattery, but I'll take it." Sarg guzzled some water. "You know, I don't care if it's February and gloomy out there. I still worked up a sweat."

Drayco glanced at the tables against the far wall and caught the gaze of a man he didn't recognize who was staring at him. Yet there was also something about the man Drayco couldn't pinpoint, the feeling he'd seen him before.

Sarg said, "What's the matter? You see the ghost of J. Edgar wolfing down his boiled chicken?"

Drayco turned to Sarg and nodded at the stranger's table. "That guy look familiar to you?"

Sarg duly looked. "What guy?"

"The one who—" But as Drayco checked again, the man was gone. "I didn't conjure him from my imagination."

"Describe him."

"Sixtyish, distinguished. A full head of hair parted on the left, square jaw, Greek nose. Pale skin, no scars or moles, so I doubt he's the out-of-doors type. Manicured hands, custom jacket, Italian shoes. Which could pretty much describe most of the men in this room."

Sarg grinned. "Maybe that's why he comes here. Blends in."

Drayco traced the circumference of his coffee cup with his finger. Had he been doing it nonstop? He was distracted, not a good sign. "I need your advice, Sarg."

"About your Mom's case? I can't tell you whether it's a good idea to look into it or not. I wouldn't blame you either way."

"Benny Baskin all but shouted I can't be objective. But you can."

Sarg chugged more water. "After you called me with your news this morning, I did some quick checking on the victim, the ex-TSA guy. Jerold Zamorra was well-liked at work, competent, no official complaints. Received a commendation when he retired. His wife—"

"Was murdered a year ago. I know. It was during a spate of ATM thefts. And both the Arlington and Falls Church police think it was random. Picked the wrong bank machine at the wrong time." Drayco took a sip of his now-lukewarm coffee and grimaced. "You said no official complaints. And unofficial?"

"A former colleague, Rena Quentin, filed a sexual harassment charge. Quietly resolved and both of them left the agency not long afterward. Oh, and Jerold was estranged from both his daughter and brother. For reasons unknown."

"Any gossip on Jerold Zamorra and his murdered wife?"

"If you mean do his colleagues think he killed her, no."

"The daughter might."

"If Zamorra was the one who murdered his wife, I'm not going to cry about his death, whether your mother did it or not. Hell, we should give her an award if she did."

Sarg paused as the waiter delivered his salad. "Every time I asked you about your mother over the years, you clammed up. Weren't you curious? Didn't you want to track her down? For that matter, didn't Brock?"

Everybody was asking that these days, an irritation he didn't need. But this was Sarg, and if anyone deserved an answer, he did. "Guess I was afraid of what I might find. As for Brock, he was so angry, he just didn't care."

The burger was dry and tasteless. And was it just him or did the grease and charred meat make the place smell like an abattoir? Drayco looked around the table, prompting Sarg to say, "Do not desecrate that lovely Angus burger with any of your weird toppings. Thank God there's no marshmallow fluff around."

Drayco took another bite, then pushed the plate over. Sarg immediately cut off a chunk and closed his eyes as he masticated it into oblivion. "Yep, perfect as is. Don't tell Elaine, she's still on the vegetarian warpath. You wouldn't want to see me get scalped, would you?"

Drayco checked the table where he saw the stranger earlier, but two women had taken his place. "I need to check out Zamorra's condo. If my mother didn't kill him, I'd like to see how the real murderer got in and out without being seen."

"It was dark. And raining."

"The weather had some help. The few details I got from sneak peeks at Detective Halabi's report said exterior lights on Zamorra's end of the building were burned out. His unit has two doors, the front and a rear entrance opening into an alley that runs the length of the building."

"Burned-out lights? Did he live in a slum?"

"The report said the maintenance man recently broke his leg, which explains the lights. And the address puts the building in a 'transitional' neighborhood."

"Transitional? What, can't decide whether it wants to be a condo or a townhome when it grows up?"

"Basically, affordable housing being torn down for expensive condos. Not a slum though the housing complex across the street has a large immigrant community. Several undocumented. Great motivation to stay below the radar and not get involved in a crime."

"Except for the mystery witness."

"There is that."

Sarg polished off both salad and burger with a satisfied burp. "Sounds a lot more interesting than the case I'm consulting on for the Bureau. You'd have it all figured out in an hour."

"Taking a trip on the hyperbole train, are we?"

"Okay, *we* would have solved it together in an hour. Batman and Robin. And since you're fifteen years younger, that makes you Robin."

Drayco gave a slight smile. "There's no way you're going to get me in yellow tights and green hot pants."

Sarg snorted. "I'd give my eyeteeth for one of those cool utility belts."

They spoke at the same time, "And the bat car."

Sarg watched him in silence then said, "You can't shit an old shitter. You're rattled by this, junior. Can't say I blame you."

"The police discovered Maura was using an alias and took a taxi to Zamorra's. Paid in cash. No arrest record. No record at all. The nonexistent woman. What am I supposed to think? She may be the woman who gave birth to me, but I know more about most Hollywood celebrities."

"What did she say when you went to see her?"

"Not much. Maybe that was my fault."

"What do you mean?"

"My mind went blank. I didn't ask her why she came back now. Or about that piece of paper with 'Brisbane' on it."

Along with a thousand other questions that arose *after* his meeting with her. Brain-warping questions, if he allowed himself to dwell on them, and he wasn't a dwelling kind of guy.

"Then, you'd say your meeting with her was unsatisfactory?"

"Make that unnerving."

Sarg finished his water with one last gulp and pushed his seat back as he eyed Drayco with a slight smile. "I'd say you need a break, maybe fly over to the Eastern Shore. Visit the Jepsons or Darcie. But I know you. That ain't gonna happen. Cut yourself some slack. It's going to take time to process this."

Sarg motioned to the waiter to bring the check to him, over Drayco's protest. As Sarg read it, he asked, "Been having any more of those hypno-paralysis-whatever dreams of yours? After almost losing Tara, I've had a few nightmares of my own."

Drayco didn't want to discuss his dreams, not even to Sarg. "Ah, the lovely and talented Tara. She doing well?"

"My daughter could out-tough a Marine drill sergeant." He counted out some bills. "Said to tell you how sorry she is, by the way. About your mother."

Drayco picked up the salt shaker and rolled it around in his hand. Sarg just had to go and mention bad dreams. He looked up to see Sarg staring at him again. "My offer stands, Drayco. I'll be happy to testify at your hearing. You told Benny Baskin that, right?"

Drayco nodded and set the shaker down. "You're on the witness list."

"Chief Onweller won't mind if I take a few mornings off, as long as I make it up later."

Drayco let that sink in. "If I didn't know better, I'd say you were offering your services on this murder case. Gratis, no less."

"When some rich long-lost relative of yours pops in with a wad of cash in hand, you can repay me. Funny, I hadn't seen you in three years, and within the span of a few months, you got me chasing impossible scenarios all over creation."

"Impossible? Always liked those odds."

Having both Benny and Sarg watching his back made it a lot more likely any gambles Drayco took would pay off. But, as usual, Sarg had read him all too well. Drayco wasn't just rattled, he'd fallen off axis. One more reason to stay away from Maura McCune, or whatever her real name was.

Yet, as much as he'd tried to hate her or push her out of his mind, it was the picture of her seated next to him at the piano that always flipped open in his mental photograph album. But the murder, the lies, the long silence—he slammed that album shut once more.

9

Weaving his way through the notorious Friday afternoon rush traffic was always an exercise in frustration for Drayco. Even more so today, with that protest Sarg mentioned adding a slew of road closures and detours into the mix.

Drayco couldn't tell what the protest was about from the glimpses of signs sporting the usual banner words, "justice, murder, action." Different day, different battle, different players. Shades of the gray life in the nation's capital—parades of protesters below and the incessant military helicopters above.

After what normally would be a half hour drive turned into ninety minutes, with "tinks" of occasional sleet on the windows and one cellphone call from Benny, Drayco finally pulled his blue Starfire in front of his brick townhome near Capitol Hill. The building didn't have the terracotta trim and marble glitz of the Mayflower Hotel, but it was as welcome a sight as a five-star pleasure palace.

Ordinarily. As he drove up in front, his elderly neighbor was standing outside chatting with a younger woman whose blond hair was tied into a neat braid, almost camouflaged against her blond leather jacket.

The neighbor, Coraline Chapman, was hard of hearing, but her eagle eye cataloged all his comings and goings as well as his visitors. After he parked the car and climbed out, Coraline asked, "Is this your new girlfriend, Scott? It's time you hooked up with someone different. I didn't like the last one, the brunette. That one's a hussy if I ever saw one."

Nelia beat Drayco to the punch. "Just a colleague, Mrs. Chapman, I'm a Sheriff's Deputy over on the Eastern Shore."

"You know what they say. Cops should marry cops because they know what they're getting. Fewer divorces that way."

Drayco had patiently tried to explain to his neighbor the difference between cops, deputies, FBI agents, and consultants, but to her, they were all cops. Like Keds or Xerox or Coke. One generic name fits all.

Nelia didn't smile at the older woman's quip but did look in Drayco's direction as she said it. A light mist enveloped them in a cold mesh of dense dampness, and when it started to sleet in earnest, Mrs. Chapman scurried inside her front door. Nelia and Drayco dashed into his place, welcoming the dry warmth from the wall radiators.

Drayco took her coat and laid it on a table above one of the radiators to dry off. "I didn't think I'd see you again, Tyler. That is, so soon." Tyler, Drayco. Always professional, just two colleagues hanging out together.

Nelia invited herself to grab a beer from his refrigerator and settled into the soft leather sofa across from the blue abstract painting on his wall. It was the same painting that matched what he saw when he listened to a Prokofiev piano sonata.

She propped her feet on the coffee table and took several swigs of the beer. He waited for her to say something, but she just stared at the painting and remained silent.

When her beer was half-drained, she finally said, "It seems we're always apologizing to each other. But I should have told you about law school."

He sat on a chair to her right, a bottle of his favorite Manhattan Special espresso soda in hand. "I didn't peg you as insane."

She opened her mouth to reply, but he continued, "Law school, working for Benny, and sheriff-ing? God knows when you find time to do your coursework."

"Georgetown has a part-time law degree. Most of my classes are at night during the week, and I get Fridays off. Sheriff Sailor's letting me work half-time and managed to convince the county bean counters it was a good thing. He's using the other half of my salary as a sort of time share to pay a new deputy, another woman. She just had a baby, so job share works well for her, too."

"Still don't see how you can do it all."

"I already know a lot more than most first-year students."

"How long will the degree take, then?"

"Four years, but it's doable. If the back-and-forth commute doesn't kill me first."

"Well then, I'll make that *mostly* insane." He rubbed his chin. "Why now?"

She shrugged. "I guess it was all those cases I've worked where I couldn't help anyone. Just arrest them. Or maybe it was your situation. With the review board."

So perhaps her disapproval with him wasn't as severe as he'd first thought. Then why no word from her all this time? Hell, he knew why. It was the five-ton pachyderm in the room. "What does Tim think?"

"Officially, he's real rah-rah. Underneath, I think he resents the time away from him."

"I could fly you over to save some of the commute time. Not sure Tim would like that idea."

"He already thinks you and I are—"

"Yeah."

Nelia looked around the room, then asked, "How's Darcie these days?"

She was probably half-expecting to find more of Darcie's lingerie lying around as she had on one occasion. Thankfully, Darcie had taken that red bow "outfit" from Valentine's Day with her when she left. He replied, "Good. I mean, she's fine. As in healthy. She's very ... healthy."

Nelia hid a smile, then exchanged the beer for her feet on the coffee table. "I was worried about you today."

"Benny assures me the hearing will be a piece of 'devil's food.' His words."

"Not that. I mean, yes that, but your mother, too. I never wanted to pry. Yet I did wonder about her. How could any woman do it? Up and leave her family?" Nelia rested her arms on her thighs. "Does she know about your sister, about Casey's death?"

"I spoke with her briefly. We didn't get into personal details. Just the murder. She says she didn't do it, by the way."

"Do you believe her?"

"I don't know."

"Do you want to believe her?"

Drayco looked at a web in one corner of the ceiling. What a lucky spider with only three goals in its little life—spin web, catch food, eat. "My father just wants her to disappear again, and part of me agrees with him."

"But you're going to investigate this, aren't you?"

"I wish I could say no." He raised his shoulders and tilted his neck until he heard a crack. He spied a bottle of aspirin on the table next to Nelia's coat and got up to take a couple.

When he returned, she motioned him over to the sofa, and he sat beside her as she said, "Turn around, so your back is facing me."

He complied and soon her hands were massaging his upper back and shoulders, expertly digging her thumbs into his sore muscles. He relaxed into her touch and closed his eyes. "God, you're good."

"Surely you've had massages before? Maybe a pre-concert massage?"

"None this nice."

"Not even the violinist who seduced your virginity away from you?"

He'd almost forgotten he told her about that. Hard to forget her reply that it was technically statutory rape since he was sixteen and the violinist in her thirties. "That was a different kind of massage."

Nelia's hands finished with one knot on his right shoulder and then stopped. "That should help a little."

He turned around to face her. "Has your husband hit you again?"

It was her turn to be tense, and he quickly added, "I'm sorry. I told myself I wasn't going to mention that. Want another beer?" He hopped up without waiting for her answer and rummaged around in the fridge. "Here you go," and handed the bottle to her.

There was safety in silence, and they sat within that safety zone for several minutes, marred only by the occasional swig from his espresso soda or her beer.

Nelia was the first to break the zone. "Benny filled me in on the details of the murder. As much as he knows right now, of course."

"As much as any of us knows. He called my cellphone while I was in traffic to tell me the arraignment isn't until Monday. Bail is looking like a no-go."

"Hope I can be there. Will you?"

Drayco rubbed his forehead. "Probably not a great idea under the circumstances. You and Benny can be my stand-ins."

She glanced at the painting again and shook her head. At his response or the painting? He didn't have a chance to ask before she continued, "What struck me is how nearly impossible it would be for your mother to stab the victim hard enough to kill and not get any blood on her. Not even her shoes."

"Unless she changed clothes."

"They didn't find any. And then to wait there meekly for the police to pick her up? She's either a patsy or a criminal genius."

Two equal possibilities, and the latter, in particular, he couldn't ignore. Was this all a calculated plan to use an insanity defense? Was she counting on Brock or her son to rush to her aid as pawns in some elaborate scheme?

He deserved answers. And tomorrow he'd begin nailing them down one by one, starting with the victim's estranged daughter and brother. The faster he could get a chance to interview some of the actors involved, the better. For Maura's sake, Benny's, and Sarg's— before Halabi pulled out his leash.

Nelia stood. "I should go. To deal with some of that coursework you mentioned."

He popped up to join her. "It's a five-hour drive to Cape Unity."

"But only a five-minute drive to the room I'm renting near campus. One of Tim's friends is cutting me a break on the price."

"Five minutes?"

"Um hmm." She walked to the front of the room and grabbed her coat from the radiator. "I have a roommate. Gary."

"Gary?" Drayco folded arms across his chest.

"He's nice. Quiet. Studious. Handsome, too."

She smiled at him as she opened the front door. Before disappearing, she added, "He's gay." And then she left.

10

Nelia opened the door to her third-floor apartment and then slammed it behind her. She eased onto the marigold chenille sofa and stared at a bare patch on the armrest. Had that always been there? Oh, well. Beggars can't be choosers when it comes to furnished apartments.

She moaned and put her head in her hands. It was a lot harder to see Drayco than she'd thought it would be. Perhaps her reasons for avoiding him the past four months weren't all that clear anymore. Perhaps it mattered and perhaps it didn't or maybe she was going to hell for all those thoughts she was having and knew she shouldn't.

When she'd told her roommate Gary earlier she was going over to see Drayco, Gary looked him up on the computer and uncovered some newspaper articles of Drayco from his previous cases. "Hubba hubba," was his sole reaction.

And when she'd told Gary about the late Andrew Gilbow and the shooting and fire at the warehouse, he'd taken Drayco's side. "The turd deserved to die. If you ask me, he didn't even deserve a mercy killing. He should have died in fiery flames here on earth and roasted in the fires of hell for all eternity."

With a sigh, she took her head out of her hands and fell back against the sofa.

A garbled male voice wafted out of the bathroom, and she glanced up to see Gary brushing his teeth as he asked, "That good a day?" Or at least, that's what she thought he'd asked. It sounded more like "Sat gouda hay?"

"Tell me again why I'm not insane to think I can do this. Law school's bad enough on its own. And I had to go and think I can combine it with a job. Make that two jobs."

Gary strolled to the kitchen sink and spat out the toothpaste. "I never said you weren't insane. As a matter of fact, I think you are certifiable."

"Thanks for that. I feel so much better."

Gary grabbed some bottled water from the counter and brought her one, too. "I also didn't say being insane wasn't a good thing. Hell, Mendel, the father of genetics was called insane. So was Semmelweis, the guy who discovered the link between germs and disease. One of Thomas Edison's teachers called him mentally ill, and everybody thought Tesla was cuckoo."

"You're saying I'm in good company?"

"Guess it depends on how you define 'good.' Semmelweis was eventually committed to an asylum because nobody believed him, and Tesla was a bit of a nut case, scared of germs and pearls. Of course, Tesla also believed women would become the dominant gender and rule over mankind like queen bees. So, buzz buzz, darling."

Nelia laughed. "Now I really do feel better."

Her renewed good mood lasted all of five minutes until her cellphone rang, and she saw her husband's number. Should she ignore it? Yeah, that would go over well. "Hi, Tim. Hope your day hasn't been too bad."

"That new home assistant we hired to make meals for me is terrible. She actually tried to feed me mussels. Doesn't she know I have a shellfish allergy?"

"Well, I—"

"And then she practically cold-conked me with the vacuum cleaner. It's not as if she can't see a guy in a big honking wheelchair. And when she was cleaning up, she put my meds in a different drawer. Took me an hour to find them thanks to the tremors. I know she's not a doctor, but it doesn't take a genius to know you have to take MS meds on a set schedule."

Nelia bit back a retort she'd probably regret later and instead replied, "Would you like me to find someone else?"

"Then I'll have to train someone new. No, I just want this person to do her goddamned job the way she's supposed to."

"Maybe we can get Barbara back." That was wishful thinking. Barbara had been a saint and tolerated Tim as well as anyone until he barked at her one too many times. Nelia doubted they had half the amount of money it would take to lure Barbara to return.

Tim growled at her, "If you were here more, this wouldn't be a problem."

"This isn't a new situation for us, Tim. We've had this commuter marriage thing for the past few years. You couldn't move to Cape Unity, and I couldn't get a job in Salisbury. And that's just the way it is. Besides, Sheriff Sailor's been amazingly supportive about everything. Not too many bosses would be."

"Yeah, well, now I'll hardly ever see you, will I? Unless that's your plan all along with this latest scheme of yours."

"That wasn't my plan at all. You know I've always dreamed of being an attorney—"

"Or maybe your plan is to get closer to Scott Drayco. Is that it? Because if it is, I have news for you. I've got spies up there in D.C., so if you do anything, I'll know."

Whether it was from the constant tip-toeing around her husband or her shitty week, she couldn't stop herself. "You're one to talk. Remember Rachel Masters? Somehow I don't think she left her monogrammed bras in our car as souvenirs."

"Are you accusing me of having an affair?"

"Years ago, yes. Before the MS got bad."

"Oh, now I'm so much of a cripple, I can't even have an affair, is that what you're implying?"

"God, Tim. You can be a real bastard, you know that? I'm the one who's always defended you to others, who makes excuses for your shitty attitude and cleans up the personal messes you leave in your wake. When I said for richer or poorer and in sickness and in health, I meant it. Did you?"

His tone softened. "I'm sorry, sweetheart. Guess it was just missing my meds."

She could tell by the slight slur in his voice that wasn't the only reason. She'd have to talk with Lisa about hiding the booze from now on. "You need a good night's sleep, that's all. I'll make sure Lisa knows your meds have to stay in the same location at all times. And I'll get one of those low-riding vacuum cleaners instead. And a feather duster."

He chuckled and rang off. When she pressed the end-call button on her phone, Gary said, "Tim drinking again?"

"Sounded more like a gin call than a vodka call."

"Most people in your situation would be talking divorce. I think it's admirable you want to stick together."

She stared at him. "You do?"

"My parents were divorced. I know how hard it was on them and me. And sometimes I wonder if they didn't regret their decision. Wouldn't want you to make a mistake by being too hasty."

She forced a smile. "Can't say I ever liked hasty pudding."

"You actually ate some of that disgusting stuff?"

"My grandmother made it once. Cornmeal mush with maple syrup."

Gary made a face. "You almost put me off my appetite. I say almost because I happen to have stopped by DreaMed and picked up kabobs and falafel. Before you say you're not hungry, let me remind you that you'll need fortification before your night class."

He was right. She did the best she could in deference to his generosity, but it didn't get the bad taste of Tim's words out of her mouth. Even the ambrosia of the gods wouldn't be enough to do that.

11

With yesterday's protest over and the traffic along with it, Sarg picked Drayco up on the dot of nine in Sarg's newly waxed Range Rover, giving Drayco time to fill him in on an earlier call from Benny. "Jerold Zamorra's brother, Edwin, has a beef with his brother's former employer. Filed a lawsuit requesting an injunction to prevent the TSA from touching private areas without reasonable suspicion."

Sarg zigzagged around some construction cones, cursing under his breath as they almost got sideswiped by a truck. "Think I could get in on that lawsuit of his and make it a class action dealie?"

"You and millions of other people. Jerold's daughter Ashley wasn't listed as a party, so that's not the reason behind *her* estrangement."

Sarg grunted. "What a lovely litigious triangle, those Zamorras. Rena against Jerold while they worked at the TSA, Edwin against the TSA."

They pulled up to a typical middle-class Alexandria home, meaning somewhere between half a million and a million dollars. That chunk of change bought Edwin fifteen hundred square feet of a half-brick, half-vinyl-siding colonial with a postage stamp yard. The interior was a bachelor-chic mix of varying hues of beige and brown.

It was the mantel that drew Drayco's attention. It wasn't every day he saw a witch doctor's mask made of wood, bone, and feathers. Hanging next to it was an antique apothecary box sporting vintage bottles bearing names like Foley's Kidney Pills.

Ashley Zamorra and Edwin Zamorra greeted them with identical frowns. When Drayco arranged the meeting, he'd said he was acting on "behalf" of law enforcement to uncover the truth behind Jerold's murder. Well, he *was* a crime consultant, and Sarg's FBI creds were impeccable. As far as Halabi was concerned, ask questions now and apologize later.

In addition to her frown, Ashley wore a tricolor headband of silver, copper, and gold crowning her shoulder-length dark hair. Her metal hoop earrings contained symbols he couldn't identify without staring, and he didn't want to make her feel anymore ill at ease than she already was. The sprinkle of freckles across her nose made her look even younger than her thirty years, especially combined with red lipstick the same color little girls use when playing dress-up.

Edwin, on the other hand, looked every bit his age. His close-cropped gray beard formed a ring under his chin like a soap-bubble beard, forming a point at the end. He was vaping away on an e-cigarette that smelled a little like green apples.

Neither of the Zamorras offered Drayco or Sarg a drink or a seat. Sarg took the latter, but Drayco stood to make it easier to prowl around the room. He spied a framed photo of Ashley standing with her arm around a woman who shared Ashley's high cheekbones and rail-thin frame. He picked it up and looked at Ashley. "Is this Ophelia, your mother?"

She nodded. "My father killed her a year ago."

She ignored Edwin's attempt to interrupt, adding, "The police don't say that. They arrested two teenage boys. My father was having an affair, and I guess he just got tired of Mom. Murdered her to be with his mistress."

"Do you know the identity of the woman he was having an affair with?"

"That woman they arrested, probably. I'll bet she's his mistress and killed him when he cheated on her, too."

What could Drayco say? It might well be true. "Your parents were divorced for a year before your mother was murdered. Why would your father wait until then to kill her?"

Ashley grabbed a pillow from the couch and hugged it so tightly, Drayco was surprised the stuffing didn't explode. "To get his hands on her money. She'd made a lot from her decorating business. And she had life insurance. After my parents divorced, she kept putting off changing her Will. Made us both beneficiaries, three-quarters to my father, one to me."

"How much did three-quarters amount to?"

"Several hundred thousand. My father squandered it away on bad investments. Lost almost everything."

Ashley blinked back tears as Edwin patted her on the shoulder. "I miss my mother every day. And I regret all the times we argued because we both had a temper."

She choked out a laugh. "Mom kept cheap dishes around for times she felt like exploding. She'd throw them at the back fence, her version of skeet shooting. I adored her."

Drayco studied the smiling woman in the picture frame. Unlike Maura McCune, this woman had years of emotions etched into her face, mostly crinkled laugh lines around her eyes. But those eyes—they didn't match her smile. It was as if someone copied and pasted the eyes and mouths from two different women.

He replaced the photo in its original spot. Other frames nearby held additional pictures of Ashley and her mother, including a couple of Edwin with one or both women. None with the victim, Ashley's father, Jerold.

Edwin coughed, then cleared his throat. "The police showed me a photo of that woman they arrested. I saw her with my brother once before. Knew she was trouble then. You can always tell with the Jezebels. Not like Ophelia, whose only fault was she was a clutter-bug."

Drayco asked, "Where did you see Maura—that is, the suspect— and your brother together? And when was this?"

"Three weeks, a month, I'd say. I stopped by his apartment as they were leaving and just missed them. But I saw them drive off together."

"Was that the only time?"

Edwin pursed his lips, releasing a little vapor cloud. "I think so. At least, that's what I told the police."

"You didn't see them together before Ophelia's death?"

"I'm not sure why that would matter, but no."

Sarg piped up from the couch. "What about Ophelia's other family members, Miss Zamorra? They also believe Jerold killed her?"

Ashley replied, "My grandparents are dead. One passed away before Mom, the other died right after, of a heart attack. Mom was an only child."

Drayco moved to a spot with a direct sight line to both Zamorras. "And your father's family, other than your Uncle Edwin here?"

"I'm not close to my dad's parents anymore. Uncle Edwin's spoken with them, but I'm not sure I want them at the funeral. Of course, they believe he didn't do it, didn't kill my Mom."

Sarg glanced from one Zamorra to the other. "When was the last time either one of you saw Jerold?"

Edwin answered first. "Two weeks. He seemed fine."

Ashley added, "I dropped off a box of stuff at Dad's condo. The last of the items he had at Mom's place. She left the house to me, thank God."

Drayco asked, "When did you drop off that box?"

She hesitated. "The day he died. If you think it's related to his murder, I don't see how. Old notebooks, ledgers of some kind. And a few odds and ends. I gave the police a list. I'm surprised they didn't tell you."

Sarg turned to Edwin. "The lawsuit you filed against the TSA. What'd your brother think about that, sir? Can't imagine he was ready to dance a jig."

Edwin straightened up. "It had nothing to do with Jerold. He didn't make the policy."

"Surely it could drive a wedge between you."

"We didn't always see eye to eye, but my brother was a good man. I regret our falling out."

"Do you work for the government too, sir?"

"I own an independent compounding pharmacy. More control, less red tape. Hate corporate bureaucratic idiocy, bean counters always looking over your shoulder." Edwin checked his watch. "I took a quick break to meet you and Ashley here, but I need to get back. Saturday's one of my busiest days."

"We understand, sir. Do you mind if we take a look at Jerold's condo? We have full police approval."

Edwin rubbed his forehead. "If you think it's necessary."

"Just trying to make sure the right person goes to jail for your brother's murder, that's all."

"I suppose it would be okay. Do you have a key?"

"We were hoping you do, sir."

Edwin disappeared into a side room, then returned and handed Sarg a key. "Very good, sir, much appreciated."

Drayco handed both Ashley and Edwin one of his cards. "In case you think of something else. Anything at all."

Back at the Range Rover, Sarg rubbed a tiny smudge off the finish. "Hate to say it. All that business about Jerold having an affair with your mother seems to be a godsend for the prosecution."

"I admit I don't know my mother, but when she talked about Jerold, she didn't exhibit the air of a woman in love who killed in a crime of passion. If she's guilty, it was some other reason."

Drayco slid into the passenger seat. "Did you notice all the photos of Ophelia and Ashley? One of the Ophelia photos seemed to be taken a long time ago. She was much younger, and there wasn't a ring on her finger. She and Edwin were standing unusually close to each other."

"You're thinking the other man, instead of the other woman?"

"Possibly. And Edwin did have a key to the condo, despite being 'estranged.' Motive and opportunity."

"I hate love triangles." Sarg poked his head through the driver's side door. "Where to next? I got a couple hours before my weekend yes-dear chores suck me back in."

"Sucking is a pretty good term for it. We get to meet Jerold Zamorra's former TSA colleague, the one who accused him of sexual harassment. She said the only time she had available in her busy schedule was at polo practice."

Sarg sighed. "I love the smell of horse shit in the morning."

"By the way, since when do we have full police approval to go through Jerold's condo?"

"After I talk with them, we will. Provided they've released the crime scene."

Drayco grinned. "Good. I was thinking of breaking and entering, myself."

Sarg narrowed his eyes. "You are kidding, right?"

"Let's hope that wax job of yours keeps the shit off the Range Rover."

Sarg groused, "If there's so much as one speck, I'm handing you a bucket and sponge, junior."

12

Sarg wrinkled his nose as they headed inside the arena. "I suppose it's better than my uncle's farm. Barely."

The powdered lime and pine oil were doing their best to hide the odor, but the earthy excrement was every bit their match. Drayco watched the two teams of three players each, one dressed in red helmets and jerseys, the other in blue, as horses and riders scrambled around the dirt track as if they actually knew what they were doing.

It seemed chaotic, a blur of legs, hooves, mallets. In the middle of it all, a tiny ball bounced around and occasionally hit a colored patch of wall leading an official to raise a flag.

This was a practice match, without an audience. But if people had been in the stands, they'd be applauding number three on the red team who seemed most at ease with her mount and quick reflexes. After she had whammed two balls in fairly quick succession into the painted goal, a whistle blew. From the hand-shaking and dismounting afterward, Drayco guessed the skirmish was over.

He and Sarg approached a bystander and asked which of the players was Rena Quentin, and the bystander pointed out red number three. They cornered their quarry before she could disappear into the back. When they introduced themselves, she called for someone named Bob, and he took her pony to the stables.

She wore tall black riding boots, knee pads, and white trousers, the standard polo getup, but everything looked new as if just bought from an expensive catalog. Definitely not Walmart. She wasn't wearing any jewelry or rings, save for a rose-gold watch sporting a designer label.

That ostentation didn't come from any government salary savings. Drayco's midnight research had uncovered the fact she received a substantial divorce settlement from her late husband several years ago. A very amicable parting or the man must have been dotty about her— the divorce was uncontested, and he later sang her praises in a magazine interview.

After they made the introductions, Rena looked at Drayco, "You are a crime consultant," and then to Sarg, "and you're FBI? I've already talked to the police. It's that sexual harassment thing again, right?"

She still had the mallet in her hand and twirled it around. "In retrospect, I wouldn't do it again. Report it that is. And not just because I was strongly encouraged to take a nice bonus package in addition to the standard retirement. Then slink quietly away, of course. Sure, I was furious with Jerold at the time. But I learned later he and his wife Ophelia were having problems. Likely explains his behavior. And certainly made me see him in a more sympathetic light."

"Can you tell us more about this behavior, Ms. Quentin?"

"Do I have to spell it out for you, Agent? If you get your jollies that way, fine. He touched my breasts and crotch and tried to kiss me on more than one occasion. And no, I hadn't encouraged him. Guess he thought since he was lonely, and I was a lonely widow, it would be welcome. Well, it wasn't."

The sound of cheers got her attention, and she glanced at a new group of players on horseback with a wistful smile. "You're going to ask me where I was the night Jerold was killed because you think I did it in retaliation. I'll beat you to it. I was shopping at Nordstrom in Tysons Corner. And no, I didn't buy anything, but you'll probably find clerks there who remember me. They have such amazing staff."

Sarg pulled out his notebook and jotted down the details. "Did you know Ophelia Zamorra well?"

"She was a fine woman, Agent Sargosian. Lovely, talented. I hired her to decorate my house. Amazing results, like something out of *House Beautiful*. I recommended her to all my friends. And as for Jerold, I even attended a recital of his after we both retired from the agency. My little peace offering, I suppose. I hate being on bad terms with anyone."

Drayco's ears perked up. "A recital?"

"He was in a small-time piano quartet. Played the viola. The four of them were together for at least five years, I believe. A pianist, whose name I can't recall. The cellist, I believe Lauralee Fremont is her name. And the violinist, Gogo Cheng. Gogo dates Jerold's daughter, Ashley. Gogo is also a martial arts instructor and they practice in a room at Kicks and Sticks where he works. I hear he's amazing at what he does."

Drayco was amazed she'd used "amazing" three times in two minutes. Maybe he'd buy her a thesaurus.

Rena wrinkled her nose. "Star-crossed lovers, Gogo and Ashley. Neither Jerold nor Ophelia approved of their daughter dating Gogo."

"Then I'm surprised the quartet didn't disband." Drayco added, "Although music groups can be a lot like families, often staying together despite hating each other's guts."

"You sound like you speak from experience, Mr. Drayco. Other than the Gogo-Ashley thing, Jerold never mentioned any disagreements. Well, nothing serious. And Lauralee ..." She paused. "I'm afraid I don't know her well."

Sarg asked, "And his former TSA colleagues, Mrs. Quentin? Any bad blood there or someone outside the agency who'd made threats?"

She sighed. "Everyone hates the TSA. Even the TSA. If World War Three breaks out, I suspect the TSA will be blamed. But you might not have to look much farther than Jerold's own backyard."

"Are you referring to Edwin's lawsuit, ma'am?"

"Just another reason for Jerold to retire. First, my sexual harassment charges. Then the pressure on him to make his brother retract the lawsuit. How could he stay after all of that?"

She used the mallet to knock dust off her boots. "We may not have been best friends, Agent Sargosian, Mr. Drayco, but I'm sorry Jerold is dead. If you have any more questions, call my answering service, and we'll set something up. If you'll excuse me, I've got to get out of these nasty clothes."

She headed through the same door where Bob and her horse vanished. Sarg made haste to exit, himself, making Drayco sprint to keep up with him. "Got a hot date, Sarg? Or should I say, an 'amazing' date?"

"As long as it's not Rena Quentin. Women who are taller than I am give me the heebie-jeebies. And yes, I know it's sexist. My hot date, as you put it, is my desk at home and a stack of files. Followed by something roof-ish or garage-ish. Haven't decided which to tackle first."

"I appreciate you taking time to lend your FBI air of credibility as a hedge against Halabi. Drop me off at Shady Grove, and I'll take the Metro on in."

"And deny me a chance to take GW Parkway?" Sarg inspected his shoes before climbing into the car. "What's the next stop on your Quixotic Quest, Don?"

Drayco opened the web browser on his cellphone and found the page he was seeking. "Kicks and Sticks. Gogo Cheng is listed as teaching Eskrima."

"Never heard of it."

"It's a type of Philippines martial arts. Practitioners use weapons. Like sticks, blades—and knives."

13

After Sarg dropped him off at his townhome, Drayco checked his messages and looked for the little stray tabby he'd been feeding. No messages, no tabby. He looked at his piano, all cold and lonely. Taking the rest of the afternoon off sounded pretty good right then.

Instead, he grabbed a late lunch of two-day-old corned beef on rye from his fridge and hopped in the Starfire. He pointed the car toward the outskirts of Falls Church and a one-story building with its exterior brick walls painted black. Guess the traditional red paint on nearby buildings, or even white, was too cheery for a martial arts studio.

Once inside, he couldn't miss the eye-catching display positioned near the entrance. It immediately drew him to the case filled with lethal-looking knives, each one labeled. They fanned out from the center weapon, a *bolo*, which resembled a machete. There were two *kampila* swords with fork tips. Then a *parabay*, like a small half-guillotine blade, next to a fish-shaped *barang* and a wavy *sundáng*.

He peeked into the large room off the lobby with pads lining the wooden floor and mirrors framing each wall. Two men dressed in red quilted armor pads and plastic head protectors with face masks were sparring with long-handled sticks. The smell of chalk dust mingled with sweat and stale rubbing alcohol.

After asking a passerby where Drayco could find Gogo Cheng, he made his way to a room in the back where he was met first by the turquoise-tipped spiky amoeboid blobs of tones from a violin and cello playing Beethoven.

Gogo looked to be a few years older than Ashley Zamorra. His muscular build from the martial arts training made him resemble a tennis player, not a violinist, especially when he lifted his sleeve, revealing a dragon tattoo. The cellist, Lauralee Fremont, appeared to be from a mixed-race background, her blue eyes setting off her smooth, creamy-mocha skin that pegged her as thirty-ish at most.

The pianist appeared to be AWOL. It took several moments after Drayco entered the room for his presence to register. When it did, he was sorry it made them stop playing.

Gogo narrowed his eyes. "If you want to sign up for Eskrima lessons, check with the front desk."

"My name is Scott Drayco. I'm a crime consultant looking into the murder of Jerold Zamorra. Your former violist, I understand."

Gogo exchanged a quick glance with Lauralee, then replied, "We were just discussing that. Have to find a new fourth now. We already put out feelers, but it'll have to wait until Kegger returns from Japan."

"Kegger?"

"Our pianist. His real name is Olen Vasey, but everyone calls him Kegger. You can guess why. He's in Japan for a month, a music exchange thing."

Gogo sized up Drayco with an appraising scan. "You say you're a crime consultant? I'm surprised the police haven't been by yet. You working for them?"

Halabi's ears must be burning right now. "I consult with various law enforcement organizations."

"So, what—we're suspects? Because if we're suspects, I want to talk to a lawyer first."

"The police believe they have the murderer in jail. I'm just here to fill in some gaps about Jerold and a possible motive for his death. What was he like to work with?"

Gogo waved his bow in the air—not unlike the stick-work of the sparring duo Drayco saw earlier—before he tossed it on the stand. "Oh, you know. He was Jerold. Played the viola well. We'll miss that."

Miss *that*, not miss *him*. Interesting. "Was he easy to get along with?"

Drayco addressed the question to both, but Lauralee stayed silent and stared at the floor, while Gogo just shrugged. This was going well. "The two of you still practice without a violist or pianist?"

"Gotta keep the fingers limber."

Drayco studied the piano. It was an upright Yamaha but full sized. The bass would be stronger and offset the too-bright timbre. The action of the Yamahas he'd played on before were a little stiff, but he didn't mind.

He sat on the bench and grabbed the sheet music on top of the piano. "Mind if I jam with you for a little?" He began playing, and it wasn't long before Gogo and Lauralee joined in.

They played all the way through the first movement, and when they finished, Gogo had a broad smile on his face. "You played both the piano and viola lines. Damn."

Drayco rubbed at a small scratch on the shiny, black finish. "I enjoy Beethoven. Not as prismatic as Bach, but depending on the piece and instrumentation, colorful."

"Sounds kind of like synesthesia. I played with a guy who had that once."

"Guilty as charged."

"Well, I've got perfect pitch. From one freak to another."

Drayco smiled. Nothing like music to break the ice. "Beethoven by night, martial arts by day. But why Eskrima, Gogo?"

"Get asked that all the time. It's Filipino, I'm Chinese. Should be Kung Fu, right? I got tired of people making Bruce Lee jokes all the time, so I finally caved and picked the first martial arts thing I saw. My parents hate it."

He looked like he'd swallowed a vinegar milkshake. "It's their fault. They told me to pick an extra-curricular sports activity when I was a kid. It was either this or tennis. I never saw the attraction of chasing a little ball around."

"My parents hate everything I do." Lauralee spoke for the first time, her voice soft and husky. She grabbed a tube of coconut-scented lip balm from her music stand and jabbed it around her lips.

Gogo shot her a sympathetic look. "Don't know what's worse—caring too much or caring too little. Or about the wrong things." He quickly changed the subject back. "Eskrima teaches close quarter weapons combat. Let's face it. Hardly anyone attacks you these days unless they have a weapon."

Drayco had researched Eskrima more before he arrived. The discipline was becoming popular in law enforcement training for that very reason. "I spoke with Ashley Zamorra and her uncle, Edwin, yesterday. You and Ashley are dating, right?"

"For two years. Jerold didn't exactly give his stamp of approval. Don't guess our parents were destined to get along, either. Jerold grew up during the Cold War when all Chinese were communists. My parents grew up under communism and don't trust authority figures."

"Like the TSA."

"Exactly. Guess some of it rubbed off on me. *Cào nǐ zǔzōng shíbā dài.*"

Drayco grinned. "Fuck your ancestors to the eighteenth generation?"

"You speak Chinese?"

"When I was in China years ago, the timpanist in the orchestra I played with taught me a few swear words."

"You toured?"

"A lifetime ago." Drayco pulled the keyboard cover down on the piano and leaned on it. "Ashley believes her father murdered her mother. And seems quite convinced of it."

"With good reason. Rumor was he had at least one affair, maybe more. Who knows?"

"Do you believe Jerold killed Ophelia?"

"I don't disagree with Ashley when she brings it up." He picked at the hem of his black t-shirt. "But, I don't know. I mean, Jerold could be an ass. And combative. And who knows why he wore those Godawful ugly golf pants all the time. Like he wanted to offend people."

Drayco tried to banish the thought of those pants getting anywhere near his mother but couldn't. "Any scuttlebutt about who the 'other woman' was?"

"Don't ask, don't tell." Gogo shrugged again. "Didn't spend enough time with him to find out. And Ashley didn't care, either. Not after her mother died."

"I was a little afraid of him," Lauralee said, blinking slowly. "He could be a dictator. Wanted things his own way. It got worse after he left the TSA."

"Did you know his wife, Ophelia?"

"Did I know his wife?" Lauralee nodded. "I was afraid of her, too. Man, she had a temper. I don't think she approved of me being Ashley's friend. Have no idea why. Ashley is ... she's generous, she's sweet, she's kind. She lets me live in the basement of her house. I couldn't afford to live anywhere near D.C., otherwise."

Drayco noted Lauralee's clothing, the wool sweater dress with a wide belt engraved with Burberry, the stylish suede boots with six-inch heels. Not far from her music stand sat a handbag with Prada on the label. Maybe if she spent less on clothes? Or was a sugar-daddy responsible?

He said, "Was Ashley the reason the quartet stayed together?"

Lauralee jutted out her chin. "Gogo, Kegger and I took a vote. We were going to kick Jerold out of the group."

Gogo added, "It had gotten worse lately. Mood swings, his condescending attitude." Gogo's cellphone chirped with a "Kung Fu Fighting" ringtone, and he excused himself to answer it, standing just outside the doorway.

Some papers behind the score on Gogo's music stand were in danger of falling off, and Drayco reached over to push them back to safety. But not before he saw what they were. Betting slips.

When Gogo first answered the call, his voice started at a whisper, but as he got more agitated, so did his tone. After what sounded like an arrangement for a meeting, he hung up and thrust the phone into his pocket.

Lauralee took the opportunity to get up, open a window, and then light a cigarette in a holder. When Gogo noticed, he put his hands on his hips and said, "I don't know why you took up smoking. You went twenty-eight years of your life without, why the hell start now?"

She tapped the ash outside the window. "I love the way it looks. Elegant. Like Audrey Hepburn in *Breakfast at Tiffany's*."

"Gaah, even your movies are old-fashioned." He laughed. "So much for that body-being-a-temple jazz. But I'll take Kegger's booze over your nicotine any day. Good to know you're not trying to hit on me."

She snorted, but her voice had an edge to it. "Hit on *you*? You know I'm not interested in testosterone types."

Testosterone types as in those who assault women, perhaps? Drayco asked, "You knew about the sexual harassment suit against Jerold?"

His companions glanced at each other briefly again, then away. Gogo nodded, while Lauralee took another drag on her cigarette. Drayco pressed them further. "Did Jerold ever push himself onto you, Lauralee?"

She said a little too quickly, "No."

Feeling the tension level rising several degrees and fearing their dialogue might soon be toast, he changed the subject. "Why isn't Ashley part of your quartet? Or I guess that would make it a quintet?"

Gogo groaned. "Oh, lord, that would be a disaster. Her ear's not tin, it's steel. Cliché intended."

Drayco swung his legs around the bench to face them. "Speaking of clichés, the police will probably ask where the two of you were the night Jerold was killed."

"Ashley and I were together. You can ask her." Gogo picked up his bow again, this time twirling it like Rena and her polo mallet.

Drayco waited for Lauralee, who took a puff off the cigarette. "I went clubbing by myself in the District. The usual places—PsychoTropics, Ultrabar, Danceskellar. Someone will remember me."

The staff member who'd given Drayco directions earlier poked his head in the door. "Your four o'clock students are here, Gogo."

Gogo grabbed his violin, closed it inside a case, and thrust the case in a corner locker. That prompted Lauralee to pack up, too, and hoist the cello case over her shoulder. As Gogo hurried out of the room, he said to Drayco, "If Kegger ever gives us the heave-ho, I may give you a call."

Lauralee tentatively stuck out her hand to shake Drayco's. "My parents would say it's a sin to be glad someone's dead."

"More so if you're the one who killed him."

She cocked her head to one side. "The Bible says an eye for an eye, doesn't it?"

"It also says if your eye offends you, pluck it out, but I don't see too many people doing that these days."

That elicited a small smile, and she gave an equally small wave as he made his exit. He paused briefly to watch Gogo, who was wearing black padded gloves, demonstrate a thrusting move with a *bolo* knife to his students and then expertly deflect an attack from a partner armed with a *daga* sword.

Gogo had the motive and skill to stab Jerold. Lauralee wasn't a martial arts expert, but she harbored her own reason to hate the victim. And to hate the victim's murdered wife, for that matter.

Throw in one vengeful daughter, an estranged brother, and possible ex-colleagues with an ax to grind, and all of a sudden, Drayco's mother had a lot of competition for the Person Most Likely to Kill Jerold Zamorra. Although it still didn't explain why she was standing over his body with a knife if innocent of his actual murder.

God, he was tired. Rock-pile-on-the-shoulders tired. Brock was probably gearing up for his usual three-day weekend, with no more worries than whether rain would keep him from going quail hunting. Or shooting hoops with his Bureau-brats gang of former agents. Drayco spent a lot of his youth out of town touring, but on those rare occasions he was home, Brock never once suggested they play a round of basketball.

And Maura McCune Drayco was alive all that time. Somewhere. Only now, he knew exactly where she'd be spending her weekend. Why did the thought of her in that orange jumpsuit safely tucked away not give him any comfort?

14

After a couple of hours running the type of errands that felt like a rat chasing cheese in a maze, Drayco finally made it home. He squinted at the sky, which was already dark at five-thirty—the one thing about switching from daylight saving time to standard time he liked. Couldn't make out a single constellation, thanks to the District's light pollution. But the moonlight was enough to show him something unexpected.

He'd developed a habit years ago of cramming a small piece of green paper between the gate on the side of his townhome leading to a small yard behind and the gate's frame. The lock on the gate was currently in place, but the paper lay on the sidewalk. It would be difficult for that paper to come loose without the gate being opened.

After easing the lock off, he made it through the gate without a sound. He navigated from one stepping stone to another until he got to the rear corner of the building. Not much of a gardener, his yard's landscaping consisted of one weeping cherry and a low evergreen hedge. No places to hide.

Seeing nothing that shouldn't be there, he started to open the back door but tripped over the cat dish. The little stray silver tabby he'd been feeding must have moved the bowl while eating, as she often did. Seems like he was always taking in strays of one kind or another, animal and human.

Drayco opened the door and entered, noted the security system was armed, and punched in his security code. His senses still on full alert, he maneuvered slowly through the kitchen and made a sight-sweep of the living area. Clear. He shrugged out of his jacket, tossed it on a chair, and removed his shoes before heading up the stairs.

He took one step when the rattle of the front mail slot startled him, followed by the "thump" of letters dropping to the floor. The mailman must be running unusually late. That was followed by another noise that made him whirl around, just not soon enough.

A giant blur of a figure shot out of nowhere, grabbed him, and shoved his face against the wall, leaving Drayco with just enough air to breathe. He struggled to twist out of the steel grip, but his assailant knew what he was doing. It was almost impossible to get out of a rear mount headlock, and struggling would only waste energy.

Drayco gulped in a couple of deep breaths and waited for King Kong to relax an inch so he could counter-attack. When the man didn't oblige, Drayco tried Stalling for Time 101 and wheezed out, "Look, if this is about that overdue gas bill, it's in the mail."

"It's about Maura McCune." The big man's voice was more baritone than bass, but his growl hit Drayco's skull like brick-colored nails. "And your investigation."

"My investigation?" Drayco's neck was going to be purple tomorrow.

"You need to let it go."

"No can do. I'm going to find out the truth, whatever it is."

"The truth?" The man's grip released a fraction, and Drayco gauged his best defensive move. The man asked, "You're not trying to prove she's guilty?"

"Not unless she is. I have no idea who killed Jerold Zamorra. Yet."

As quickly as he'd ensnared Drayco, the man half-picked him up in a move that a WWE wrestler would envy and launched him into a nearby chair. He pulled out a large knife that would put one of those Eskrima *bolos* to shame. "Thought you'd be like your father. Wanting Maura to take the fall."

Drayco was getting a good look at his attacker now. At least six-seven, maybe six-eight, mostly bald save for a wrap-around thatch of neatly trimmed blond-gray hair, with matching beard and mustache. Squinting green eyes, a triangle-shaped strawberry birthmark on the right side of his head. And dressed all in black.

"My father and I don't agree on a lot of things. But he doesn't want his former wife to 'take the fall,' as you say. He doesn't care what happens to her."

"And you do? Even after she abandoned you?"

Drayco stared at him. "Who are you? How do you know my mother?"

"Iago, and she's a friend. That's all you need to know." The knife in his hand didn't waver one centimeter. "Detective Halabi and the police have it wrong. Maura is innocent of murder. She may have stabbed him once, but she didn't kill him."

Now that was information few people outside the police department knew. Unless Halabi had a mole burrowing into his ranks. "I've talked to several people who have good reason to hate, maybe kill, Zamorra. But when I talked to my mother, she refused to tell me squat. I'm not sure how anyone can help her as long as she takes that line."

"She and Zamorra were colleagues. In a business of theirs. A very successful business. He was two-timing her, and it made her angry. Argue-angry, not kill-angry."

"And I'm just supposed to trust you on that?"

"If you know what's good for you. Besides, you said you wanted the truth, and that's the truth."

"What are the chances of you telling me what this business venture was?"

Iago glared at him, staying silent.

"Right. Well then, I will help her, and therefore you, *if* she is innocent. And that's all I can promise."

Drayco's visitor thought for a moment. "Okay." He lifted his arm as he folded up the knife and returned it to his pocket. As he did, Drayco glimpsed a tattoo on the man's right forearm, the letters ICYHWM. "If I find out more, Drayco, I'll contact you. And I expect you to do the same."

"How will I find you?"

Iago didn't answer and let himself out the front door. Drayco jumped up to follow him and peered outside. No car, but the man had vanished.

Whoever Iago was, he knew a lot about security systems. He'd managed to counteract Drayco's state of the art anti-jamming software and rolling code transmitter. Even more effective than Darcie's sweet-talking-the-neighbor scheme.

Small, greenish dots on his doorstep caught Drayco's eye, and he bent down to scoop them up. He examined them in the light. Pepita, or pumpkin, seeds. Did Iago accidentally drop them? Or were they his calling card?

Drayco grabbed one plastic bag from his kitchen to seal the seeds in and filled another bag with ice. Then he headed for his computer but stopped when he spied a small white square of paper half-hiding underneath the chair were Iago tossed him earlier. Part of a bus ticket.

Setting the ticket next to the computer, he tapped on the keyboard with his left hand while using his right hand to hold the ice bag to his neck. Time to find out who this Iago character—if that was his actual name—really was. What the hell did he have to do with Maura McCune? And what kind of "business ventures" were she and Jerold involved with? Somehow, he doubted it was door-to-door cosmetics sales.

He trawled through every online database he had access to, growing more frustrated by the minute with the big, fat zero that summed up his results. It was rare he couldn't find anything on a person, let alone two, in this day and age of Big Brother Internet. There weren't many people powerful enough to wipe their computer traces clean.

He threw the ice bag across the room and watched with more than a little perverse pleasure as it split open, spilling water and ice cubes all over the floor. Agent Rodriguez wouldn't call him *Sereno Drayco* right now. "Mister Serene" was no longer on the scene. With a sigh, Drayco went to the closet to grab a mop.

15

After his late-night mopping exercise, Drayco had tackled a Chopin ballade with such force, he'd apologized to his piano afterward. Maybe that was why the instrument had sounded off, lacking its usual colors, almost flat, even though he'd had it tuned two months ago. His unsatisfying playing had been followed by more failed research attempts that kept him up until three, making him oversleep this morning and barely making it to his appointment on time.

Sarg didn't look too irritated at the fifteen-minute delay in picking him up from Union Station, giving Drayco's Starfire a little pat before he climbed in. "You should treat me to a second breakfast. Let me guess—I'll bet you had a fluffernutter. Or some equally awful creation."

"I'll have you know I had sausage, eggs, and a biscuit."

"The Sunday morning McDonald's drive-through special?"

"Microwaved. What did you have, caviar toast points?"

"Tarragon omelet. After the Army, I swore I'd never eat crap-on-a-cracker food again."

That was an image Drayco didn't need. "Didn't the Rangers get special chow?"

"By special you mean MREs? You should take a cooking class, junior."

"They'd throw me out. Though I might sail through Can Opening 101."

Sarg grinned. "It does my soul good to know you suck at something."

After navigating through surprisingly heavy traffic on Route 50, they made it to an eight-story, glass and concrete tower in Arlington that looked like every other glass and concrete tower developers erected in the region these days.

The sign outside this particular line of condominiums said *Glencroft Shores*—another bit of developer whimsy. The nearest body of water was a good six miles with Lake Barcroft to the west or the Potomac River to the east. The unit prices didn't reflect that, starting in the upper six figures—if Jerold was broke, how could he afford one of these?

A light blue Ford sedan pulled in next to them, a woman with blond hair behind the wheel. She rolled down the window and called out, "It is all right if I park here?" Drayco pointed to another guest space, and she headed for it.

Sarg peered at him. "Not that I mind, because I like her—but what's Deputy Tyler doing here?"

"She's getting a J.D. part time and came into town early this weekend to cram for a test. She's helping Benny out, Benny's helping me out. I told her she could come along." When Sarg peered down his nose with one of his "are-you-shitting-me" looks, Drayco added, "It's not what you think."

Sarg muttered, "I think it's exactly what I think."

Drayco ignored him and pulled out the key to Jerold Zamorra's condo. Like the police report indicated, it had a back entrance opening out to a wide alley that led to an underground parking lot. It was daylight, meaning it wasn't possible to see burned-out lights. But due to the building's overhang, if the closest exterior light were out, it would make for a dark scene. Easy to get in and out unnoticed.

Unlike Jerold's brother's beige-y neutral place, this one was painted in odd color combinations, green, purple, orange. The few furniture pieces looked like Ikea catalog rejects, and the floor was a faux-wood vinyl. A musty, rancid smell similar to decaying meat filled the air, but it was competing with the pungent scent of Pine-Sol.

The police report showed the forensic techs had used oblique lighting and electrostatic dust lifters looking for latent shoe prints, but other than those of the police crew, they found only Jerold's and Maura's. The same as with the fingerprints.

Nelia gave a quick glance around, "The police have already been through this place? And Ashley and Edwin, too? Can't imagine there'd be any clues left."

Sarg replied with a bow toward Drayco, "But The Brain hasn't been through it yet." He opened a small box he'd brought with him and passed it over to Nelia and Drayco. "Don't forget your gloves, kids."

Drayco started with the kitchen, the site of the murder. Despite someone mopping up most of the blood—the crime scene techs or maybe a cleanup crew Ashley had hired—it was easy to tell where Jerold fell. The bottom cabinets still had dried blood stains, and a few flecks lined the cracks in the tile grouting. That explained the odors.

Despite Halabi's prickly attitude, the man had a stellar reputation, and his crew had done their job well. Not seeing anything of interest, Drayco returned to the living room to rejoin Sarg and Nelia.

He walked over to a wall with a frame holding a matted document of some kind. Upon closer inspection, he saw it was a pair of state lottery tickets. Some kind of joke? Had Jerold won one dollar and framed the winning ticket on a lark? The date on the tickets went back three years.

Sarg pulled out his notebook to write down the numbers, prompting Drayco to ask, "Why not type them into your cell?"

"Because this notebook doesn't need charging and doesn't have any parts that can fail." Sarg returned the small pad to his shirt pocket. "By the way, that Iago guy you told me about over the phone this morning? I ran his description through various channels. Nada. Should be easy enough to track one NBA-sized thug. Or so you'd think."

Hearing Sarg had also struck out made Drayco feel a bit better. And even more intrigued. "Like Maura McCune, a man who doesn't exist."

Sarg picked up a succession of three glass snow globes, examining each in turn. "Doesn't mean he's not our murderer."

"Why threaten me if he thought I was trying to prove Maura guilty? Her conviction would take him off the hook."

Nelia stopped next to an aquarium and pointed. "Funny you should mention hooks. Dead fish. I thought it smelled a little, well, fishy in here."

Drayco joined her and bent over to look inside the tank. Then he pushed up his sleeve and reached into the tank to grab something from the bottom.

She scrutinized the object in his hand. "One of those fake rocks. How did you know? This one is the best I've ever seen—it's so realistic, you can't tell it apart from the real ones."

"Not just a fake betta boulder, either." He flipped it over and pried open the bottom, pulling out a key hidden inside.

She said, "A small key like that—"

"Safe deposit box, storage unit, gym locker? Must be hundreds of banks and storage units in the area."

"Perhaps Ashley or Edwin Zamorra might know something."

Sarg piped up, "Or Drayco's mother."

Nelia headed to another glass tank in the corner of the room and pulled out a snake. "A bloodred corn snake. And it's still alive."

Drayco and Sarg looked at each other with raised eyebrows. Seeing their reaction, Nelia glared at them. "I like snakes. And no penis jokes, please. As the lone female deputy in my department until recently, I get plenty of those."

Sarg stifled a smile, but Drayco sucked in a breath. The thought of Nelia being subjected to sexual harassment made his blood boil. She was respected by her colleagues for the most part, but one of her fellow male deputies recently got a stone-stud earring and suggested she call him "the stud." He'd have to talk to Sheriff Sailor about that.

"This little guy should get fed once every four or five days. Someone must have been here. Guess they don't like fish as much." Nelia placed the snake inside its enclosure. "About that key. I don't see a computer anywhere, so I'm assuming the PD carted it away. Maybe there's a note explaining the key's purpose on the hard drive."

Sarg replied, "Halabi's crew are working on the computer as we speak. Also took away an old-fashioned Rolodex. He kept a list of passwords on it. And get this—he filed it under 'P.'"

She laughed. "Seriously? And this from a former TSA executive."

"Had me scratching my head so hard I drew blood. The PD haven't found anything in his e-mail. Just a few messages from former colleagues, the how ya doing, want to meet for dinner variety. Cellphone was also a dead end. More standard TSA contacts and family. All leads the police are following."

Drayco made a note to buy Sarg that extra breakfast or lunch later. With Halabi wanting Drayco as far from the case as possible, Sarg was using his more "official" channels to follow the police investigation and keep Drayco up to date. It wasn't a position he enjoyed being in, having to rely on Sarg and Benny Baskin to keep him in the loop.

The trio spent an hour checking through the rest of the condo, with Drayco adding more details about his "guest" the previous evening. Sarg put his hands on his hips. "Sure would love to know what Mystery Goon was up to. Guess if he'd meant you harm, you wouldn't be here right now. Gave you a little souvenir, though, didn't he? That's a lovely bruise on the right side of your neck."

Nelia stopped riffling through a set of books when Drayco mentioned Iago and bit her lip but didn't say anything. She picked up another book and examined it. "I have more mysteries for you. Benny wormed it out of Halabi that the witness who called police the night of Jerold's murder used a mechanical device to disguise his voice."

Drayco finished checking a desk drawer, slamming it shut with more force than he'd intended. "Definitely sounds planned, not a heat-of-the-moment thing at all. Luckily, I have a couple more people to add to Jerold's anti-fan club." He filled them in on his meeting with Gogo and Lauralee.

When he described Gogo's dragon tattoo, Sarg chuckled. "Appropriate. *Drayco*, the dragon."

They re-converged in the front room, where Drayco fingered items on a table that included a miniature Nikon camera, a toy stun gun, toy handcuffs. Another joke on Jerold's part? He studied photos on the same table, a picture of Jerold, Gogo, Lauralee, and a man who must be Kegger, the pianist, all with their instruments. Jerold was standing away from Gogo, close to Lauralee. Nowhere in the condo did Drayco see any mementos of Ophelia, Jerold's murdered ex-wife.

Sarg nodded at the key from the aquarium in Drayco's hand, "I would do some checking on that for you, but—"

"It would appear too much like an official FBI case."

"And I'm tippy-toeing around the line as it is."

As Sarg uttered those words, Drayco heard the sound of a key being inserted into the front door. A woman walked in, haloed by the bright sun behind her. She took one look at them, put her hand over her heart, and toppled to the floor.

16

The elderly woman, who told them her name was Imogen Layford, sat on a sofa in Jerold's living room, fanning herself all the while she apologized. "I musta gave you folks a scare. More'n you gave me."

Nelia handed her a paper cup of water they'd scrounged for her out of the kitchen. "Just glad you feel better now."

"Oh, I do, I do. Jerold's my neighbor. Was my neighbor. Still can't believe he's dead and murdered. He was gone a lot, you know. Asked me to take care of his fishies while he's away. No one's told me to stop, so I just keep doing it." Her voice had a slight twang, and she added a little "uh" at the ends of words ending in "T."

Nelia looked over at the tank with the fish floating on top. "From the looks of it, you might not have to do that anymore."

Mrs. Layford followed Nelia's gaze and put her hand over her heart again. "Oh, dear. I had a spot of the stomach flu. Didn't think an extra day would hurt."

Drayco said, "I doubt his family will mind. Did you ever meet any of them? His daughter Ashley or his brother Edwin?"

"I met Ashley once, not long after Jerold moved in. Seemed like a pleasant young thing, and she had that nice Chinese boyfriend with her." Mrs. Layford lowered her voice. "I wasn't spying, mind you, but I heard a little yelling. Thought perhaps the daughter didn't get along with her father. Love or money, isn't that what it usually boils down to?"

Drayco sat beside her. "You said Jerold was away a lot. Did he say where he was going so frequently?"

"A bit of a mystery, that. He didn't say, you see. But he didn't take a suitcase, neither."

She took a few sips of the water from the paper cup. "Jerold was such a nice man. Said hello and would joke about my little bichon. Or ask if I'd won the lottery yet. He tole me I should enter Mrs. Senior America." She gave a little cackle.

After the cackle turned into a coughing spell that made her drink more of the water, she apologized and continued, "Now Jerold's brother, Edwin. He's a nice man, too. I switched to Edwin's pharmacy 'cause it's close by. I didn't have nothing against my old pharmacy, but I can take a bus to this one, it's just two stops down. Guess I need my meds changed, 'cause I've been taking a turn for the worse since. Old people don't like change, you know."

Drayco smiled. "Old is relative, and change can be overrated."

She reached over and patted his cheek. "Aren't you a dear boy." She smiled sadly. "Poor Jerold. Used to joke about my chewing tobacco, too. Gave him some to try. But he started gagging, and his nose turned red like one of those cartoon characters with steam coming out their ears. Such a sensitive stomach he musta had."

"Did you witness any other arguments involving Jerold?"

"Not a peep out of him, ordinarily."

Drayco was glad to see Imogen had recovered the pink in her cheeks but was disappointed she didn't have anything newsworthy to tell them. He wasn't ready to give up. "Did you see anyone unusual or hear anything odd the night Jerold died?"

"The police asked me that, too. Unfortunately, that's my bingo night, you see. We have a bingo club here at the condo. In the rec room."

She frowned, her face pensive. "I forgot to ask the police something, though. That lottery thing never panned out. Sent in the money as I was told, but never got one whit back. It's been three months. You think I should call Canada?"

Sarg coughed, and Nelia's eyes widened.

Drayco asked, "How much money did you send?"

"Close to three thousand, as I recall. Put a money order in the mail, just like they told me to."

Right now, Drayco was betting he, Sarg, and Nelia were thinking the same thing. Getting Mrs. Layford back the money she'd been scammed out of could be next to impossible.

"Do you still have a copy of that lottery notice?"

She shook her head. "I hate clutter. I threw it away."

That would make it harder to track down, but he made a mental note to call a friend at the FTC, to at least add it to their database. There wasn't enough evidence for the FBI and the U.S. Postal Inspection Service to get involved. Canadian lotteries, Jamaican, Costa Rica, Nigeria ... the victims of the fake schemes had been scammed out of billions over the past couple years alone.

The trio walked with the elderly woman back to her condo to make sure she got in safely. Then Nelia took leave of the two men to head for a study group session, but not before she aimed one parting shot in their direction. "Her story reminds me of a man who scammed elderly women out of home repairs on the Eastern Shore. The sheriff nabbed him, thankfully. Sleazebags. Castration's too good for them."

Sarg watched her drive off. "Remind me not to get on her bad side."

Drayco didn't have a chance to add just how fierce she could be because his cell rang. It was Benny Baskin with another update, bless his overworked hide—Drayco had found out after the fact the attorney already had a couple of other high-profile cases when he agreed to defend Maura.

He listened to Benny's news and replied, "You sure? Good work. And thanks, Benny."

After hanging up, he explained to Sarg, "Benny learned Jerold's Will left everything to Ashley. All two million dollars of it, spread out over several bank accounts. If he lost everything via 'bad investments' as she said, where did all that money come from?"

"Do tell," Sarg rubbed his hands together. "Sounds like it's time to interrogate the newly rich estranged daughter again, don't you think?"

"I'll arrange it." Drayco looked back at Mrs. Layford's condo. She waved at him through the window. The FTC guys had heard countless stories like Imogen's lottery fraud before, but it was still worth a try.

17

"Halabi's not budging from his belief your mother killed Jerold?" Sarg's hand hovered over the door handle to Kicks and Sticks, where Ashley had agreed to meet them. "Despite the fact Ashley hated him and just inherited a cool couple mill?"

Drayco shook his head. "Not according to Benny's sources."

As they entered the studio, Drayco pointed out the weapons display to Sarg, who gave a low whistle. "Those could do a world of hurt."

They stopped to watch Gogo wrapping up a session, then followed a staffer to the same room where Drayco met Gogo and Lauralee the other day. Like Lauralee with her cigarettes, Ashley seemed equally determined to flout the fitness discipline in the place, polishing off a candy bar with a gulp from a sugary soda.

Gogo followed on the heels of Sarg and Drayco and took a chair next to Ashley as he used a towel to wipe the sweat from his face. "I just saw you two days ago, Mr. Drayco. What is it this time?" He wasn't the least bit out of breath.

Drayco introduced Sarg, then replied, "Jerold Zamorra's Will. Which I understand was read to Ashley yesterday. She told us her father squandered his money, yet he left her a little over two million dollars."

Gogo didn't let Ashley answer. "So? Maybe he stole something and sold it. Maybe he finally found a winning stock market formula. Ashley told you she and her father weren't exactly on speaking terms. She wouldn't know how much money he had."

Sarg asked her, "Is that true, Miss Zamorra?"

She crossed her legs and propped the soda bottle on top of her knee. Her foot jiggled back and forth making the liquid in the bottle slosh around. She didn't seem to notice. "That Will must be old. My father invested all the money he got after my mother's death into stocks. Lost a lot of it. Hell, I thought he'd lost all of it. And besides, even if he did have money stashed away, I'll never see a penny of it. The creditors will snatch it."

Sarg pulled out his notebook. "That inheritance from your mother—where did she get her money?"

"My mother's business was good. She knew my father wasn't Mr. Financial Guru, so she also took out a term life insurance policy. In case something happened to her. Well, something did happen to her, didn't it? He killed her."

"About that life insurance policy and the rest of her inheritance— if she was afraid of Jerold, why leave him two-thirds? Why not bequeath it all to you, Miss Zamorra?"

Ashley hesitated. "I never said she was afraid of him." She glanced sideways at Gogo. "And for all his faults, he could be charming. Persuasive. He had her fooled."

"Had us all fooled," Gogo said to Sarg, staring at the little notebook where Sarg was taking notes. "Ashley trusted Jerold, too. He invested Ashley's share of the money she inherited from her mother for her. Gone, just like his."

Drayco studied Ashley, her quivering lip, the jiggling foot. She hadn't been this nervous last time he spoke with her. "You knew your father was bad with money. If you also believed he murdered your mother, why entrust your money to him to invest?"

"Guess there was part of me that still thought of him as Daddy." The quiver increased. "Sure looks like I inherited his bad-money-sense gene, doesn't it?" She uttered a harsh, brown-forked laugh that made Drayco wince and seemed to surprise even Gogo.

Sarg moved closer to the younger man so that he was staring down at him. "You had no idea Ashley stood to inherit that much money?"

Gogo whipped the towel off his neck and matched Sarg's stare with one of his own. "I know that game, what you're implying. That I want to marry Ashley for her money or would kill Jerold for it. If you think that, you're as insane as Jerold was."

Ashley's quivering lips formed a slight smile as she turned to Gogo. "Marry? But your parents want you to find a nice Chinese girl."

"I don't give a shit what they say. Or what the police say. Doting, honorable Asian son, my ass. No one tells me what to do."

Sarg quipped, "From the looks of those nasty-looking blades out front, I can see why."

"And no one's accusing anyone right now," Drayco added. "As I mentioned earlier, the police don't have you as suspects, and we're just shooting for the truth."

Gogo was still frowning as he reached over to squeeze Ashley's hand. "That woman they arrested for the murder? You said the police are certain she did it. Don't blame Ashley. Blame that bitch."

Sarg looked over at Drayco and said quietly. "If she's guilty, then she'll stay behind bars."

Gogo added, "And frying, too. I mean Virginia has the death penalty, right?"

Drayco tried to keep his face neutral, but Gogo was correct. The state also held the dubious honor of executing the highest percentage of death row inmates, something he didn't want to dwell on. After years of picturing his mother dead, he'd hate to see her die that way.

He forced his attention back to his current companions. Perhaps it was Ashley, operating alone or with Gogo, who made the decision to carry out their own form of execution?

Gogo's cellphone chirped with the same "Kung Fu Fighting" ringtone Drayco had heard on his first meeting with the young man. Gogo hopped up and went out into the hallway to take the call. This time, he didn't bother to lower his voice, mentioning Lauralee by name. As it became clear that's who was on the other end, it was equally clear both of them were upset.

Drayco gleaned a few details, the words "arrested," "police," and "bail" catching his attention.

Gogo hung up, stalked back into the room, and threw the phone down on his chair. "Goddamn it. Lauralee got picked up for shoplifting. She needs bail and a ride home. But I've got another class in ten minutes."

He glanced at Ashley, but she shook her head and said, "And I've got to get to work by three o'clock. Inheritance money or no, I can't afford to get fired."

Gogo pulled some bills out of his pocket and counted them, then thrust them at Sarg. "You're cops, right? She's at the Arlington Detention Center."

Drayco looked at Sarg, who shrugged and then grabbed the bills from Gogo. Time to do their impression of bail bondsmen.

∂ ∂ ∂

Drayco entered the Arlington Detention Center, this time with Sarg along for the ride. That fact came in handy when Drayco spied Detective John Halabi and sent Sarg along with the money to bail out Lauralee.

Sarg didn't seem too upset to be dispatched solo. As Drayco watched him vanish around the corner, it struck home how close in age Lauralee and Sarg's daughter Tara were. Where was Lauralee's father right now? Why hadn't she called him instead of Gogo?

Detective Halabi's narrowed eyes and scowl showed how he felt about seeing Drayco. Halabi motioned for him to follow as they headed into an empty interrogation room where he closed the door.

"You've been talking to people. Asking questions."

"A few. Enough to discover there are plenty of motives and shaky alibis going around." Drayco didn't sit down. Neither did Halabi.

"I thought we were clear on that issue. I realize this is your mother, but I shouldn't have to remind you that interfering with a police investigation is a crime."

"Did you get the autopsy results?"

"Now there you go asking *me* questions. Again." Halabi sighed. "Benny Baskin will get hold of that info, anyway. The M.E. found four stab wounds to Zamorra's chest, plus the dent in his head that matches the shape of the base of the cabinets. He was stabbed and fell, unconscious. Probably died within a couple minutes."

"All four stab wounds made by the same knife?"

Halabi paused. "Apparently. Three were deep. One more shallow. The shallow one had less bleeding and—"

"It means Maura McCune's story could be true."

"Or she stabbed him a fourth time after he was dead. Doesn't prove a damn thing."

Drayco walked over to a dark window he guessed led to an observation point on the other side. Was someone watching them right now? "What about Ophelia Zamorra's killers? You said it was allegedly a random attack?"

Halabi scratched the back of his head. "Don't see how that's related to the McCune case. But yeah, the sixteen-year-old punks were caught on camera at two other robberies using stolen ATM cards. Good thing criminals are morons."

"Were they also caught on security cameras at the bank where Ophelia Zamorra was murdered?"

"An hour before, according to the M.E.'s time of death."

"They used a stolen ATM card, left, and then returned later and decided to kill someone? Why?"

"Who knows? Maybe they dropped something and came back to get it. Saw an opportunity and took it. If you want to read the novel, go bother the Falls Church PD."

Drayco ran his finger along the top of one of the chairs. Cold, hard steel—like Halabi's face right now. "And these 'punks' weren't caught on camera in the act of murdering Ophelia?"

"She was slain outside the camera's range." Halabi bent over to place his hands on the table. "What does it matter to you?"

"That camera business is awfully convenient. Did these two suspects admit to murdering Ophelia?"

"Why would they? Less damning proof, smaller sentence."

"How was she killed?"

"Hit over the head with an ordinary baseball bat left at the scene."

"Prints?"

"None."

"Anything else unusual about her murder? Something that doesn't fit?"

Halabi pulled himself up to his full five-eleven and folded his arms across his chest. "As I said, go read the novel. But if you must know, they crammed the victim's debit card down her throat."

Drayco leaned against the wall as he weighed that bizarre detail. Not that he liked second-guessing police officers, but overworked cops plus overzealous prosecutors often added up to mistakes. "Did the suspects wear gloves in those other two robberies? The ones caught on camera?"

"Noooo. But they could have this one time. Got the idea from old *Law and Order* episodes or some other TV show."

"Let me get this straight. Someone wearing gloves brings a bat with them to a bank, waits for the victim, bashes the victim over the head, steals her money, and then crams the ATM card down her throat. That's a pretty big M.O. change for our two young 'moron' thugs. Seems much more like a copycat and premeditation, not random."

"Still—"

"Plus, seems like the killer planned the attack specifically to stay out of range of the security cameras. What did her autopsy reveal?"

"Cause of death was blunt force trauma. Plus asphyxiation—the killer inserted the card while the victim was still alive."

Drayco pictured the crime scene in his head. Did the killer know Ophelia was alive at that point? If so, the card was what—malice? A statement? Torture for the fun of it? "Did you ask Maura McCune if she had an alibi for that night?"

"You kidding? She refuses to tell us anything about where she's been for the last thirty years, let alone one itsy bitsy night."

Halabi moved toward the door and held it open. "Look, I can't order you not to talk to people. Note that I said talk, not interrogate and not harass. If you come across something, anything, I expect you to let me know. I can still charge you with impeding an investigation."

Drayco fingered the key in his pocket from Jerold Zamorra's fish tank. "If I come across anything important."

Halabi's brow was a furrowed field of suspicion, but he waved Drayco on.

When Drayco located Sarg, he wasn't surprised to see Sarg was successful in helping Lauralee get released on bail. Luckily for her, the watch she stole was under two hundred dollars and "only" a misdemeanor in Virginia. If it were her first offense, Lauralee could probably plead guilty in exchange for restitution and community service.

They decided to buy her a drink before dropping her off at her room at Ashley's house. They grabbed a table at Northside Social and let her get settled with her Masala chai latte and cheddar chive scone. The aroma of freshly roasted coffee mingling with fresh-baked bread made for an olfactory orgasm.

After a few tentative bites, she wolfed down the scone and made quick work of the latte. Drayco took note of her appetite, coupled with her waif-like frame—despite her penchant for high fashion, it was clear she wasn't spending much money on food.

She took one last bite, then spied a crumb on the table, picked it up and swallowed that, too. "If this gets back to my parents, they're going to kill me. You don't have to tell them since I'm an adult, right?"

Drayco shook his head, and her shoulders relaxed. "My parents adopted me when I was a baby. They took good care of me. Well, physically. They're very strict. It's an Apostolic church thing."

She gave a short laugh, then reached into her purse to pull out the tube of coconut-scented lip balm, making liberal use of it. "They disapprove of everything I do, even the string quartet because it's not church music. Too frivolous. Loathe the way I dress. And the cigarettes? I'm going straight to hell."

Sarg got up to get her a refill of her latte, leaving Lauralee alone with Drayco. He asked, "What kind of watch did you shoplift?"

"What kind of watch? Oh, it's rose-colored gold. At Nordstrom's. Starving musicians can't buy stuff like that. Oh, Gawd, if Gogo knows, Ashley does, too."

As she said Ashley's name, a smile played about her lips, and she fiddled with the necklace around her neck. The necklace was also rose-colored gold, with what looked like a small ruby pendant. Maybe that watch wasn't the only thing Lauralee had filched.

Her little smile made him remember her comment to Gogo at Kicks and Sticks, about not liking testosterone types. More like male types in general—Lauralee had a crush on Ashley, or maybe more than a crush.

Sarg returned with the latte which she accepted and started sipping immediately. When the lid popped off, causing some of the liquid to spill onto the table, she said "Damn," and almost looked like she was going to lick the table. Sarg pushed over a napkin and gave Drayco a fleeting "WTF" look before asking, "Miss Fremont, how well do you know Gogo and Ashley?"

"How well do I know Gogo and Ashley?" She had a habit of repeating what someone said and then answering as if she wasn't sure what she'd heard. Or was buying some time.

Maybe a little shock therapy would take care of that. Drayco asked, "Could they be capable of murder? They both hated Jerold and had reason to want him gone, permanently."

She put the unfinished drink down, her eyes flashing with a spark he hadn't seen before. "Ashley wouldn't. She couldn't."

"And Gogo?"

She licked her lips and looked at the door as if she wanted to bolt. "Why are you asking me this? They know who did it. Look, I'm grateful you bailed me out and all, but I don't feel comfortable answering these questions."

"You like Gogo, don't you?"

"Do I like Gogo?" She hesitated. "He's a skilled musician. And good at that whole martial arts stuff. I mean, we all have our faults. I smoke, he gambles, whatever."

Her comment reinforced the betting slips Drayco had seen on Gogo's music stand. "Did Gogo owe Jerold money? For his gambling habit?"

"Maybe. I don't know. Everybody's been acting weird lately. Must be something in the air." With the excuse of having to "recycle some latte," she headed for the bathroom.

Sarg waited until she disappeared. "Gambling? Those betting slips you told me about?"

"Killing someone you owed a lot of money is one sure-fire way to clear the books."

Drayco filled Sarg in about his hypothesis about Lauralee's crush on Ashley, which Sarg mulled it over. "If she told Jerold, I'll bet that went over well. I mean, if Jerold didn't want an Asian son-in-law, don't think he'd appreciate a woman hitting on his daughter. But would Lauralee have killed him over that?"

Drayco leaned back in his seat. "Maybe. Then there's her five-fingered discounts. Could indicate a pattern. She says she has no money, yet all her clothes look new and expensive. Maybe she stole something from Jerold and was discovered."

He sighed. "What is it with women and fashion? I guess pink-gold's one of the hot crazes right now. First Rena's watch, now Lauralee's."

"It's like those Caveman Ugly boots all the women drool over. Tara had a pair. I asked her why the hell she'd want something that looked like kids made it at a summer camp."

"The soul of tact, you are."

Sarg grinned, patted his pocket, and took out the little notebook. "By the way, I checked those lottery ticket numbers. The ones from Jerold's condo."

"Didn't win, did they?"

"You already looked? Should have known, Mr. Eidetic Memory. I guess it was an inside joke of Jerold's, after all."

"Possibly. Although did you notice how few tchotchkes he had lying around? Each one should carry more emotional weight, wouldn't you say?"

"Touché." Sarg gave a longing look over at the pastry counter. "After we drop Lauralee off and I return to my Quanticube, what's on your agenda the rest of this lovely day?"

"Got a meeting with Benny. We have to go over the upcoming hearing."

Sarg and Drayco both stood at the same time, but Sarg placed a hand on Drayco's shoulder, holding him back. "About that hearing thing. We've never really discussed it—Gilbow's shooting. Self-defense, mercy killing, whatever it was. Just want you to know you did the right thing."

Drayco smiled. "Thanks." Having Sarg and Nelia's vote of confidence meant more to him than anything the review board could say. Technically, he hadn't quite gotten Nelia's yet, but her visit to his townhome the other day spoke volumes.

What he didn't tell Sarg was that the nightmares he'd had over the past several months of shooting the burning man in the warehouse were morphing into ones starring a middle-aged woman with graying auburn hair—as she stabbed Jerold Zamorra, over and over, while mystery man Iago stood by and laughed.

18

Iago narrowed his eyes as he caught sight of his target in the dim light of a near-dead street lamp. He'd tailed him for blocks, through some of the back alleyways of Logan Circle. He thought he'd lost the guy until the other man ducked down a half-flight of stairs, disappearing into a basement garage. Perfect. Iago followed him into the space.

Ulysses Porro was not a particularly well-suited name for a bookie. As far as Iago knew, the only heroic act this Ulysses had taken was beating the spread on a longshot NFL team. The man didn't even look the part dressed in a pair of brown polyester pants and a tan shirt from Discount Whatever that sported a mustard stain on the pocket.

Ulysses' eye twitch went into overdrive when he spied Iago. "I'd remember your face if I'd seed it afore, and I ain't, that's a fact. If it's money you be after, you got the wrong guy. Must be some other poor schlub. You can scuttle right back out the way you come."

Iago stepped closer. Twitch-twitch-twitch-twitch. It was like watching a pair of caution flags flapping in the breeze. "Not here about any bets."

"There, ya see? Wrong place, wrong guy."

"Right place, right guy. Or so says a good source who pegged you at the Glencroft Shores condos in Arlington. Night of February thirteenth."

"Glencroft Shores? Arlington? Not my usual stomping grounds. I got no reason to be there, then or now."

"My source says you were. And that you saw something and phoned it into the police. In disguise."

"Police? Now, why would I do that?"

"Maybe because you knew the guy who'd just been whacked. Jerold Zamorra. Name ring a bell?" Iago took a step closer, within inches of Ulysses.

The guy didn't back up, to his credit. But Iago was pretty certain from the smell coming from those brown polyester pants that Ulysses wasn't as tough as he wanted Iago to think. "Zamorra? I don't know. Maybe."

"Let me give you a refresher. You handled some bets for Jerold Zamorra. Several bets, as a matter of fact. Dating back a year or two."

Ulysses licked his lips. "Now you mention it. Yeah. Guess I might've. The guy was a true addict, you know? The kind that's easy to suck dry. But I don't know nothing about no murder."

"Funny, that. Because my source swears he saw you in that area that night."

"So what if I was? I'm a businessman. And it's a free country." Ulysses uttered a horsey laugh. Iago didn't join in.

With one swipe of his big paw, Iago grabbed the other man by the throat and lifted him high into the air. Ulysses gurgled and coughed, the spittle dribbling down his jaw. After thirty seconds, Iago let him go, and the man sagged against the concrete wall behind him.

"One more time. You sure you didn't call the police that night? You sure you didn't see who killed Jerold Zamorra as they left his condo?"

Ulysses' hoarse voice replied, "I didn't see nobody. Honest."

Iago frowned. His source was usually correct. But if Ulysses was seen near the area of Jerold's condo, then the source hadn't been entirely wrong. "Were you there taking bets with Jerold earlier that night? Is that why you were there?"

Ulysses nodded and croaked out, "An addict, I tell you."

"And you didn't see anyone else there? Before or after?"

Ulysses shook his head.

Well, that was that. Another dead end. Time to give his new "friend" a little extra incentive not to mention Iago's visit to anyone. "Okay, then. Just remember one thing—I was never here." Iago whipped behind Ulysses, circled his arms around the man's trachea, and squeezed both sides of his neck.

Ulysses did his impression of mercury on a cold day and dropped, all the way to the ground. Iago took the opportunity to stroll out of the basement, back up to the alleyway above. The guy would only be out for maybe thirty seconds, sixty tops. No need to hang around any longer than necessary.

It took a bit over twenty minutes to walk back to his car, and once inside, Iago dialed up his employer. "It was a bust. The so-called witness didn't see anything. He just happened to be there earlier handling some bets for Jerold, but that was the extent of his involvement in the murder."

The baritone voice on the other end said, "You didn't kill him, did you?"

"When was the last time I did that? Besides, you said to keep a low profile."

"And I trust you will take that command to heart. Making yourself a target of the police won't help Maura. You would do well to remember that."

"You wound me. You know no one wants her freed more than I do."

There was a long pause on the other end. "We all want this nonsense behind us."

"And Drayco?"

"Which one?"

"The younger."

"Keep a close eye on him, as usual. If my instincts are correct, he'll be our best hope of success."

"You that sure he won't spend all his time trying to nail Maura?"

"His father might. But our young detective, I believe, is on our side."

"And if it turns out he isn't?"

Another long pause. "We'll deal with that if and when it happens. Keep me posted."

After they had hung up, Iago pulled a photo out of his wallet and rubbed his finger over the picture of the woman with the graying red hair. He didn't relish the idea of harming her son. Still, if it came down to a choice ... He replaced the photo and drove off.

19

Monday, February 18

Drayco yawned and looked at an online cookbook. Who knew there were so many types of omelets? Spanish, Japanese, Dutch, French, Southwestern. He found his target, a recipe for a tarragon omelet, but his hopes of making one to shock the hell out of Sarg were cooked as soon as he read the instructions. He flipped off the monitor. McBreakfast to the rescue.

The meeting with Benny last evening had turned out to be more of the same rah-rah legal coaching session. But despite Benny's outward show of confidence, Drayco had known Benny long enough to sense the attorney was worried and not just about the upcoming board hearing. Benny's first meeting with Maura McCune was about as enlightening as Drayco's. She was angry; she didn't kill him. No info on why she was there or why she was upset with Jerold.

Benny was already considering a plea of involuntary manslaughter. More than ever before, Benny was counting on Drayco's ability to hunt down witnesses, evidence, anything he could use to defend his client.

After dropping some melatonin last night, Drayco felt a little better rested this morning. He briefly entertained the idea of stopping by O'Greavy's for one of their gourmet omelets as a substitute brag fodder for Sarg the next time he saw him, but he didn't have the stomach for it. He couldn't remember the last time he was truly hungry.

After his drive-through breakfast, he headed to the Rebekah Hasendahl House, one of the oldest buildings still standing in Fairfax County. The original log-cabin school, later remodeled and expanded, now served as a shelter for battered women.

It was also, as he'd learned, Ashley Zamorra's "day job." For once, he wanted to get Ashley alone, apart from Edwin or Gogo. Of all the possible suspects so far, she alone had the strongest motive and greatest access to her murdered father.

She was surprised to see him but welcomed him in. He'd only taken a few steps inside the place when someone lunged at him from the left. His instincts kicking in, he twisted away to the other side, and that's when he saw he was facing a woman holding a kitchen knife. Her voice was as cold as the Potomac waters in February. "I told you I'd cut you if I ever saw you again."

Before he could react a second time, Ashley slid in front of him, putting herself between him and the woman. She said slowly and calmly, "Belinda, this is Mr. Scott Drayco." She sounded out his name again, slower this time. "Scott Drayco. This isn't Tomás. Mr. Drayco is our guest, and he won't hurt you."

Belinda blinked her eyes, lowered the knife to her side and whispered, "Sorry. So sorry." Dropping the knife, she ran off toward the back. Ashley nodded at another staffer who retrieved the knife and hurried after Belinda.

Ashley ushered Drayco into a small side room with soothingly bland, blue walls where they could talk in private. "Belinda ran away from home when she was twelve. It's been one abuser after another, although Tomás was the worst. Guess you reminded her of him. That's the thing about sexual violence. Never leaves you alone as long as you live."

Drayco nodded. He'd seen it all too well in other people before. He looked around, taking note of the frayed edges of the camel-tan carpet and the cracked window blind. Funds for the shelter must be tight.

Ashley settled into a brown metal folding chair that squeaked when she sat down, and he sat across from her. She wore the same neon-red lipstick as when he last saw her and the same earrings that he could now tell were astrology symbols. Scorpio, to be exact—the scorpion.

She studied him with a look of suspicion in her eyes. "Why are you here? Uncle Edwin and I told you everything we know."

"I just had a few more questions."

"Couldn't it have waited until after work? Belinda was doing so much better, and I hope her little relapse won't set her back."

"If you'd like me to meet you later—"

"You're already here. We'll just have to make the best of it." She fiddled with the ends of her French-braided hair. "Although this will have to serve as my break."

He softened his tone. "I apologize for the interruption. How long have you worked here?"

"Only a year, but I enjoy it. Most of the time. I feel like I'm helping these women, if in a small way." Her voice grew quieter. "Guess personal experience helps."

Personal experience. Now that was unexpected. "Are you referring to Gogo or did your father abuse you?"

She inhaled a sharp breath. "Gogo? Despite the martial arts thing, he's a teddy bear. No, it was my ex. And my father never hit me. He did hit my mother, but she could give as well as she got. I grew up in a very dramatic family, Mr. Drayco."

"You indicated you were close to your mother, isn't that correct?"

She bit her lip. "I miss her every day. She wasn't just my Mom, we were best friends."

Maybe it meant more to daughters to have a mother they could count on. Drayco thought of the photos in Edwin's home of mother and daughter together, laughing. Right next to the photos of Edwin and Ashley's mother standing so close—intimately close—together.

He almost hated to ask, but he had to know. "Ashley, was your mother in love with your Uncle Edwin?"

She stared at the camel carpet for a few moments without replying. She didn't raise her head when she finally said, "I often think how different it would have been if she'd married him instead of Dad. They both pursued her, but Dad won."

When she looked up at Drayco, her eyes were soft with pain. "I admit I wondered, more than once, if Uncle Edwin and Mom had an affair. Maybe part of Mom's constant fighting with Dad was because she'd realized she made a mistake. Should have married Uncle Edwin."

Drayco studied Ashley, comparing her to Jerold and Edwin. The brothers shared a strong family resemblance, so it wasn't easy just by looking to tell if Ashley was Jerold's daughter or Edwin's. But it would explain why Edwin was protective of her.

"What can you tell me about your parents and their habits or routines? Or even hobbies."

She shook her head. "I don't understand why you'd ask about that. What does this have to do with that woman they arrested?"

"Sometimes connecting the dots takes you into some strange territory. Motives aren't always straight-forward."

She sighed. "Well, they were pretty boring. At least, to me. Mom was kinda OCD about her business. Spent long hours on it. Lots of satisfied customers." Drayco knew this himself, having checked with some of her former clients and consumer complaint agencies last evening.

"Dad had his quartet, as you know. He also liked to play golf at the East Potomac Park course. He was bitter he wasn't a high enough mucky muck to bypass the long waiting list at the Washington Golf and Country Club."

"Do you recall your mother's behavior changing at all before her murder?"

Ashley blinked her eyes several times and got up to grab a tissue from a box on a counter. "Sorry. It's bad enough to remember she's dead. But thinking about how she died ..." She dabbed at her eyes and clutched the tissue in her hands. "She seemed normal to me. Happier, even, after she got divorced from Dad."

"Was your father happier, too? You said you thought he cheated on your mother. Maybe he was in a new relationship with his affair partner or someone else."

"As I said, I hadn't seen him in a year or so. Just to take over his things that one day."

A young woman dressed in faded jeans and a red sweater two sizes too big for her opened the door and stepped a foot in. "Everything okay, Miss Ashley?"

Tendrils of the woman's dark hair fell in curtains across the right side of her face but couldn't completely hide the yellow-green-purple skin peeking through. She glared at Drayco.

"I'm fine, Tanya. Just chatting with a friend."

The woman huffed but withdrew and closed the door.

"Most of the women here, like Tanya, are victims of domestic violence. They're understandably suspicious of men. One reason we don't allow many men in here."

"I'm sorry. I didn't want to upset your residents." He thought of Rena Quentin and her sexual harassment case and how much difference money and clout can make.

"It's why I brought you in here where we could be out of sight."

"Nor did I want to upset you. I have a feeling Gogo would have something to say about that—he seems very protective of you."

She sat in silence before adding slowly, "Gogo and me, we have our ups and downs. Nothing major, mostly lots of little things. He loves to haunt all those tacky dollar stores run by Chinese in strip malls. You know, the ones filled with cheap, flimsy trinkets. And I hate Chinese food. Tried to get him to go vegan like me, but he's into all that animal protein stuff for his training, whey, egg, even fish protein. But I love him."

"It seems mutual."

She gave him the first smile he'd seen from her. "Now, if we can get his parents on board, we'll be all set. First, my parents were against him, then his parents against me. It's so twentieth century."

"I knew your father disapproved, but your mother too?"

"My father wasn't the one who disapproved that much of Gogo. Well, he did at first. Before he got to know him better in the quartet. They didn't get along, but it wasn't that. Mom was dead set against us dating."

"Did she give any reason?"

"Not really. Just protective, I guess. He's eight years older than me." She rubbed her forehead. "The ironic thing is I never told her I'd married once before. One of those quickie Vegas weddings to a man twenty years older. The day after our 'honeymoon,' he started hitting me. And come to find out he was already married but hadn't bothered to get a divorce."

"You got it annulled?"

"Faster than you can say fraud." Ashley clutched the crumpled tissue in her hand even tighter.

"Why didn't you tell your parents?"

"The same reason you didn't tell your parents about every stupid thing you did."

Drayco had to agree with her there. A guilt sandwich wrapped in shame washed down by a lecture. Not exactly a happy meal. "Sounds like your parents cared. That's a lot rarer than you'd think."

He got up to get her another tissue. "I need to ask you more about the days before your mother's death. Did she seem afraid or mention any stalkers? Or perhaps she had problems with one of her customers?"

"Zilch on all counts. That's why I know my father killed her. Who else hated her that much?"

"The police think it was a random robbery."

"You don't?"

"Maybe. I don't think your father's murder was random, however. It was someone with an ax to grind. Or who stood to gain from his death."

"You still think I killed him? For his money?"

He took a deep breath and chose his words carefully. "I believe you hated him. But if everyone killed the people they hated, half the population on the planet would die each year."

"Meaning you haven't decided yet."

Score one for Ashley being smarter and more perceptive than he'd first thought. It was a reminder he had to push past any feelings of sympathy for her and remain objective—cold, calculating killers were often terrific actors.

Still, without knowing more about his own mother's past, Ashley's motivations might pale in comparison with Maura's. It was time he did something about that knowledge gap.

20

After checking on the Generic Silver Camry he kept in the garage beneath the small and woefully overpriced office he rented near Capitol Hill, Drayco hunched over his laptop. His initial efforts after he first talked to his mother hadn't been of much use, but in the time since, new possibilities had percolated through to his conscious mind. He drilled down into the internet's labyrinth, trying the dozens of databases he had access to, then started tunneling through more obscure websites.

The white and mostly bare walls surrounding him weren't much of an inspiration. The framed degrees, especially the criminology doctorate, even seemed to be mocking him. Maybe he needed to get a potted plant.

He started with "Brisbane," the name found with Maura at the time of her arrest. Through Benny and other sources, he'd learned Halabi and company had struck out with their Australian line of investigation. But Brisbane, the city, was named after Sir Thomas Brisbane, a Scotsman. Brisbane was a Scottish surname going back to at least the thirteenth century. And Maura was allegedly Scottish. Or so she'd told Brock.

He pored over birth and death records, police records, newspaper articles. There were a lot of accounts of noble, law-abiding Brisbanes, but the skeletons in the family tree interested him more. One branch seemed to follow a gypsy-esque lifestyle, not true Roma people but never settling down. There was very little information about them. Ghost people.

It was in this line where he came across a link to a Maura Brisbane, born at a time that would make her a contemporary of his mother's. It was just one tiny mention, and it referenced a fraternal twin brother, Alistair. If this were the same woman, now he knew where he and Casey got the twin gene. And it also meant he had an uncle he'd never known—unless the man was dead.

Drayco didn't find immigration records for Maura, but he did see a brief record for Alistair, who'd moved to the U.S. thirty-six years ago. That would be the same time Maura McCune allegedly did, marrying Brock a year later.

Drayco next researched Alistair Brisbane, who appeared to be very much alive, if the same man. Of Alistair's time in the U.S., there was one brief news item about him and his role as a power broker, but that was from over a decade ago. The man apparently liked to keep a low profile. Nevertheless, his name popped up once or twice in the same paragraph as a senator or lobbyist or judge.

No arrests or blots on his record as near as Drayco could tell. Or much of anything in any record, for that matter. He'd have to get Sarg to run his name through the FBI databases, but it looked like invisibility was the man's specialty.

He came across only one photo of Brisbane, and it was blurred, with Brisbane half-hidden behind a congressman from New York. Despite the poor quality and the fact its subject was fifteen years younger at the time, Drayco could see traces of Maura in Alistair. He'd also seen this man before—it was the same mystery man who'd stared at him in the Mayflower Hotel's cafe.

≈ ≈ ≈

Blades of the late-afternoon sun managed to stab through the cloud layers as Drayco stood outside a small duplex, one unit painted white, the other gray. Nice and neutral. As if the building were shrinking back from the road in hopes no one would notice it.

Being midafternoon, the occupants of the white half appeared to be away. Since the duplex sat at the end of a side street with homes spaced relatively far apart, he figured picking the door lock to the gray side's door would go unnoticed.

Thanks to Benny, Drayco had gotten a peek at the list of tenants the police compiled of homes, apartments, and condos within a few miles of Jerold's place, hoping to find where Maura McCune had been staying. What they hadn't noticed, but he had, was that the gray duplex was rented under the name of Isolde Ian—a combination of Casey's middle name and Drayco's middle name. After chatting up the landlord and learning "Isolde Ian" paid her rent in cash, Drayco figured he had a winner.

His conscience pricked him a little as he pictured Sarg's disapproving look, but at least he'd brought along nitrile gloves. He slipped them on.

Essentially a one-bedroom apartment, it didn't take long for him to conduct a sweep of the place. Making it even easier was the lack of belongings, something you'd expect from living the gypsy lifestyle. One lightweight suitcase lay in the bottom of the bedroom closet, with conservative, nondescript women's clothing hanging above. Even the one small trash can was empty.

No computer, no TV, no dishes other than paper plates and plastic ware. One small potted plant sat in the kitchen window, wilting from neglect. On an impulse, he picked it up and gave it some water from the sink. At least, there weren't any dead goldfish around.

He returned to the bedroom and sat on the bed close to the nightstand so he could open its lone drawer. Inside were four driver's license IDs from different states with different names beside her photo. He made a note of each, knowing it was just a matter of time before Halabi and his people found this place. He'd do some checking on those IDs for his own edification and let Halabi waste his own time.

Next to the drivers' licenses sat a burner "dumb" phone, possibly the one she used to call Jerold. He checked recent calls and found Jerold's number, but no others. Either this was a new phone or Maura was careful to change out the SIM cards frequently. He'd love to pocket the phone and let the FBI techs dig into the SIM card, but decided to let the proper channels run their course.

The only other items inside the drawer, beside some receipts for food and cleaning supplies, were two decks of Tarot cards and the sole piece of jewelry around, a necklace with a half-heart pendant that had PAH engraved on it. Risking more of Halabi's wrath, he slipped that item into his pocket. Act now, apologize later.

An invisible woman, an anonymous life. No roots, no identity, no real existence. Thirty years since she left her family, and this was all she had? Or perhaps she had a storage unit somewhere, also paid for in cash.

He scanned the receipts again. The receipts went back almost two years—living in the area for two years, and she never tried to contact him? Had he passed by her on the street and didn't even know who she was?

A couple of poetry books graced the top of the nightstand, one by Robert Frost, one by E.E. Cummings. He checked the Frost book first. No notes, no inscriptions, no secret pieces of paper or numbers anywhere. He picked up the Cummings book, flipped through the contents and noted the poem "I Carry Your Heart With Me." Then he flipped to the front of the book and saw an inscription in all block letters, ICYHWM, the same as Iago's tattoo. The inscription was signed simply, "I."

21

They sat in the Range Rover in the dark, headlights off. Drayco looked over at Sarg. "You didn't have to come along."

"Just happened to be coming to town when I got your call. Dropped Elaine and a friend of hers off at the Ken Cen for one of those crappy musicals."

Drayco grinned. "This from a man who likes polka?"

"It's a cultural thing. With a small 'c.' You sure you got the right info from Gogo Cheng's phone call at his studio?"

Drayco pulled out the mini-flashlight he always carried in his pocket and flicked it on for a few seconds to look at his notes. "This is the date and time he mentioned. The place is a bit of a guess. The coded words he used on his end of the conversation fit a boat supply joint, and there aren't many of those around."

"And the betting slips you saw are his tickets to the wide world of illegal sports betting."

"Could be dangerous. Remember the task force that took down the multi-million dollar gambling op at the Eden Center a few years ago?"

"How could I forget? The Bureau was part of that one. Vietnamese gangs, as I recall. Don't know which are worse around here, them or MS13."

Drayco nodded at the back door. "Shall we go in?"

The cars lining the street around the boat supply building and the lights in the basement all but confirmed Drayco's theory, as did the unsmiling face of the man covered in tattoos who answered the door. Drayco couldn't tell if they were gang tattoos, but since this was a betting joint, he'd bet they were.

"You're not invited to this party," the man said, standing in the center of the doorway.

Drayco took advantage of his six-four height and got just close enough to tower over the man, his hands on his hips to show he wasn't holding any weapons. "Looking for Gogo Cheng," he said.

Tattoo Man's fierce stance wavered a fraction. "You cops?"

"He owes me money," Drayco replied. "And I need it. Now."

The other man nodded. "Yeah, we hear that a lot. I'll get him."

Through the door, Drayco could see TV monitors tuned to sporting events around the world. Ice hockey and basketball in the U.S., tennis in Mexico, horse racing in Australia, cycling in New Zealand, cricket in New Delhi. The interactive computer betting consoles were another tip this was not an amateur set-up.

When Gogo arrived at the door, shock didn't begin to describe the look on his face. He swallowed hard but said loud enough so Tattoo Man could hear, "I said I'd get you the money tomorrow. Couldn't it wait?" and he stepped outside and closed the door.

Drayco nodded at Sarg's car, and the trio climbed inside, Gogo and Drayco in the back, Sarg in the front. Drayco conducted a quick scan of Gogo's body and clothing, but he didn't appear to have any Eskrima weapons on him.

"It's not what you think." Gogo's voice ordinarily had green forks that stabbed at Drayco, but tonight those forks had hard black edges.

"Then, what is it, sir?" Sarg's own voice dripped with more sarcasm than usual.

Gogo's words came out in a rush. "Years ago, my parents gave me a painting of Chinese calligraphy. Some Song Dynasty thing. Been in our family for generations. I took it for granted, didn't realize its worth. Jerold Zamorra said he was having a big party and wondered if I would loan it to him. I said, sure, and didn't think anything of it. Until he didn't give it back."

His hands, balled into fists, pounded the seat. "Found out later he'd sold it to pay for his goddamn gambling debts. And that it was worth over fifty grand. Then I decided to find the painting by tracking down the buyer."

Drayco kept one eye on Gogo and another on a car parked near them until two people got in and left. "Do your parents know?"

"Hell no. That's why I've got to find that painting first. Then I won't have to tell them."

"Why not go to the police?"

"The police would want to talk to my parents. Then they'd find out."

Sarg spoke up from the driver's seat. "When was this alleged party of Jerold's?"

"About six months ago."

"So, Mr. Cheng, you're telling us you're just here to find out if any of these delightful, upstanding gentlemen know who Jerold sold that painting to, is that right?"

"I've been coming a couple times a month. Betting a little here and there. Just enough to gain their trust. That's all, I swear. I'm not rich, but I make enough from the studio and concerts."

"Don't forget Ashley's money, Mr. Cheng."

Gogo glared at Sarg's profile. "How many times do I have to tell you people I don't give a shit about her money? When I first started dating her, hell up until a few days ago, I thought she had less money than I do."

Drayco waited for another car to empty its passengers into the building. "I take it this sport betting operation moves around—thus the meeting details over the phone at Kicks and Sticks?"

"That's how you knew? Man, I thought you were psychic. Yeah, it moves every couple weeks."

"Did you find what you were looking for—the name of the person who bought your painting?"

Gogo sat straighter in his seat. "Sorta. Some guy called Marchand. Faust Marchand. But that's gotta be a fake name, right?"

Sarg wrote down the name in his notebook. "We'll check out your story. In the meantime, I'd strongly suggest you stay away from this group."

"Hell, if you can help me get back my painting, I'll do anything you say."

Drayco replied, "No promises, but we'll see what we can do." He added, "Does Ashley know about any of this?"

"Not the painting nor the gambling. I'd like it to stay that way."

Drayco put a hand on his shoulder. "Why don't you go home and tackle some Bach. Always clears my head."

Gogo took the hint and scrambled out the door. They watched as he went to his car, hopped in, and peeled away. Sarg put his index fingers to the sides of his head and said, "I have a feeling there's going to be a raid on that outfit very soon. I must be psychic."

Drayco switched out of the back seat into the front passenger side. "Then I hope Gogo takes our advice."

Sarg grunted. "Jerold swiping, then selling, a painting worth fifty grand—I've seen wimpier motives for murder. And despite what he says, I don't buy that whole 'I didn't know about Ashley's inheritance' bit."

Drayco said, "Hmm," as he drummed his fingers on the dashboard. "During my quick glance inside that joint, I didn't see many women. But there were a few."

"You're thinking Maura was involved in part of this? The gambling, the painting, both?"

"Iago said she and Jerold were business partners in something, but I don't know. Maybe I'm the one who's being played."

"Then they don't know betting against a Drayco is the definition of insanity." Sarg started up the engine. "What's up with that name he got, this Faust Marchand guy?"

"It may be a fake name someone gave Gogo, as he suspected. 'Marchand' is French for dealer or broker. And Faust—well, I guess when you play dice with this guy, you make a deal with the devil."

22

Drayco knew he wasn't alone the second he stepped inside his townhome. Every muscle in his body tensed as he looked around for signs of Iago. Or someone worse.

From the kitchen came sounds of the freezer door opening and ice cubes being dropped into a glass. Since most intruders wouldn't help themselves to his food supplies, he relaxed a bit as he headed to the kitchen. Maybe Darcie was back with more lasagna? And if she was wearing that red bow again ... He headed into the kitchen.

Brock straightened up and turned around so fast that he almost fell over. His tie was partially undone, his jacket and pants rumpled, and he squinted at Drayco through a half-sloshed fog. Drayco walked over to him and picked up the bottle of Scotch that was nearly full when Drayco left this morning.

Brock grabbed the bottle from him, tipped his glass in salute, and staggered to the sofa in the den. "Hate being on the receiving end of an interrogation. Halabi and his 'minions,'" Brock made quote marks in the air, "had me in for a couple hours today. Who, What, Where, Why, When, Which, Whatever."

"I thought they grilled you already. Unless this has to do with some kind of illegal scheme they uncovered?" He wasn't about to bring up Iago. Not yet.

"No, but it wouldn't surprise me one whit."

For one microsecond, Drayco entertained the idea Brock had him totally snowed all this time and was in cahoots with Maura, but a microsecond later dismissed the idea as preposterous. "I think this is the first time I've ever seen you drunk."

"Drunk? This is stewed. Rhymes with screwed. Next is smashed, rhymes with trashed. Then on to drunk. Drunk, drunk ... oh, yeah. Funk. Or Flunk." He took another sip. "Last time I was screwed-trashed-drunk was when *that woman* disappeared. Now she's back. You do the ..." He belched. "Math."

Brock sagged into the sofa as he balanced the Scotch in his hands. He sat there without saying anything or taking another drink for several moments. Finally, he said, "I lied."

Drayco had just decided to head to the kitchen and make some coffee, but Brock's words stopped him in mid-stride. "You lied to Halabi?"

"No." Brock sipped some of the Scotch and tilted his head to let the liquid trickle down the back of his throat. "To you."

"When? What about?"

"I had your mother declared legally dead to tie up all the legal mumbo jumbo. Closure. Hell, to me she *was* dead. Then I got a letter. When you were fifteen. From her."

"You sure it was from her?"

"Didn't have the handwriting analyzed, but didn't matter. I knew."

Drayco stood over his father, trying to rein in his anger. "Do you still have it?"

"Threw it away. But I 'member what it said. She knew she was declared legally dead. She wanted to stay that way as far as everyone was concerned. 'Specially you. Said it was for the best."

"Why didn't you tell me?"

"I agreed with her. Better she stay dead."

Screw the coffee. Drayco needed another bottle of Scotch all to himself. "Casting aside—for now—the million reasons you should have told me, why would she bother contacting you at all? What did she gain?"

"Hell if I know. Why'd she leave in the first place? Why'd she even marry me? What makes oranges orange and blueberries blue? Why are sofas so damn hard?" He pounded the one he was sitting on.

Brock's hand shook, and he dropped the drink on the table. Rivulets of Scotch flowed over the edge and onto the area rug. He said,

"I wish you better luck in prying anything out of her," then got up to rummage through Drayco's cabinets to get another drink while Drayco mopped up the spill.

Drayco called after him, "Don't you think you've had enough?"

Brock stopped making the drink, then lurched forward and stood close to Drayco. "I'll tell ya what I've had enough of. This." He gestured at the space between the two men. "This distance. It's always there. You. Me. An ocean between. The Arctic Ocean, with little icebergs circling around."

"And you blame me for that?"

"I blame the whole fuck-sucking universe for that."

"Let me guess. This is the point where you tell me I'm adopted."

"You may wish you were. Hell, I may wish you were, after all of this." Brock pushed on Drayco's chest. "We should duke it out. Right here and now."

He raised his other fist, but even though Brock was still fit and only a couple of inches shorter than his son, Drayco easily grabbed his father's hands to interrupt his half-hearted attack. "Some other day. With a boxing ring and gloves. Right now, we need to put you to bed."

Brock deflated faster than a child's balloon and allowed his son to cart him off to the guest bedroom. Brock mumbled, "Waste of your time and skills, this thing. Won't even get paid for it. Leave it alone."

Drayco managed to wrestle off Brock's shoes, jacket, and tie. Brock always wore ties. Maybe even to bed, for all Drayco knew. Drayco flipped off the light to the guest room. He wandered out to the den and sat in almost-silence as the faint snores from his father wafted out to him.

After Drayco's piano career was cut short, he'd always thought he chose to go into law enforcement due to his father's influence. Was it really that? Or had part of his subconscious dragged him into it because deep down, he never accepted his father's story of Maura just up and abandoning them without one word?

Maybe he blamed Brock but never admitted it to himself. For not going after her, for not trying to seek the truth. All part of the distance between them, and now, another lie. Lies on top of lies.

In the cosmic pool of irony, it would be fitting if this case destroyed the relationship he had with his father, even as he got reacquainted with his mother. Had everything in his life been one gargantuan, universe-sized lie?

The mostly empty bottle of Scotch stood on the table, but Drayco didn't make a move toward it. Despite himself, when the snoring from the guest bedroom stopped, he got up to make sure his father was still breathing. The snoring started up again, and suddenly tired beyond words, Drayco stumbled up the stairs to his own bedroom. Following his father's example, he fell onto the bed, clothes and all.

23

By six a.m., thousands of day laborers congregated in Home Depot and 7-11 parking lots spread throughout the metro area— hopeful penitents at the Feast of St. Paycheck waiting for a blessing. Wearing patched coats and shod in steel-toed construction boots, they scarfed down coffee, breakfast taquitos, and yellow and pink pan dulces while keeping an eye on every single vehicle passing by.

If the men were lucky, they'd get hired for the day at minimum wage and not be stiffed or become a victim of crime. When they swarmed around Drayco's car as he stopped to ask if they'd seen his quarry, he hated to disappoint them. But he got what he was seeking.

The man Drayco had tracked down was not likely to be a crime victim, more than able to hold his own. And thanks to another of the day laborers who'd been helpful—in exchange for a couple of Andrew Jacksons—Drayco now knew the man's full name.

Drayco spied his pray, a man dressed all in black. He rolled down his car window to motion for the man to come over. "Looking for a job? Hop in."

The man hesitated, then joined Drayco and immediately slid his seat all the way back. Drayco also had problems in cramped spaces with his long legs, but he wasn't six-eight. "Greetings, Iago Pryce. I could pay you for the day, but I have a feeling you don't need it."

Drayco pulled his Generic Silver Camry into a parking garage in Shirlington and turned off the engine. Iago crossed his arms over his wide chest, no small feat. "Howdja find me?"

"You dropped a bus ticket stub at my home. Plus, you had dirt under your fingernails like a workman and mud on your shoes despite the fact it hasn't rained in a week. You also had the distinct aroma of sewage cologne, so I looked at the bus line and scoped out day laborer spots near the water pollution control plant. A day laborer job is a perfect cover for someone who moves around a lot. And you do move around a lot, don't you? Following Maura McCune?"

Iago didn't reply, grabbing a handful of pepita seeds from his pocket and tossing them into his mouth.

"Has she been in the U.S. for the past thirty years or just the last two?"

Still munching on the seeds, Iago replied, "Like you said, moving around."

"And you follow her. Are you some kind of official bodyguard?"

Iago turned his head sharply. "How much do you know about her?"

"Not much, which is why I'm here. If you're supposed to be keeping Maura out of trouble, why don't you just go to the police and say—truthfully or not—Maura was with you and couldn't have committed the murder?"

Iago uttered a derisive laugh. "Even if it was true, I don't exist."

"That means you weren't with her that night. How can you be so certain she's not guilty?"

More silence, except for the sound of Iago's chewing.

"I'm guessing you have several identities like she does. Okay. What's with ICYHWM and E.E. Cummings?"

"You found her apartment." Iago picked at his nails, but it would take a lot more than that to get the dirt out. "I met her at a poetry slam, went for one date. She said she wasn't interested in pursuing anything. I followed her, found out what she does for a living, who she is."

"That's more than my father discovered."

"He doesn't care like I do."

Bodyguard or stalker, Iago still represented the first crack in the wall of mystery surrounding Drayco's mother. But he wanted more.

Much more. "Let's talk about what she does for a living. Petty theft, cons, fraud. Am I warm?"

"What difference does it make? Everybody gambles with something. It's all in the cards or numbers. Sometimes you win the lottery, sometimes you don't."

"It matters because you said Jerold was a 'colleague' of Maura's. And she was angry with him for two-timing her."

"Maybe they were partners, maybe they weren't. It's not relevant. She didn't kill him over it. Look, I'm your friend as long as you try to help her. But if you change your mind and try to prosecute her, you'll see me again, all right. But you don't want to see me again that way. Trust me."

Drayco ignored the threat. "Maura arrived in the U.S. about the same time as her twin brother Alistair, isn't that right?"

Iago pushed open the car door and stepped out, bending down so he could see Drayco, still inside. "Best you forget that name. Throwing it around can be bad for your health."

He didn't slam the door but shut it quietly and deliberately. By the time Drayco started his car and pulled out of the garage to follow, Iago was nowhere in sight.

So much for tailing the guy. Drayco had a pretty good idea Iago wouldn't return to this location and gave it his best shot, driving around for a half hour. No luck. Maybe he should have followed on foot, but if Iago hopped onto a bus, Drayco would have been spotted right away.

He wasn't surprised Iago would know about Alistair Brisbane, but did Brisbane know about him? Or about Maura, for that matter. Iago didn't fit the circle of powerful friends Drayco glimpsed from that one newspaper article. How did all the puzzle pieces fit together?

He pulled the car over to text a message to a friend he hadn't seen in a while. He needed answers, and he needed them soon. Taking into account the time difference between the States and Scotland, it was only late morning there, so no tirades about waking up his friend. But if anyone could track down a phantom in the Scottish netherworld, it was Brody McGregor.

First, he had another meeting with the ghost from his past.

24

Maura McCune clasped her hands together on the little desk across from the glass. It was déjà vu as Drayco observed her in his second meeting at the detention center, with one exception—this time, Benny Baskin sat next to him. Since Benny's prior solo visit with Maura had proved frustrating, or as Benny put it, "like talking to Mt. Everest," he'd decided to let Drayco take the lead.

Drayco studied Maura, his gaze falling to the scar on her neck. He hadn't paid that much attention to it on their first meeting. It was definitely an old scar, almost a W-shape, like one left over from a burn ... or maybe a hot poker. She caught him looking at it and tried to pull the top of her orange jumpsuit up to cover it, but it was hardly adequate for that.

After he stared at her for a few more moments without saying anything, she finally blurted out, "As jails go, it's a pretty decent one. There's even a library. I'm reading that new thriller by Simon D'Avanzo."

"And how many jails have you been in?"

She just bit her lip, then shook her head.

"I'm not sure what I should call you. A gypsy? A nomad? Or is con woman more accurate?"

Her pale skin turned a mottled crimson. "I cannae expect you to understand, Scotty. I couldn't tell you the troth, could I? To know the kind of person I was." Until now, her accent was a mere shadow of its former self. But the more agitated she got, the more it spilled out.

"You abandoned us when Casey and I were five years old. You don't want to know what I think of you."

She clasped her hands tighter, the knuckles turning white as Drayco continued, unable to keep the words from pouring out. "When Casey lay dying in the hospital with me and Brock by her side, she cried out for her Mommy. Did you know that?"

Maura turned her head away. She cleared her throat and released one of her hands long enough to dab at her eyes before turning her attention back to him. Her voice was so soft, it was almost a whisper. But this time, she spoke each word slowly, sounding more like she had on his first visit. "I can't change the past. Only the present."

Despite his promise to stay silent, Benny piped up, "You can start by telling us your relationship to Jerold Zamorra."

"We found out we were in the same line of work and hooked up as partners. Turns out, it was a bad idea on my part. I've trusted few people in my life and here I'd trusted Jerold, and he was going to double-cross me."

Drayco asked, "With someone else, a new partner?"

She nodded. "I don't know who."

"That's why you called him and arranged the meeting right before he was murdered?"

"Aye. And when I found him lying there, dead, I was furious. He'd betrayed my trust, and now he'd robbed me of my chance to get back at him and his new partner."

Drayco leaned back in his chair. "I asked you before if you and Jerold were lovers. You didn't answer."

"We weren't lovers like you think. It was just one time. And no, this wasn't a lover's tiff."

"Do you even know anything about love? Why did you marry Brock?"

She smiled a sad little smile and avoided answering the question.

Benny shot him a "stick to the case, you idiot" look. Drayco gritted his teeth and pressed on, "Describe this work partnership, this scheme of yours and Jerold's."

She clenched her jaw. "It doesn't matter now."

"Of course it matters now. It can help prove or disprove your case. Is it that you don't trust me, either? You're afraid I'll use the information against you?"

A sigh escaped her lips. "Ah, Scotty. Please don't ask me that."

"Why shouldn't I? Don't you owe me that, at the very least?"

"I can't. Don't you see? I don't want to exchange a sentence for a murder I didn't commit for a sentence for something else."

"You're all but admitting you *have* done something illegal. Look, if you don't help us on the murder charge, nothing else will matter. You'll be put away for life." He ran a hand through his hair. "Tell me how we're supposed to help you?"

"Find the person who did this."

Drayco counted to three and took a couple of deep breaths. "It will be a lot easier if you'll help me. For instance, Ashley and Edwin Zamorra, Jerold's daughter and brother. Did you meet either one of them?"

"I saw Edwin once, from a distance. Ashley, no."

"Did Edwin or Ashley know of your partnership with Jerold?"

"I don't think so. He didn't say."

"How long were you partners with Jerold?"

"About six months."

"Did he ever mention his deceased wife, Ophelia?"

"I'm sorry, Scotty. We didn't talk about much other than our plans. Even when we made love that one time, I didn't feel like he was there. Like his mind was on other things. Things he chose not to share."

Drayco almost said *takes one to know one*. He tried to read her body language but wasn't sure if he was seeing her as she was now or how she was three decades ago. "You've been in the area two years. What have you been doing all this time?"

"Making a living. Trying to stay busy."

"Does that living have something to do with Tarot cards?"

Her eyes widened, and she paused before answering. "You and I used to play cards when you were little. Do you remember? But you always beat me. You had such a remarkable memory, even as a lad.

Always knew what everyone else had drawn or discarded and could guess what was left in the deck."

He remembered. Even then, he'd suspected she cheated a little. "I could use your various ID cards as a deck, there are so many. Want to tell me about them?"

"The police haven't asked me about those." She blinked at him then smiled as the light bulb went off. She knew he'd been to her apartment, but the PD hadn't—and Drayco hadn't told them. "It's just a game, Scotty. That's all."

"Like Guess-Who-You?"

"Exactly." Her smile grew wider.

He'd have to explain to Benny later about Guess-Who-You, the role-playing game he and his mother had made up, where each had to pretend to be someone else while the other guessed their identity. But at least, he and Maura seemed to be connecting a little again. "It seems fraternal twins run in the family. Casey and me, you and Alistair. I've been talking to Iago Pryce and—"

Her demeanor changed immediately. "On second thought, I've said everything I have to say. You don't need to help me any further. Consider yourself off the case, both you and Mr. Baskin. You can just leave me alone from here. Besides, I stopped caring about you or anyone else long ago."

She pressed a button to signal for the warden to come and take her to her cell, leaving Drayco to stare at her now-vacant seat. The warden returned a few minutes later and motioned for Drayco and Baskin to be escorted back to the front desk. Turning his head to look at the impassive face of the warden, Drayco hauled himself up and picked his way out of the building, with Baskin following closely behind.

"What was that all about?" In addition to sounding like a bull terrier, Benny even looked like one with his hands on his hips and his stocky legs splayed out to either side. "You think it's related to this shady Brisbane guy you told me about?"

"Not sure, but I aim to find out. And Maura's still your client until I tell you otherwise."

"Sure, sure, boy-o. You Draycos are such fun to work with."

Drayco scowled in reply. No one wanted him on this case, not even his mother. That should be a sign, right? He wasn't superstitious and certainly didn't believe in divination, but he had a sudden compulsion to pay a visit to a cemetery.

25

The trip south on I-95 to Fredericksburg was a helluva lot easier in the early afternoon than during rush. A mere ninety minutes later, and Drayco was in front of his target. He'd changed his mind at the last minute, not about going to the cemetery, but about making another stop first to a place he hadn't visited in eighteen years.

It would look almost the same as when he'd last seen it, if it weren't for the boarded-up windows, peeling shingles, and overgrown yard filled with brown ivy, shotweed, purple deadnettle, and lichen-covered fallen branches. The tilted "For Sale" sign looked like an afterthought erected half-heartedly by a ghostly hand that wanted the place left as is.

Drayco had been on one of his European concert tours when he'd heard from Brock his father was selling the place and moving his son's belongings to the new digs. Then came the carjacking. Then it was in the FBI, then out of the FBI, and he'd never had the chance to say goodbye.

Maura was the one who'd chosen the home, making it surprising Brock didn't dump it soon after she left, just as he'd dumped everything else associated with her, except his children. At least, technically.

The crumbling front door was about as secure as Drayco's townhome these days, and he easily shouldered his way past. The place didn't look half-bad on the inside, not unlike how the Draycos left it years ago. The families who'd lived there since had done little to change the interior. Even the paint in the living room was the same pale green he remembered.

Why was he here? That question dogged him all the way up the stairs to the second floor, where he peered into his empty boyhood room before heading to the attic. Happy memories, sad memories, or something else altogether?

A thick layer of dust coated the attic, and any previous insulation was long gone. That made it easier for him to find the little compartment in the wall above the floorboards, partially obscured by joists. This attic is where he'd hidden for an entire day after his mother left because he didn't want to be found, wanted to be left alone. During his "escape," he'd stuck something inside that little hiding place. Surely it couldn't still be there after all this time?

He reached into the hole and grabbed a yellowing sheet of paper, the type of wide-ruled paper schoolchildren use. There was a crude drawing of a woman with red hair, and a child's handwritten scrawl spelled out the words, "She said I will always be with you. She lied."

The day before Maura left them, she was extra nice to him and Casey. Taking them to the county fair, his first time ever on a Ferris Wheel. They ate so much ice cream and hot dogs and cotton candy, he threw up. It was that night she'd said those words to him, *I will always be with you.*

Why had he hidden the little paper here? Why had he not wanted Brock or Casey to see it? His reasons were long forgotten. But he'd always liked hiding places, which is why he often looked for secret compartments on cases, a habit that had come in handy more than once. He started to put the paper back into its former coffin but thrust it into his pocket instead.

Feeling a bit silly for having come here on some psychic mystery quest he couldn't identify, he made his way back down to the living room. With one last look around the place, he turned to leave but stopped when he spied something under one of the windows.

He knelt down next to the floorboards and picked up the little pieces scattered there as if they'd fallen out of someone's pocket. He'd seen those before and recently, at that. Iago's pepita seeds.

જ જ જ

Still mulling over the possibility—or rather, the likelihood—Iago had been to the Drayco childhood home for some unknown reason, Drayco drove to the cemetery with its familiar low brick wall topped with an arching gate made of concrete and wrought iron. He'd been here a lot more recently than his old homestead.

But on his last visit, it was in the mid-90s and people were already setting off firecrackers in the distance, preparing for the Fourth of July celebrations later that day. If only the drive to Fredericksburg from D.C. weren't so long, he'd come more often. At least, that was what he told himself.

He bent down on one knee to trace his finger over the engraved letters on the headstone, Casey Isolde Drayco. He said, "Sorry I haven't been here in a while."

He looked at the flowers on a grave over to his right. Plastic. He hated those. He wished he'd brought some lilies, her favorite flower. He'd never bothered to wonder why Brock didn't purchase a grave marker for Maura, but now he knew.

"Mom's alive, Drasee." When they were quite young, he thought it was funny to call her Drasee Drayco. She hadn't seemed to mind, but he was the only one who got away with it.

"Turns out, she may be a murderer. Or at least, a criminal. You can imagine how Brock is taking it. Oh, and she has a twin brother, just like us. Name's Alistair, and it appears he may be a bit shady, too. I haven't told Brock about that tidbit yet." Why hadn't he? He wasn't even sure himself. Maybe it was all the lies in the air taking their toll.

The cold from the ground seeping through his slacks made Drayco stand up and dust off blades of yellowed grass. The truncated shadows falling in parallel lines behind the grave markers were like rows of soldiers standing at attention waiting for a call. To what, life? Resurrection? Someone to remember them?

"I could use a little advice, Drasee. I don't usually have problems committing to a case, seeing it through. But I've dragged some friends into this, putting their reputations on the line. The deeper I dig, the more it appears she's guilty."

Maura McCune's story, unless she skillfully fabricated the whole thing, did check out on one level, though—that she stabbed him once, likely after he was dead. But why did Maura suddenly clam up at the mention of Iago's name? And had she really spent that much time in Jerold's company and bed without him saying anything about his daughter and brother or other personal details?

The mild weather from the first two weeks of February was morphing into a chilly reminder it was indeed still winter. He stuffed his hands into his pockets to warm them as he gazed at the tombstone. He started to walk away when the largest crow Drayco had ever seen swooped down from a tree and landed a few feet from him.

It seemed totally unconcerned by Drayco's presence, even looking up at him and emitting a loud cry that might sound like a simple "caw" to most, but sent lines of mulberry-colored metallic chain loops to Drayco's ears. Small chains like on a necklace Ophelia wore in one of the photos displayed in Edwin Zamorra's home.

He squinted at the crow. "I guess it wouldn't hurt to talk to Edwin again." The crow flapped its wings and flew away.

Quantico was on Drayco's way back to D.C., but he decided against bothering Sarg. The man was likely knee-deep in paperwork with a phone glued to his ear, anyway. He'd already helped out quite a bit using his contacts and databases to follow-up on several of the suspects and leads in the case. Not to mention volunteering his valuable time.

Even after three years away from the Bureau, Drayco sometimes looked over at the passenger seat en route to questioning a witness or client, half-expecting to see Sarg sitting there. He was surrounded by ghosts from his past everywhere he turned. As he left the cemetery, he turned to take one last look at the small grave. "Thanks, Drasee. Next time, lilies."

26

Drayco had to wait until Edwin closed his pharmacy at six before meeting him at his house. Edwin explained the timing, "It's only me and one clerk most times. Occasionally, it's just me. Small business, small staff."

Drayco sat near the fireplace, with a good view of the witch doctor's mask and antique apothecary box on the mantel. They weren't the only artifacts in the room—unlike Jerold's Spartan condo, every surface and wall sported a photo, painting, art piece, or some other knick-knack.

Edwin sat on the edge of a chair opposite Drayco. "You didn't say why you wanted to see me, Mr. Drayco. Not to appear unwelcoming, but I don't see how I can help you further with Jerold's murder case. If that's why you're here."

"Just a few questions to clear up a thing or two. Shouldn't take much of your time."

Edwin shrugged. "The police have my statement."

"According to the police report, you were working late the night of Jerold's death?"

Edwin fiddled with the buttons on his white lab coat he was still wearing. "My clerk had left for the day. And it was after we'd closed. No customer witnesses if that's what you're implying."

"We ran into one of your customers the other day. Mrs. Imogen Layford. She was a neighbor of Jerold's at his condo."

Edwin pulled an e-cigarette out of his pocket and started vaping as the green apple aroma swirled around him. "I have several customers who live in that complex. But yes, yes, Mrs. Layford is a customer and a fine woman. Lost her husband ten years ago to Parkinson's or ALS. Or possibly MS. One of those hideous neurological conditions."

A quick image of Nelia Tyler flashed into Drayco's mind. He'd never met her MS-stricken husband, Tim, or seen a picture of him. Just heard his voice over the phone when he was in a drunken stupor—the same night he'd left bruises on Nelia. Hopefully, Mr. Layford had never hit Mrs. Layford out of frustration.

"Did you know about any fraud schemes Jerold was involved with?"

Edwin pressed his lips together in a thin line. "Fraud? What, like a pyramid thing?"

"Not sure yet. I have a source who says he may have been involved in something illegal."

"First I've heard. The police didn't mention it."

"They will. And when they do, they might suggest you wanted a piece of the action. He refused, so you killed him."

Edwin's laugh was a staccato goat bleat. "I assure you, I knew nothing of it."

"What about Ashley?"

Edwin's eyes flashed. "What about Ashley? Surely you don't think she was involved in something fishy. Not our Ashley. And don't wave that inheritance thing around, either. She's a sweet girl—she'd never get involved in fraud or murder."

"Ever hear the name, Alistair Brisbane? or Iago Pryce?"

"Don't ring any bells."

Edwin jumped at the sound of a knock on the door. He got up, looked out the window, and unlocked the door long enough to grab a pile of rubber-banded mail. "He's late today." Edwin didn't look at the envelopes and tossed them onto a table, next to a copy of the *PDR Drug Guide for Pharmacists*.

Drayco wasn't ordinarily jumpy, himself, but Edwin's late mail and his reaction to the knock were reminiscent of the night Iago "dropped by" his townhome. He started to touch his neck but stopped himself. Fortunately, the bruises were fading, and he'd stopped getting funny looks from other people.

Drayco could see the top envelope on Edwin's pile, not the address, but it was hard to miss the all-red Past Due lettering. "Was the lawsuit you filed against the TSA the beginning of your estrangement with your brother? Or did it start long before?"

Edwin cleared his throat. "I'm truly sorry about Jerold and me. About our relationship going south. Despite what you said about that fraud thing, he was a good dad to Ashley and a fine musician. Even Rena Quentin, his former colleague who filed that harassment charge, told me she respected him."

"Before or after she filed the charges?"

"She called the other day, to see how I was doing. She's feeling horribly guilty now that he's dead. That's what happens after people die, isn't it? We appreciate them more."

Edwin rubbed a hand across his forehead. "Rena told me something else interesting. She researched you. Wondered why you were asking questions after the police had already done the same."

"And she found out the accused murderer is my mother, is that right?"

Edwin nodded. "Rena got curious. Once a security wonk, always a security wonk. But after learning that, not sure I should be talking to you."

"I'm more estranged from my mother than you were from Jerold. I'm only seeking the truth, and if she's the murderer, so be it. You told Agent Sargosian and me you'd seen the suspect, Maura McCune, with Jerold once?"

Edwin chewed on his lip and seemed to be considering Drayco's words. Finally, he replied, "Once, yes, from a distance. She's an attractive woman. I can see why Jerold would succumb to her wiles." Unlike the last time Drayco had visited, the man was fidgeting, with his right foot tapping out a rapid rhythm on the floor.

Drayco looked around the room, noting unusual glazed clay pots with Matisse-style patterns. He pointed them out. "Local artist?"

"My sister-in-law was very creative and not just at interior design. She made those for me."

"You and your sister-in-law were very close." Drayco got up and walked over to one of the pots with vivid purple, green, and orange shapes, holding it up to the light. "Were you in love with her?"

Edwin stopped the perpetual foot motion. "Now see here, Mr. Drayco—"

"Jerold didn't have any photos of her at home. Yet, you do."

"So? Jerold and I didn't see eye to eye on a lot of things. Including Ophelia. He never treated her right."

"Your niece practically said she wishes you were her father instead of Jerold." Drayco put the pot down and moved to a shelf filled with books and games—Life, Monopoly, playing cards. And one Tarot deck.

"Ashley said that?" Edwin resumed the tapping again, slower this time. "Guess since Ophelia and Jerold are both dead now, it won't hurt to tell the truth."

Drayco put the pot back on the table. "I'm listening."

"It was love at first sight for me. I never stopped loving Ophelia, not until the day she died. No, no, not even then. I still can't imagine being with anyone else."

"Did you and Ophelia have an affair?"

"We ... we had a one-night stand."

"When was this?"

Edwin chewed on his lower lip. "A long time. Years."

"Did Jerold ask for a paternity test? To see if Ashley was his?"

"What? No. Oh, no no no no. He didn't know about us. The chasm between us was mostly his creation. Had nothing to do with Ophelia."

Edwin jumped again when the phone rang. He didn't make a move to answer it and let it go to voice mail. "I hear they've released Jerold's body to Ashley. Took long enough. Now we can move forward with the cremation and funeral."

"I'm surprised Ashley wants a funeral at all, considering she believes he killed her mother."

"My parents requested it. It's their son, after all."

"I didn't think Ashley was on speaking terms with your parents."

"I confess I talked her into it. Didn't seem right, him not having a proper send-off with all his family and friends there."

"All?"

"Well, we won't have to rent out Westminster Abbey." More goat-bleat laughter.

"Will the surviving members of the quartet play? Or maybe you?"

"Don't think the quartet is up to it. And me, I'm tone deaf."

After Drayco made his exit, leaned on his car in the now-darkness. Edwin's house wasn't close enough to the Alexandria waterfront for Drayco to see it or hear it from here. When the winds were from the east like tonight, though, you could get whiffs of the Potomac River's fishy, rotting compost odor that was minus its sometime-chaser of sulfur or sewage. The river couldn't hide its presence, no matter how hard it tried.

The Potomac should take a few tips from Edwin. Because Drayco would wager his beloved Steinway that Edwin was hiding something.

27

When Drayco had left home earlier in the day, Brock was still sleeping off his alcoholic stupor. Drayco wasn't surprised his father was long gone by the time he made it back to his townhome after dark. No note. Nothing on the home answering machine. No cellphone call. No surprise, that. In danger of losing a bet once, Brock changed the rules in his favor so he wouldn't have to admit he was wrong.

Drayco took a quick shower and did a minimal towel off before pulling on a pair of sweatpants, then hurried down to the den where he flipped open his laptop and dialed up his friend, Brody McGregor. It was after midnight in Edinburgh, but Drayco wasn't surprised Brody-the-night-owl had suggested this time for a video conference call.

Brody held up a bottle of Balvenie single malt Scotch whisky and poured a glass. His Scottish brogue always deepened after he'd had a few. "Wish I could hand you one through the screen, Scott, 'cause I think you're going to need it." He took a sip. "And put a shirt on, would you? Don't need your manly abs mocking me at this hour."

Drayco grabbed a t-shirt he'd thrown onto a chair and slipped it over his head. "Happy?"

"Happier than you're gaunnae be. But you're the one who asked me to check into Maura McCune."

Drayco steeled himself against the news. Whatever Brody had dug up, it was bound to be the truth. The ex-Interpol agent was as thorough in his private career as he'd been at his old job, where his former bosses were still trying to get him to return.

"Good or bad, I want to hear it."

"Aye, then. You already know her family name, Brisbane, via her twin brother. A lot of the records have gone missing over the years, but the Brisbane family has a history of run-ins with police. Mostly small-time stuff. They were what we call Scottish lowland gypsy Travellers."

"Like the Romani gypsies?"

"Can be, or at least, share a common history. Also, share cultural beliefs. The importance of family, a hatred of working for anyone else, and of course the nomadic bit. In Scottish Gaelic, they're known as the Ceàrdannan or Craftsmen. Or, if you're one of their critics, 'tinkies.'"

"Tinkies?"

"Short for tinkers."

"Ah. Tradesmen."

"Of a sort. Often found around circuses and fairgrounds."

"Apparently, they peddle more than honest wares, if they're having police run-ins."

"Exceptional con artists or confidence tricksters, that lot."

That wasn't surprising at all, considering what he knew about Maura and Alistair. Perhaps it was in their genes. Or they'd been doing it so long that they didn't know how to do anything else. "You said small-time crimes. That doesn't sound like anything that would make me need a whisky."

Brody took a sip from his glass. "The records are a wee bit spotty, but I came across one of a man named Dugald Iverson. Found dead thirty-six years ago. Blunt force trauma. No one ever arrested."

"Suspects?"

"The police records daednae list any. Found a couple of elderly former neighbors of Iverson's who gave me a name. His teenage ex-girlfriend, Maura Brisbane."

Drayco wiped his still-wet hands on his t-shirt. "And yet she was never charged or arrested."

"Neighbors never saw her again. No one did. Poof, vanished just like that."

"Until she turns up in Virginia under the name of Maura McCune."

"And marries your faither. Sorry, Scott. Wish I had better news. I'll keep on digging. Always more than one side to a story."

"So they say." Drayco wished he had that glass of Scotch whisky right now. "Thanks, pal. Next time I'm in your neck of the woods, I'll buy you some haggis or something."

"You do, and I'll puke all over you. Never liked that shite. Now hamburgers, on the other hand ..."

"Blasphemy, my friend."

"Not if it's McDonald's, aye?"

"Funny man." Drayco didn't feel like laughing upon hearing Brody's bad news about Maura, but he was grateful for his friend's attempts at softening the blow.

After Brody signed off with that promise to do more digging, especially on the Dugald Iverson case, Drayco sat with the laptop while staring at the blank screen. What had he ever known about his mother? Zilch, mostly. And apparently, Brock hadn't either. Or else Maura really was a masterful con artist who had everyone fooled.

The immigration records he'd checked on this side of the Atlantic produced paltry results, and even his usual reliable sources had found nothing on Maura Brisbane, Maura McKewen, or Maura McCune. What name did she use when she landed here? And how did she get here? Fake passport? Stowaway on a boat? It was a lot easier to do thirty-six years ago before the days of 9-11 and the TSA.

He headed to the kitchen, pulled a Manhattan Special soda from the refrigerator, and looked for something to eat, the empty shelves reminding him he hadn't made it to the store in a while. Grabbing a carton of leftover takeout rice, he added some pickle relish and hot sauce. Dinner was served.

While munching on the rice, his gaze fell on the necklace he'd taken from Maura's apartment, now lying on his table. Halabi would have his nuts on a skewer if he knew Drayco pocketed the jewelry. He picked it up, turning it over in his hand as he studied it. He was pretty sure he'd seen something like it before.

He put down the rice and made his way upstairs to his attic where he dug through a box of old cards and trinkets he'd almost forgotten. His probing fingers touched what he was after and then grasped a smaller, white box.

It was a box he'd rescued from the trash when he was five, a box he'd seen his father throw away in anger along with an album filled with photos. Right after his mother left. Drayco didn't know why he'd rescued it or why he kept it. Other than his piano playing, for years it was the only real tie he had to his mother.

From the box, he pulled out a near-identical necklace to the one from Maura's apartment—with a half-heart, this one engraved with MIZ on it. He went back downstairs and put the heart from this necklace next to the half-heart from the apartment. Together, they completed a heart figure and spelled MIZPAH.

He sat back down at the computer, and it didn't take long to find what he was after. *Mizpah*, originally from Genesis, an emotional bond between people who are usually separated, a way of keeping the other person in your memory. Even sometimes used on headstones.

She kept her necklace?

He picked up the two necklaces and let them dangle from his hand, the gold glinting in the overhead light. He carried them with him to the piano and laid them on top, then started playing the Intermezzo in A Major from Opus 118 by Brahms.

When he was first learning how to play, his mother told him it was one of her favorite pieces. That had spurred him to learn it, practicing it over and over while she hummed wordlessly along with the melodic line. One of the saddest little pieces in a major key there ever was.

He closed his eyes as he played, easing into the complex harmonies that fired every region of his brain, hearing the music with its grooved fuschia sandpaper sheets sliding across his skin even as his mind thought about the case and how it seemed out-of-tune, just like his Steinway had lately.

He reached the hymn-like passage in F# major that used hints from the composer's *German Requiem,* partly inspired by the death of the composer's mother. It was the segment from the fifth movement where the voices sing verses from Isaiah, "As one whom his mother comforts, so will I comfort you."

He stopped playing, jumped up from the bench, and began pacing. After a few minutes of that, he headed to the kitchen to grab what was left of Brock's bottle of Scotch but stopped. He didn't want to play, and he didn't want to drink.

Instead, he flopped down onto the sofa and stared at the dust on the ceiling fan as his thoughts swirled like the fan blades. Jerold, Edwin, Ashley, Maura, Ophelia—he stopped on that one. Why did the ATM thieves change their M.O. and bash in Ophelia Zamorra's brain with a baseball bat, then cram the bank card down her throat?

Ashley said her mother hadn't been acting strangely prior, with no hints of fear or stalkers or business woes. Unless Drayco's mother were lying and her relationship with Jerold went back several years, and she decided to get rid of her romantic rival.

He hardly knew Maura McCune, and he owed her virtually nothing. Why did the truth matter so much now?

He started to pick up the TV remote when something caught his eye. A switch plate in a back corner of the room was ever-so-slightly crooked. His housekeeper wasn't that vigorous. He grabbed a screwdriver to unscrew the plate and peered inside with his flashlight as it illuminated something that definitely shouldn't be there.

Using the screwdriver again, he gently freed a small metallic device no bigger than one-fourth of an inch across and held it up to the light. It was one of the most sophisticated bugs he'd ever seen, and he had a pretty good idea of who'd put it there.

There were probably more, but he was too tired to make a sweep of the house. Besides, as high-tech as this little baby was, he'd probably need his bug and wiretap detector that went up to ten gigahertz, which was currently living at his office. He lay back on the sofa and settled on a sports channel. He hoped his listeners liked ice hockey.

 و ود ود

Iago popped some pepitas into his mouth as he stood in the shadows of a building far from the nearest street light. He stared at the detention center, its concrete, steel, and glass facade looking colder and deader in the dark light. Even the clouds seemed determined to prevent any moonlight from bathing the building in a more welcoming glow. Maura was in there, somewhere. Was she cold? Was she frightened? If they were in certain other countries, he could just plant a small bomb and waltz right in and grab her. It had worked well in Lagos.

He let the rest of the pepitas fall from his hand to the sidewalk and whipped out his cell. When the baritone voice answered, Iago said, "Got the bugs on their phones. Benny Baskin's was easy. Scott Drayco's was a little trickier, but they're working good. I put the tracers on both of Drayco's cars and a couple in his home and office."

"Excellent. I also have another associate carefully monitoring Detective Halabi's whereabouts. I hear he's rather fond of fish and chips."

Iago grunted. "Then you've got something in common. What about the senior Drayco, Brock?"

"He won't be a problem."

"Are you sure?"

"I'm sure he could be a problem if he chose, with his high-profile connections. But he has no interest in either helping or hurting Maura."

"Good. One Drayco is a handful. Or at least, the younger one is."

"I suspected he would be. I have followed his career with great interest. I was surprised when he left the FBI, but after learning his reasons, I understood. I think he was mistaken, but it works to our advantage now."

"He's asked his former partner, that Sargosian guy, for help. Might have to worry about the FBI getting involved after all."

"Aye. But I'm preparing for that possibility, just in case." The man on the phone coughed. "Sorry. A touch of a cold, I'm afraid. Do you need more money?"

"I'm good. You taking something for that cold?"

"A little rowanberry wine."

"Sounds better than menthol crap. Maura would probably give you some of her whisky-honey-vinegar cure."

"Yes, well, hopefully, we'll have her back soon. Do keep the faith, old friend."

"Faith? I prefer action. Think I'll check out that Gogo Cheng kid. Had plenty of reason to hate Zamorra, and he's got that martial arts thing going."

"And yet I doubt he could take you on and win."

Iago chuckled. "Your confidence in me warms the cockles of my heart."

"Warming—a lovely idea. I think I'll have Hazel heat up some chicken soup for me. And your talk of bugs reminds me I need to check that latest sweep to make sure we're clean."

"Time for me to switch to a new burner phone."

"I'll see to it. Do keep me posted on our detective friends."

Iago hung up with his employer and gave one last look at the detention center. At least Maura was safe, for now. No telling if Zamorra's real killer would be gunning for her, too, if she were out on the streets. With a heavy sigh, he headed off in the direction of Clarendon. He had a sudden hankering for fish and chips.

28

The late-morning sun beat down on the white bubble dome that stretched out like the top of a giant Moby Dick. Rena Quentin didn't allow one single blade of grass a chance at life under her active feet, which is why Drayco was meeting her at the East Potomac Tennis Center. He'd never been inside, although he liked Hains Point, the little island between the Washington Channel and the Potomac River. The tip of the island and nearby Gravelly Point were two of the best places to watch planes take off and land at DCA.

He was early, so he meandered through the center's pro shop. Tennis balls, tennis shoes, tennis clothing. Imagine. He picked up a tennis racket, a graphite-tungsten Babolat, and looked at the price tag. Two hundred dollars. Yikes.

Heading to the indoor courts, he spied Rena and watched as the instructor worked on her strokes with her. Hardly a bead of sweat crossed her brow, and her clothes looked dry. Not that she wasn't working hard, her skin just wouldn't dare to perspire.

All that exercise seemed to be paying off, with the near-sixty retiree running around like someone a few decades younger. Even when she was just walking, she moved like a dancer, springing, pirouetting, with controlled movements.

After she wrapped up her lesson and approached him, he could see her hair better this time sans polo hat, dyed chestnut with a hint of gray at the roots and sprayed into submission. She wore a navy blue tennis dress and white shoes with a navy stripe. Her racket also had navy trim and looked suspiciously similar to one of the Babolats in the pro shop.

Rena looked up at him. "You're much taller than I remember."

She nodded at the wall, and he followed her to a sports bag she opened to stuff her racket inside. "Men think women love horses because it's an orgasmic thing. But it's not. It's the controlled power in horses, their magnificent energy and strength that I can control with a flick of my legs and feet. They're such amazing animals."

"Horses can turn on their riders."

"Mine don't." She smiled at him. "So, you're trying to prove your mother isn't a killer."

"Edwin Zamorra said you'd checked on me. You do that with everyone you meet?"

"You have to admit it was odd having you show up like that. Besides, once a security wonk, always a security wonk. Edwin's words, not mine." Rena patted her hair. "It must be difficult having your mother be a suspect in a murder."

"I haven't seen her in thirty years. I hardly know her."

"Then we have something in common. I didn't get the chance to know my mother, either. My cop father pushed her down some stairs in a drunken rage when I was eight. Broke her neck. I'd love to have just one more day with her. She was my entire universe."

She zipped the bag, and as they walked to a bench, added, "Is your mother like you remember her?"

"Her voice is."

Rena bent over to tie her shoelace tighter. "No disrespect intended, but if she's convicted, maybe she'll try the suicide route. I would in her shoes. Jails are so messy."

Drayco caught a stray tennis ball that bounced in their direction, almost hitting his chest. He threw it back. The young girl who'd missed her shot twirled around and covered her face with her racket, peeking through the strings. Drayco waved.

"Not that I'm not thrilled to see you again, Mr. Drayco. But I'm surprised you didn't just call me on the phone."

"Disembodied voices give me the willies."

She laughed. "It's all about that body language thing, isn't it? There was such a controversy about using profiling at the TSA."

"I know you and Jerold weren't on the best of terms. But did you ever get a hint he might be involved in gambling?"

"Gambling? Most people play the lottery, I suppose. Or bet on their favorite sports team if that's what you mean. Nothing else."

"What about something illegal?"

She used the towel in her hands to wipe the non-existent sweat. "He's one of the last people I'd expect to pull such a stunt."

"I stopped by the East Potomac Golf Course on my way here. One of Jerold's regular golfing buddies said the same thing."

"There you go. Maybe he cheated on his taxes, maybe he took candy from babies. Few things surprise me these days. My job, you know."

"Underwear bombs and passengers smuggling exotic birds in their bras?"

"Why, Mr. Drayco, you must read the news. Thank you for not including pat-down mishaps."

"There's the matter of Edwin's lawsuit."

"Edwin's a dear man, but he's a prude. One trip, one pat-down and suddenly he's the victim of assault. Not at all like my case against Jerold. Ironic, though, don't you think?"

"It was an effective way to embarrass his brother."

Just then, a plane taking off from DCA veered too far off the legal flight path. Its loud engine noise made Drayco pause. "An MD-88."

"However would you know that?"

"The sound of the engines." He got tired of trying to explain his synesthesia to other people. It was like explaining breathing to someone without lungs. "You said last time we talked that Jerold didn't get along with Gogo. And Ashley didn't get along with her father."

"The couple in cahoots, you mean? Gogo is into martial arts as I understand. It's possible. But they're both adults. They didn't need Jerold's blessing."

"Maybe they needed his money."

She laughed. "Jerold was terrible with money. Always splurging on things he couldn't afford. I doubt he had any left to give them."

"Two million dollars actually."

Her eyes widened. "Now I understand all your questions. My, my."

"Ever heard of a man named Alistair Brisbane?"

She thought about it. "No. And it's a memorable name, isn't it?"

She looked at her watch, the same expensive one she wore last time. At least, it wasn't navy. "I don't want to appear heartless, Mr. Drayco. Your mother is the prime suspect in a murder, and that's hard. But I learned early on how difficult it is to survive in this world. Even more being a woman in a man's world. You put on a cloak of emotional armor every day you wake up."

Moving as if she had a plane of her own to catch, Drayco had a hard time keeping up as he walked her to her car. She opened her car door and added, "Look, if I think of anything, I promise I'll give you a call. I'm beginning to enjoy these chats of ours."

As Rena's Lexus screeched out of the parking lot, he tried to imagine Jerold trying to get close enough to her to harass. His judgment must have been way off even to consider it.

Rena said she hadn't heard of Alistair Brisbane, and yet she'd ended their conversation shortly after his name was brought up, the second time that had happened to him. Maybe there was one name that frightened even the self-confident Rena.

Had she crossed paths with him while she was at the TSA? Maybe Uncle Alistair's long, multi-tentacled reach stretched farther and deeper than Drayco could begin to imagine.

29

Drayco double-checked the address. Towne Centre Estates. Were developers just not trying anymore when it came to names? Add an extra "e" to town, reverse the "er" in center, throw in "estates," and you got a generic pretentious subdivision. Still, Ashley's mother must have been a good businesswoman because the price for houses this size here could buy three homes in outlying areas like Manassas.

But it wasn't Ashley he hoped to see—it was her lodger, Lauralee. After parking a couple of houses up the street, he'd just unlocked the car door when he saw the young woman pop out from a basement entrance. Her crisp navy dress and stylish high heels screamed high-end department store. Shoplifting must pay well these days.

After one look at Lauralee's ducked head and hurried movements, he decided not to get out of his car, after all. He was also grateful for the hedge partially blocking his car from her sight line. But he could still see she carried what appeared to be a violin case that she thrust into the trunk of a red sedan before looking around briefly, jumping into the car, and peeling away.

Drayco started his engine and began to follow as they wove through the streets of Falls Church and into the even tonier areas of McLean, with multi-million dollar gated homes. Beyond the gates, the lawns were uniformly green, even in February, like rows of Stepford houses.

After Lauralee had parked in front of a tudor faux-castle, she got out, retrieved the item from the trunk, and rang a bell on the gate. When it buzzed open, she disappeared up the walkway and into the house.

He briefly contemplated doing a little friendly trespassing but nixed the idea and waited for the better part of a half-hour. When he spied her familiar brunette ringlets reappearing, sans the violin case, he eased out of his car over to hers and leaned on the passenger side facing the house.

Her smiling face faded as she spied him, and for a minute, he thought she might make a run for it. But she walked up to him with folded arms and said, "I could report you for stalking. Or harassment."

"You won't." Drayco pointed at the mansion. "Unless you want me to march up that driveway there and speak to those nice folks about what you handed over."

She glanced back at the house. "Do we have to have this conversation out here in front of God and everybody?"

He pointed to her car. "Would that be better?"

She sighed and unlocked the doors with her key remote. Once inside, she made sure the windows were all rolled up before she said, "It's not what you think."

"Right now, I don't have any thoughts on the matter whatsoever. Why don't you enlighten me?"

She ran her hand along the steering wheel. "Jerold had some musical instruments, violins, violas, that had some value. Not on a Strad-level, but pretty good. He gave them to me for safekeeping when he moved to his condo."

"After his divorce from Ophelia?"

She nodded. "He didn't have the space. And he thought I knew enough about the instruments to take care of them, keep them safe."

"I don't remember seeing them itemized in his Will."

"Guess they weren't. I mean, Ashley didn't mention them. I don't think Jerold ever told her I had them. They were still estranged, you know, him and Ashley."

"And when he died?"

"I thought about telling her. Then I heard about that two million he left her. Figured maybe Jerold wanted me to have these, you know?"

Drayco studied her. She avoided looking at him, picking at the fraying edges of the worn fabric seats. When he'd first spoken with her at Kicks and Sticks, along with Gogo, she'd mentioned her parents in the same breath as sin and the Bible. He had a good idea what they'd think about this little scheme of hers. "You've been selling the instruments and pocketing the money?"

She bit her lip. "I've only sold a couple so far."

"How many instruments are there?"

"How many total? Fourteen. He liked to collect them. And he sometimes played them in our concerts, depending on the rep."

"You called them 'not Strads,' but what does 'pretty good' mean?"

"A Guadagnini. And Sacconi, Degani, Corsini, Hardie."

"Italian school makers except for the Scottish Hardie. I've seen similar instruments sold at auction for anywhere from three grand on up to ten or even twenty. How did you get these potential buyers to believe the instruments' pedigree?"

She glanced in his direction, then away again. "I drew up some papers, okay?"

"Forged some papers, you mean?"

"I might have made up some previous owners and sales and things like that. But they're good instruments. I couldn't lie about that."

"Surely it wasn't that easy?"

"I set myself up as a dealer of rare violins and violas. I have a business address, business cards, everything."

"You conned them?"

"Like I said, they're good instruments. I didn't lie about that."

"Were you and Jerold involved with some other creative 'business dealings' before his death?" An image of Jerold's elderly neighbor popped into his head. "Some type of lottery fraud?"

She turned to look at him directly, her mouth open. "Lottery fraud? What the hell do you mean by that?"

"You tell me."

"All this talk of fraud. If you think I killed him because he was going to rat on me or something, think again. I was just one of the few people he felt he could trust with the instruments. That's it."

Drayco didn't know whether to believe her or not. Shoplifting, selling instruments that technically weren't hers, misrepresenting herself—she wasn't making it easy for him to swallow her story.

Lauralee glared at him. "Jerold gave them to *me*. That makes them mine. And I need the money—I'm already working two jobs. Besides, everybody's a scam artist. Whether it's love, money, jobs, résumés, whatever."

"And that makes it all fine?"

She gripped the steering wheel. "Are you going to the police or what? Because I'd like to know my options right now."

Options? Well, he didn't have any proof of her story. Neither was there proof those instruments had belonged to Jerold if they weren't listed in his Will or there weren't receipts among his papers.

He unlocked the door and unfolded himself from the cramped seat, relieved to stand. "You should think about buying Ashley a nice wedding present if she and Gogo end up getting hitched. A *really* nice wedding present."

He leaned over and poked his head inside to add, "And maybe you should make that instrument resale business of yours legit. You know, an LLC, a tax ID number ..."

She blinked at him. "You're not turning me in?"

"Depends upon what else I find out. If you and Jerold weren't doing anything more illegal than not paying taxes, I don't care what business you're in."

Her eyes widened as he added, "Of course if you killed Jerold so you could keep those instruments for yourself, that's another matter altogether."

He tapped the car on the hood and headed toward his Generic Silver Camry. Maybe he should have been harder on her, but right now his mind was focused on someone else, especially after his earlier conversation with Rena. Thanks to his contacts and an assist from Sarg, Drayco knew where he could find his mystery uncle at this time of day. It was time to introduce himself.

≈ ≈ ≈

Finding parking near the center of the free world, the Capitol building, was a challenge at any time but especially on a weekday. Thinking he'd have to park at Union Station and walk back, Drayco slipped into a metered spot right across the street from his target, amazed at his luck. Some poor schlub who'd given up his spot to go and get supper for his colleagues was going to be pissed.

The building was actually five blocks from the Capitol office complex, one of the thousands of lobbying firms crammed into every block in downtown D.C. like novelty-snakes-in-a-can. This firm dealt primarily with medical industry clients, the big boys in health care, insurance, and pharmaceuticals.

The meeting he was interested in started in ten minutes, according to his sources. He was early, but so was the individual climbing out of a limousine. It was getting dark, and Drayco was farther away this time, but it was the same distinguished-looking man who'd stared at him at the Mayflower's cafe.

A second man exited the limo after Alistair Brisbane, and Drayco almost didn't recognize him in his black suit and tie and charcoal-gray Homberg. Iago Pryce. Now he knew where Iago got his money to live on, the day laborer gig a smokescreen, as Drayco had suspected. A great excuse to explain away his presence, no matter where Iago needed to be, as a mere handyman.

No wonder Iago was so protective of Maura McCune. And he certainly hadn't simply "met her at a poetry slam" and gone on one date. Brisbane paid him to be his sister's bodyguard. So, where was he the night of Jerold's murder?

Both men entered the building, and the limo disappeared. Drayco settled in for a long wait until the meeting ended and he could tail Brisbane, but his cellphone rang. He picked it up, expecting Sarg or Benny, but it was a phone number he didn't recognize.

The voice on the other end dripped with amethyst-colored filaments. "I would invite you up for a glass of wine since our hosts are running a touch behind schedule. But perhaps this isn't the right time to meet my nephew. Iago was right about you. You are quite resourceful."

"Answer me this, Brisbane. How is it possible you ordinarily keep such close tabs on your sister, steering her out of trouble and thus protecting your reputation, and yet she's sitting behind bars as we speak?"

"Iago is quite good. But my sister is also resourceful. Runs in the family, you might say. She made an unwise decision, a hasty one, and Iago didn't make it in time."

"You're saying she did kill Jerold Zamorra?"

"If I believed that, I wouldn't be talking to you."

Drayco took a moment to process his comment. "All right. If she didn't kill him, who did?"

"And if I knew that, she wouldn't be in jail. That's what I'm counting on you for."

"So you stay under the radar."

"You are a bright lad, I must say."

Drayco grimaced. Maybe not so bright if he were being used as a pawn. "I know less about you than I do her. How can I be certain you didn't have something to do with Jerold's death? And that you're willing to let your sister hang for it?"

Brisbane sucked in a breath and exhaled slowly. "I've had to do a lot of things of which I'm not particularly proud. But neither I nor my sister killed Jerold Zamorra. You're just going to have to trust me on that, Scott."

Drayco heard a rustling in the background on Brisbane's end, and his uncle said, "It appears we're ready to start now. I'm afraid I can't chat any further. Don't give up on Maura yet, Scott." And then Brisbane hung up.

30

Nelia Tyler had half-mast eyes set above dark-circle pools, the look of someone who'd gone without sleep for days. Drayco had worried her grueling schedule would catch up with her, even as he respected her strength and resolve.

As they drove away from her apartment near the Georgetown campus, he handed over a cup of coffee. "Your morning dose of uppers."

She smiled, then popped off the lid and took a big gulp. "You said you needed a respectable-looking lady partner, but I'm not sure I qualify right now."

"Sure you do. I'll just tell our target I wore you out from 'partnering.'" She looked more than respectable, in her form-fitting powder blue sweater dress with a chain-link belt and knee-high cream-colored boots.

He quickly added, "It may be a wild gander chase."

"Gander chase?"

"Do I look like a goose to you?"

She laughed, then shot him a sideways glance with a slight flutter of her eyelashes. "How do I know if you have the right anatomical qualifications?"

He grinned. "I think I have my papers around here somewhere."

She feigned horror. "Don't tell me you've been neutered."

"Last time I checked, no." An image of Darcie and her red bow made him suddenly uncomfortable.

As if sensing his thoughts, Nelia changed the subject. "I take it our quarry's real name isn't Faust Marchand."

"No, but that's the name he's known by in the trade. Even uses it at his gallery in Fairfax."

"I'm surprised Gogo Cheng didn't turn Jerold Zamorra in for theft. Who knows? Maybe if he had, Jerold would still be alive, safely locked away."

That notion had crossed Drayco's mind, too. "We don't know if Gogo's story checks out yet. He may be the one who's lying. Even if he's telling the truth, it could cut both ways. Might help give Gogo more of a motive. Or less. With any luck, this little outing will help track Jerold's movements and methods."

"The fraud scheme he and your mother were involved in?"

"Maybe it was art theft. Maybe something else." He hadn't told her about Alistair Brisbane yet. He hadn't told anyone, save for Sarg and Benny. Until he knew just how much of a player his uncle was in D.C. power circles, it was best to keep Brisbane off everyone's radar—and vice versa.

"Who knows what Jerold, and by extension, my mother, were involved with. After talking to Lauralee yesterday, I have to wonder if she was right when she said everyone is a scam artist of some kind."

Nelia smiled. "I've got a lovely piece of property in Bermuda I can sell you." Then her smile faded. "You called Maura your mother just then."

He shook his head, confused.

"You've called her Maura McCune or 'that woman' until now."

Her words caught him off guard—he thought the wall he'd built to keep Maura out of his inner sanctuary was solid. He was grateful for the distraction when they reached the art brokerage, its no-nonsense white brick facade with plain black trim suddenly comforting.

If Faust Marchand made a deal with the devil, he should ask for his money back. He was already half-way to his eventual skeletal form, and everything else about him seemed designed to match, from his pencil-thin yellowing silver mustache to the bone-white shirt and jacket. When Nelia stood next to him, he barely reached her nose.

"May I help you?" Marchand's voice, on the other hand, was deep enough to reach down into the fires of hell.

Nelia looked around the gallery. "We were hoping to find Asian pieces for our dining room walls. I'm leaning toward Japanese, but my husband has his heart set on Chinese. Maybe some calligraphy. Isn't that right, dear?"

Drayco slipped his arm around her shoulders. "I know how you love Japanese landscapes, honey bun, but I think a calligraphy would set off our china better." He leaned over toward Marchand and added, "It's china that's really from China. We can't afford anything from the Song Dynasty, but we've budgeted seventy-five thousand for it."

Marchand tented his fingertips together. "Let me show you what I have," and he proceeded to walk them through a room filled with Asian ceramics and wall hangings.

Drayco and Nelia made a show of conferring over a few of the items in Marchand's collection, but Drayco finally shook his head. "I hoped you'd have something dramatic, fairly large." And he proceeded to describe Gogo's painting.

"I did have something similar to that. A man brought it to me a few months ago, and I ended up selling it and a few others to another art dealer. Unfortunately, Mr. Nardello has since passed away and his business with him."

Drayco didn't have to pretend to look disappointed. "The man who sold it to you in the first place, can we talk to him? He might have other paintings to sell."

Marchand's stiff posture indicated how affronted he was at the idea. "I have strict privacy policies at my shop, Mister ..."

"Brock. Name's Brock."

"I'm sorry, Mr. Brock, but unless it's the police who do the asking, all transactions remain anonymous. Even then, they'd better come armed with a search warrant. I'm sure you would appreciate the same courtesy." He tried to rescue a sale. "Perhaps there's something else I can interest you in today?"

Drayco turned to Nelia, who shook her head, and the two left Marchand the way they'd seen him when they arrived, obsessively straightening his paintings.

Nelia waited until they were out of earshot. "Honey bun?"

He shrugged. "I'm hungry." To his surprise, he really was.

"Starved for information, maybe. Sorry to come away empty-handed."

"Maybe not. We have the name of the other broker, Nardello. And although we can't prove it was Jerold who sold Gogo's painting, it was brought in by a man at around the right time."

Nelia looked back at the white brick building. "Jerold's actions before his death reek of desperation. Stealing from his future son-in-law, gambling debts, the mystery fraud scheme."

"Desperate men get careless."

"And leave trails."

Drayco's cellphone rang with another unfamiliar number, but it wasn't Brisbane this time. It was Ashley Zamorra, who'd kept the business card he gave her. She was working at the shelter again and wanted to see him as soon as possible. Remembering his unwelcome male presence last time, he turned to Nelia, "You up for one more, Tyler?"

"Absolutely, sugar pie."

31

The woman who'd poked her head in to check on Ashley and Drayco when he was here three days ago was the person who greeted them at the door. She wore the same faded jeans and too-large red sweater, although her hair was swept back this time.

The woman bristled upon seeing Drayco but relaxed a bit when she noticed Nelia, making him doubly glad Nelia had agreed to join him. Drayco saw Nelia glance at the fading purple bruises on the woman's face.

Drayco had explained the whole situation to Nelia on the way over, and she initiated the conversation. "We're looking for Ashley Zamorra. Can you take us to her, please?"

The woman led them to the same room as his last visit. Before turning to leave them, she looked up and seemed to realize how tall Drayco was. She took a step back and a look of panic washed over her face before she scurried off.

Ashley, who'd just walked in, noticed the exchange and explained. "Her boyfriend is tall, like you." Ashley sighed. "This is the third time she's been here. Always ends up going back to that jerk."

Drayco was beginning to think he needed a haircut or contact lenses or something if he reminded so many women of former abusers.

Nelia didn't take a seat right away and stood looking through the doorway. She shook her head, then shut the door softly. "There's a shelter like this on the Eastern Shore. I've been there many times. Since I was the sole female deputy until recently, they always sent me."

Ashley said, "You're a deputy? You don't look like one."

Nelia smiled briefly. "A friend of mine ended up in a shelter like this years ago. One of the reasons I decided to go into law enforcement."

"What happened to her, your friend?"

"Her boyfriend ignored the restraining order, found her, and choked her to death. I couldn't believe she allowed him back into her home. But she did."

Ashley nodded, as one who'd seen it all first-hand. Then she picked up something that looked like an answering machine from a counter and placed it on the table in front of Drayco. "I use this old thing at home as a backup, but it broke down several weeks ago. Just now got the thing fixed. When I turned it on, there was a message on it—must have come around the time the damned thing went haywire. Thought it was a wrong number. Well, I guess it is. It's for my father."

She plugged in the cord and played it for them. It was someone identifying himself as Dr. Mark White who said it was about that "urgent matter" they'd discussed and it would cost more than he'd initially thought. And he needed an answer by February twenty-first. "That's why I called you. I mean, since he mentioned today's date and all. Don't know if it's important."

"Why didn't you call the police?"

"That Halabi guy bothers me. He's rude. He's the one who didn't take my concerns seriously. You know, about Dad killing Mom."

Drayco wrote down Dr. Mark White's phone number from the machine. "Ashley, were you aware of your father's gambling habit?"

"Gambling? He wasn't just a bad stock picker? Guess that would explain him losing all his money."

"Did you notice any of your belongings go missing? Items he might have sold?" He hadn't promised Gogo *not* to tell Ashley about the painting but now wasn't the best time. Nor was he the best message delivery boy.

"Seriously? I'll have to go through my things and check. Good God, how irresponsible he was." She wrapped her arms around her in a self-hug, staring at the answering machine as if it would explode.

Then she looked at Drayco and sighed. "When I told you I inherited my father's bad-money-sense gene, guess I was right. I mean, that's why you're here, right? You checked my bank account and want to know if the money I took out is for gambling, too."

Drayco and Nelia exchanged glances but didn't say anything. Ashley didn't notice and continued, "With me, it's scratch-off tickets. Sounds silly, I know. It was just a few dollars a day, then ten, then fifty. And now I have all this money coming to me in the Will."

Her voice tapered off. "I read this news story. A woman embezzled a couple million bucks so she could play the lottery and hang out at casinos. That got me scared. So, I joined Gamblers Anonymous a couple months ago."

Her eyes were pleading. "Please don't tell Gogo. I can get it under control."

Drayco could taste the blood from where he'd bit his tongue. Every day was an exercise in control of some kind for most people who only wound up conning themselves. Lauralee was definitely right. Exercise, eating habits, booze, sex, drugs, running red lights, stealing from the office pool. Everyone flunked at least one test, maybe more.

"I won't tell Gogo. But *you* will. If he loves you, he'll understand."

She nodded and looked like she was going to add something else, but the red-sweater assistant called her out for some minor crisis. Drayco and Nelia headed back to the car, and as Drayco punched Dr. White's number into his phone, Nelia asked, "You really believe what you told her? That Gogo will understand?"

"They should stop lying to each other. He didn't tell her about the painting, and she didn't tell him about her gambling habit."

He stopped talking when a voice answered his call, "Sunshine Animal Hospital."

Drayco frowned. "Is this the number for Dr. Mark White?"

"Yes, it is. He's one of our veterinarians."

"Could I speak with him?"

"When he gets back. He just left for a ten-day vacation to San Juan and won't be reachable until then."

"You say he just left. Perhaps I can still call him at home?"

"I'm afraid not. As we speak, he's on Metro heading to the airport to catch his plane. And he said he was turning off his cellphone. You know, that whole get-away-from-it-all thing."

Drayco thanked her and hung up to check the airline schedules, figuring he could make it. Barely. "Change of plans," he told a bemused Nelia and began to sing, "Our mystery doctor is leaving on a jet plane, and I don't know when he'll be back again."

She glared at him.

❦   ❦   ❦

What Drayco hadn't counted on as he and Nelia hopped into the car to make a mad dash to the airport was a frantic call from Benny Baskin. "Where are you, boy-o?"

"Heading to DCA. Why?"

"Hope you're not skipping town. Because you'd better be at your evidentiary hearing that starts in a half hour or you might as well change careers right now. Become an airline pilot, why not, since you're la-ti-da-ing to the airport."

Benny's voice was even louder and more pointed than usual, making it easy for Nelia to overhear his end of the conversation. She had a stricken look on her face. She'd forgotten the date, too.

"I'll see what I can do, Benny."

Neither he nor Nelia exchanged a word as Drayco headed to the courthouse. He pulled in front where Benny Baskin happened to be standing, looking at his watch. Drayco turned to Nelia. "Stall him, stall the board. I just need a few extra minutes."

She gave him a you-owe-me slow burn. Right before she closed the door and Drayco pulled away, he heard Benny yell, "Where the hell is he going?"

Strains of Chopin's "Revolutionary" Etude played in his head at an even faster clip than he usually performed it. By the time he made it to the airport, his mental turntable had flipped through the Minute Waltz and a few other agitated pieces.

Still in speed mode, he nabbed an hourly parking spot, ran to the terminal, and homed in on the gate he'd matched to the flight number.

He pulled out his cellphone and checked the veterinary hospital's website, which had a photo of Dr. White.

A group of people poured out of the corridor that led into the cavernous lobby with its soaring ceilings and high-window views of planes waiting for passengers. Such a group might just have exited the Metro. Sure enough, he spied a man who matched the website photo and quickly cornered him.

"Dr. Mark White?"

The man blinked several times. "Do I know you?"

"I'm investigating Jerold Zamorra's death. His daughter, Ashley, said you'd left a message on her answering machine, a message intended for her father, by mistake. The message said you needed an answer to an important question by today. It may have something to do with the case, it may not, but do you mind telling me what this urgent matter was?"

White was still blinking. "I heard about his death, and I'm truly sorry. But I don't see how they could be connected. You see, Jerold had his eye on an expensive pedigreed dog owned by a friend of mine. The bitch was to have her puppies about now, and the owner had several buyers already lined up. I told Jerold I'd need his answer by today."

Drayco tried not to show his disappointment. "How much is this puppy worth?"

"Ordinarily German Shepherd puppies go for between one and twenty-four thousand, but this one's from guard dog stock. Those can fetch up to fifty grand."

"Why was Jerold not able to give you his answer sooner?"

"Said he was going to be coming into more money soon." The vet smiled. "Guess he was planning on winning the lottery."

Dr. White sneezed six times in a row and sniffled his apology. "Damned allergy meds aren't working like they should." He took a bottle out of his pocket and popped another one into his mouth, swallowing it dry. "Often wonder how you know you're getting what it says on the bottle. What with Chinese fakes these days."

White sneezed one more time. "Hell, I almost mixed up meds for one of my patients recently, myself. You think medications cost a fortune—try a lawsuit."

White looked over at the line forming through the snaking gates at the TSA security checkpoint. "It's been nice talking to you, Mister—"

Drayco handed him one of his cards, and White took it. "Dr. Drayco. Jerold Zamorra was a good customer. I took care of his snakes, you know. Look, if you have any more questions, call me in a couple of weeks. Or leave a message with my receptionist."

Drayco watched him enter the security line, then glanced at the clock on the wall. He now had about ten minutes to get back to the courthouse in time. Then pray Nelia and Benny were successful in stalling for a few extra minutes.

As he sprinted back to his car, he dialed Benny's number to give him an update. But his mind wasn't on the hearing. He couldn't stop thinking about Dr. White's comments about his medications.

32

Drayco traced a line around the rim of his glass, watching the beads of condensation drip down the sides. Drip, drip, drip, turning his paper napkin coaster into a transparent, pulpy mess. Fitting, that. He'd made it to his hearing in time, but almost wished he hadn't. Three hours of grilling made him realize what a barbecued steak feels like.

He motioned for the bartender to fill up the glass, as a voice boomed over his shoulder, "That your second or third?"

Drayco glanced up at Sarg, "You stalking me?"

"Didn't have to. How many batshit cases did we wrap up and 'celebrate' in pseudo-seedy dives like this one? I lost count. Figured this is the place you'd come after that board hearing farce today."

Drayco raised his now-full glass in Sarg's direction. "Thanks for speaking on my behalf. You and Gonzo made me sound like I deserve a halo. Spread it on a bit thick, didn't you?"

"Both Detective Gonzalez and I know better than to crown you with a halo, junior. All of us burned our Boy Scout badges years ago. This kind of job'll do that to a guy."

Sarg had the bartender bring him a soda, and Drayco pointed to it. "No beer?"

"You took a taxi, I gather, or otherwise you wouldn't be drinking. I didn't."

"Elaine's not going to like you coming home this late. It's what, ten?"

"Ten-thirty, but who's counting. Had some work downtown after the hearing, anyway. I can go into the Bureau late tomorrow."

Sarg raised his voice to be heard over both the growing bar crowd and the music as it cranked up a notch. "I think those two board members, Peggs and Scarpato, won over Saul Bobeck. Despite his shady ties to Mayor Kozell. Got a good feeling they'll rule in your favor."

Drayco shrugged and looked around at the sea of bar patrons, not uncommon in this part of Adams Morgan along 18th Street. Some of the bars were more frou-frou, not like the Black Heaven's brick-and-steel decor and its fried fare in finger form. But rivers of alcohol plus uncaged cubicle tigers mingling with the hip-hop crowd made for an electric atmosphere and frequent brawls.

Sarg swirled the soda around in his glass. "Used to wonder why you liked this place. You called it one of your 'people watching' spots. And something about the negatively charged energy attracting you."

Drayco studied Sarg's paper coaster. Still nice and dry. "Didn't feel like going home, that's all. Too quiet."

"You'd usually pound the piano after something like that hearing mess."

"Didn't feel like that, either. Haven't been near my piano in two days."

Sarg squinted up at one of the nuclear-bright red lights behind the bar that was aimed right at his face. He looked like a zombie escapee from a horror film, and Drayco almost laughed.

As if reading Drayco's mind, Sarg got up to move his bar stool. "Two days away from the piano. A lifetime for you. You usually take something like this sham hearing in stride."

"Haven't been sleeping much lately."

Sarg nodded and guzzled some soda. "More nightmares?"

"Some."

"You ever see a doc about that?"

Drayco shook his head.

A group of young men at the back of the bar erupted into loud cheers as a couple of young women got up on the tables and started dancing. Sarg raised his voice again. "You didn't tell me much about your second meeting with your mother. Still not talking?"

"Said she'd trusted few people in her life. She trusted Jerold, then he double-crossed her with a new partner. She doesn't know who."

"That's more than she's said before. So, that's why she set up the meeting with him the night he was murdered?"

"Allegedly. But being dead meant he'd robbed her of her chance to 'get back' at him."

"And she stabs the corpse instead. Oh, brother. You believe any of that?"

"I don't know."

Sarg tugged on his ear. "Would help to know where she's been all this time. Any luck tracking her?"

"Not much, but I have a friend in Scotland working on that end." Drayco peered at Sarg over his glass. "Have you?"

His former partner smiled. "You knew I couldn't *not* try, didn't you?"

"Would have been surprised if you hadn't."

"Too bad I've been every bit as productive as you. Bupkis. She doesn't exist as far as the databases go. Pretty rare these days. Especially with zero social media presence. And Brisbane is so clean, he probably doesn't have fingerprints."

Sarg took a swig from his soda. "Maura mentioned a new partner, eh? Maybe Gogo's hatred of Jerold was all an act. Maybe Gogo was Jerold's new wheeler-dealer."

The cheers at the rear of the bar grew louder as more patrons poured through the door, and the room began to resemble a newly opened can of sardines that smelled as bad. Drayco uttered a laugh that sounded to his ears like it had come from someone else. "She said she didn't want me to know what kind of person she was."

"Meaning?"

"I mentioned the phrase 'con woman' once, and she didn't correct me. My Scottish ex-Interpol connection told me the Brisbane clan are part of a group known as Scottish lowland gypsy Travellers. And that the Brisbanes have a history of minor run-ins with the law."

"We should find out where Alistair Brisbane lives. March right up the front door. Bring him some cupcakes or something."

"I already know."

Sarg frowned. "Yeah, when did you find that out?"

"Last night. Just in case I lost Brisbane's limo after his meeting near the Capitol, I made another call to a well-placed connection—don't ask me who, he's allergic to law enforcement types—and dug up the address. It was bought under an LLC based in New Mexico that isn't tied to Brisbane publicly."

"You check out the address in person?"

"I'd need to hire a helicopter or boat."

"He lives on an island?"

"Private. Sixteen acres with a beach, Federal-style main home, guest house, office, and a boat dock and helipad. Only twenty minutes from there to Potomac Airfield via a chopper. The previous homeowner was a Rockefeller."

"Why didn't Maura live there? That's one way to keep her out of trouble."

"Guess she didn't want to. Maybe even Brisbane isn't so controlling he'd be willing to keep his sister a virtual prisoner."

Someone bumped into Drayco, but that wasn't what made him turn around. The fevered pitch from the rowdy group had taken on a different tone, a sound creating bubbling brown blobs of tar to his ears. That sound usually meant one thing—the aural equivalent to him of a dog growling with a mix of anger and fear. Sure enough, the cheers morphed into screams, and fists started flying.

Drayco slammed his glass down, stood up, and headed for the group. But a bear lock around his chest that rivaled Iago's held him back, and he felt himself being hauled toward the door and outside into the cold air. Sarg only let go of him to half-push him down the street and into a quieter bar where he deposited Drayco into a chair at a table.

Drayco rubbed his arm. "What was that all about?" Sarg still had a few impressive moves left over from his ex-Ranger days. Almost put Iago to shame.

"I saw that look in your eye. You weren't headed for that crowd to stop the fight. You were going to join in, weren't you?"

"Why would I do that?"

"Negatively charged energy. You know you're not an ion, right?"

Drayco managed a slight smile. "Anion."

"What?"

"If an atom gains electrons and has a net negative charge, it's called an anion."

"Whatever. You've got bunches of particles in you, yay for you. But that brain of yours is supposed to have evolved beyond that whole limbic animal stuff. Getting rounded up by cops isn't going to help your board case or your mother."

Sarg signaled for the waitress and ordered a couple of black coffees and some water. "I saw it a lot in the Rangers. Hours, days, weeks of staying focused. Being expected to keep it together despite the world going to hell around you. That pent-up human magma has to blow some time."

"I'm fine."

"Like hell you're fine."

Drayco stared at the table. "Maybe Richard Feynman was right."

"Who's he?"

"Famous physicist who said, 'The first principle is you must not fool yourself, but you are the easiest person to fool.'"

The waitress returned with their cups, prompting Sarg to pull a bottle out of his pocket and hand it over.

Drayco picked it up. "Aspirin?"

"That beer you were on was at least your third, maybe fourth or fifth. Take the aspirin, drink the coffee."

"You don't usually carry aspirin with you."

"I came prepared."

That prompted a small smile from Drayco. "You know this bromance thing could never last."

Sarg grinned. "Just take the damned aspirin, would you?"

Drayco did and then grabbed his coffee to pour some salt into it. He stirred it in and took a sip. Just right. When he reached for the aspirin bottle again, Sarg said, "Two's enough."

"I know. This made me think of something the veterinarian said."

"That Dr. White guy you almost missed your hearing for?"

"He said he wondered how you knew what you're really getting, thanks to Chinese fakes. And that he almost accidentally mixed up some meds once."

"Not following. Drink more coffee."

"I'm not drunk. It's something Jerold Zamorra's elderly neighbor said. And putting two and two together, I'm getting five."

"Drink. Now. You'll feel better and think better in the morning. And try some of that melatonin when you get home. You need your sleep. Maybe we'll stop by the grocery on the way to your place. Elaine swears by tart cherry juice. Even better than melatonin."

Drayco relaxed and felt the negative energy draining away. Sleep sounded pretty good. And while five might sound like the wrong number, he had a sinking feeling it would turn out to be the right answer in the end. He took another sip of the coffee and plotted a con artist scheme of his own.

33

Drayco took big gulps out of the thermos of black coffee he'd filled up at the 7-11 and checked the time. He didn't want to start knocking on doors before nine. As he sat in his car waiting, he thought about his less-than-steller evening after Sarg dropped him off last night. He'd been up late again doing research and then a little attempt at the piano. A failed attempt.

He'd needed a strong dose of Bach, but found he still couldn't bring himself to play anything. Not one teensy little scale. He'd just sat there staring at the thing until he almost fell asleep on the keyboard.

One thing was sure—he owed Benny and Nelia big time for working their magic yesterday with their effective stalling. After the hearing, Benny was grumpily optimistic and Nelia cautiously worried about the outcome. In answer to their questions as to whether his plane-chasing side trip paid off, Drayco had hedged with his reply.

He couldn't give them an answer until he dug a little deeper into his new hypothesis. And for him to be able to answer that, he needed to get closer to his roots and use some of those Maura Brisbane McCune Drayco Whatevername genes to play con artist.

At the dot of nine, he drove past Edwin's small pharmacy building, within walking distance of the condos where Jerold had lived and died. He parked and headed for his first objective and knocked on the door. While waiting, he checked his image in the window to make sure he looked professional, no dandruff, no wrinkles. He'd even donned one of his hated ties.

Imogen Layford opened the door, her smile hesitant at first. Then, as recognition glinted in her eyes, she opened the door wider. "You're one of those folks who was looking at Jerold's place the other day."

"Scott Drayco, Mrs. Layford. I wonder if I might have a few moments of your time?"

She guided him to a green and blue paisley-print chair and poured him a cup of something amber. After all that coffee, he didn't want anything else but accepted it politely.

"Yerba mate," she pointed at the cup as he took a tentative sip of something that tasted a little like a cross between weak coffee, smoky wood, and flavored hay. "It'll put hair on your chest. A good sex tonic, too."

He almost choked but gulped another sip down. "Last time we spoke, you mentioned a Canadian lottery notice but hadn't kept the envelope. I don't suppose you've received another one since?"

She motioned for him to wait while she disappeared into a back room. He could hear drawers being opened and closed, and then she returned and handed him a letter. "It was sweet of you to remember that. I haven't gotten another, no, but I did find the one I told you about. I'd so appreciate it if you'd look into it for me. Jerold said he was going to."

 She sat on the sofa and stared at her teacup. "I guess he wasn't able to before he died."

Drayco put down his cup and looked over the form letter. A typically worded sham notice, "You must act now or the winnings will go to an alternate," and "Send money to cover taxes and processing fees," with instructions on where to send the money. But those instructions said to put a money order in the enclosed envelope. An envelope long gone now, and there was no address on the actual letter.

"Mrs. Layford, did any of your friends receive a similar notice?"

"Well now, I don't recollect as such. Least, they didn't say." She put her feet up on an ottoman, where it was more obvious she was wearing high-heeled boots. When she saw him staring at them, she grinned. "If you wear heels for decades, you can't just stop, or you won't be able to walk. Besides, everyone has their little vanities."

"I must confess I know very little about women's shoes."

"Most of my friends wear ugly flat things. And they complain all the time about their feet. If there's one thing I can't stand, it's belly-aching old people. If you make it to seventy, you've had a pretty good go at it, so stop complaining, I say."

He reached over to grab the cup of yerba matte but decided against it. If he wanted a sex tonic or any kind of tonic for that matter, he'd use the old standby, alcohol. "Are you feeling any better? You said you'd taken a turn for the worse lately."

"No U-turns yet, I'm afraid. Need to ask my doctor about upping my dose. Not that I'm complaining." She winked at him.

"You switched to Edwin Zamorra's pharmacy recently, isn't that right?"

"Such a kind man. Calls me whenever my refills are ready, without me having to ask."

"I passed by that pharmacy on my way here. It's certainly convenient. Do a lot of people at these condos get their meds there?"

"There's Twyla Sweet, for one. She lives in 208. And Inez Bruce. She's in 316. Oh, and Marta Aguayo. She's on the first floor in 119." She rattled off a few more names. Drayco filed each one away in his memory.

"You know, Mrs. Layford, maybe that medication of yours is just a little out of date—having to be shipped long distance, sitting on a shelf for a while. While I'm doing some checking, I'd be happy to have a friend of mine who works at a lab look into it for you. If you wouldn't mind parting with one of your pills that is."

She didn't hesitate to retrieve her medicine bottles. She had three with her and gave him one from each bottle. He noted the names on the bottles and pulled a little notebook out of his pocket. Grateful that Sarg wasn't here to see him with that notebook, he copied the name of each prescription and the dosage and then placed one of each pill in a little baggie he'd brought.

She sat back down again and drank some of the now-cold tea, not seeming to mind. Drayco handed her a photo from his wallet. "Did you ever see this woman with Jerold?" He'd gotten Benny to make him a copy of Maura's mugshot.

"That nice police detective asked me that, too. I did see her once, coming out of Jerold's place. She was angry and said if he ever did that to her again, she'd grab the nearest knife and cut him into pieces. The police seemed very interested in that."

Drayco could see the self-satisfied look on Halabi's face now. If it were up to the detective, Maura McCune would already be on death row.

Drayco chatted with her a little longer about those "obnoxious" boys on their skateboards at all hours, and then she surprised him with a cogent and insightful take on the latest stumbling blocks in Mideast peace initiatives. Most of all, she just seemed happy to have someone to talk to.

It was the same with all the other women he visited after he left Mrs. Layford's condo. Like her, they were elderly and lonely and would have kept him there all day if he hadn't maneuvered his way on to the next woman as politely as he could.

He briefly stopped by the rec room in the complex, where a group of mostly senior women were playing bingo. Lots of disposable income, lots of time on their hands. They were the throwaway people, so easily preyed on. One baitfish after another in a silver sea.

His next "interviewee," Twyla Sweet, had the same complaint about her medications not seeming to work as well after she'd switched to Edwin's pharmacy. Drayco got her to give him a sample, too, using the excuse he was conducting a survey on the quality of area pharmacies. So did Mara Aguayo, who talked about how her children didn't call and how she felt like she'd become invisible. Both women had also recently received Canadian lottery notices.

Inez Bruce, a smoker who'd had her voice box removed and talked via a TEP prosthesis and stoma, greeted him with a lighted cigarette in hand. In her mechanical voice, she told him he was such a handsome pup, he'd never have to worry about getting the ladies. That prompted him to draw up his sleeve on his right arm to show her all the scars. She was silent at first, then said with a wicked grin, "You got more you can show me?"

All the women gave him medicine samples, and he carefully cataloged each. As he did, he recalled Edwin's comment the first time Drayco and Sarg met him, about Edwin switching to his own independent pharmacy for more control, less red tape. No bean counters always looking over your shoulder. No corporate oversight wonks checking your books.

Maybe Drayco's hunch was way off, but the weight of coincidences threatened to tilt the scales of both medicine and justice down to earth with a thud.

❧ ❧ ❧

Drayco met Sarg in a parking lot in Dumfries, not too far from Quantico. Better to keep this part of his investigation from looking FBI-official for now, until if, and when, it needed to become an FBI case.

Sarg climbed out of his car saying "This is all cloak-and-dagger, junior. What's up?"

Drayco pulled out the baggies he'd labeled with prescription types and doses and placed them on the top of Sarg's Range Rover. "See if you can get these tested. Might need to get the FDA's OCI involved."

Drayco explained how he'd spent the earlier part of his morning, and Sarg looked at him with raised eyebrows. "These little old ladies just let you inside their homes, no questions asked? You'd make a great con artist, junior."

"The ole apple and tree cliché."

"What, you think Edwin was scamming his clients, Jerold found out, and Edwin killed him? Or he and Jerold and your mother—maybe even Ophelia Zamorra—were all partners in one loving family scam? A scamily, as it were? And where do Iago Pryce and Alistair Brisbane fit in?"

"When I saw Brisbane and Iago the other day, they were heading into a lobbying firm, one that deals with health industry clients like insurers."

"And pharmacists."

"Exactly," Drayco replied, as Sarg handed over a bottle of something reddish. "What's that?"

"You remember our favorite diner not far from here? They're bottling this stuff now. Pomegranate tea. Figured you haven't been staying hydrated, and that's why you're wasting away."

"Diner as in the one run by Michael and Michael II?" Or M&M, as they were known—who'd owned the place while Drayco was at the Bureau. Always kept an eagle eye on the wait staff to make sure they lived up to the M-squared's high standards. Obsessing over every detail, down to the always-fresh white carnations on the tables.

Drayco held up the bottle. "Good marketing move. The Michaels never leave anything to chance, do they?"

"Guess not. When you're in charge of your own destiny—"

"You mold that destiny to your will. Take our friend Alistair Brisbane, for instance. You might expect him to keep tabs on all the players in his little dramas, wouldn't you?"

"From what I've learned of the guy, sure."

Drayco opened his car door, reached inside, and pulled out a small object he handed it over. He closed the door again, making sure it was tight.

Sarg held it up to examine it. "A bug?"

"That one's deactivated. I found others at home and in my office, in both my cars, and I'm sure there are others tapping my phones."

Sarg looked at Drayco's cellphone on the driver seat of his car. "That's why you left your phone in there." Sarg rolled the device around in his hand. "Need help removing the others?"

"Not going to."

"You're joking, right?"

"I'll get a burner phone for times I don't want my new friends listening in. But the others, no. Let him think he's doing so undetected. Could work to my advantage."

"Better be careful which dames you bring into your love nest, then, lest you end up on YouTube."

Drayco nodded at the bug. "You can keep that one as a souvenir. In case something happens to me."

Sarg frowned at him. "Don't like you toying with this Brisbane guy." He put the bug in his pocket. "Even the little we've dug up points to Brisbane being some kind of shadow puppet master. More clout than mere politicians who come and go. You said he'd been in the country for thirty-six years, right?"

Drayco eyed the pomegranate tea in his hand. Maybe later, when he could savor it. "Mr. Big swears neither he nor his sister killed Jerold."

"And you believe him?"

"The question is, do I want to?"

Sarg picked up one of the pill baggies on his car. "These might be ordinary, genuine pills."

"Nothing would make me happier."

Sarg added the baggies to his growing pocket collection. "I'll see what I can do."

"Any way to put a stat order on it? Like, maybe, today?"

"I got some techs at a lab working with OCI who owe me a favor. A big favor. What's next for you?"

"I'm going to a funeral at five."

"Jerold's? Were you invited?"

"No."

Sarg grinned. "Sticking your head into the lion's den. Sounds like fun. If I didn't have a shitload of paperwork, I'd go with you."

"You think it would be gauche if I texted you details during the service?"

"Better yet, take some photos with a flash. And some selfies. And hold up your phone to video the whole damn thing. You'll fit right in."

34

Edwin Zamorra was right when he said there wouldn't be enough mourners to fill Westminster Abbey. Drayco estimated the three ranks of pews could seat close to five hundred people, and the place was only half full. He saw a familiar face and slid into the pew next to her in the back.

Rena Quentin looked up in surprise. She whispered, "Didn't expect to see you here."

"Ditto."

"We outcasts should stick together."

"I didn't know Jerold was a Unitarian Universalist."

"He comes from a long line of lapsed Baptists, and his wife Ophelia came from a long line of lapsed Catholics. I guess the Unitarians are the only ones who'd have them."

Churches were like foreign countries to Drayco. Maura was a devout Presbyterian when she married Brock. When she left him, he'd left her religion—in fact, all religion—behind, and so did his son.

Drayco took in the church's architecture and decor, a modern-traditional hybrid of stained glass and Bauhaus looking like a Puritan woman wearing makeup. The piano upfront was a seven-foot grand—maybe someone would play it during the service so he could hear what it sounded like. Thus far, the only music was from a small electronic organ. He shuddered.

Edwin Zamorra sat in front with two elderly people Drayco assumed were Edwin's—and Jerold's—parents. Ashley Zamorra was seated in a different area next to Gogo Cheng. Drayco was fairly certain none of them would be happy to see him here, a suspicion confirmed when Lauralee Fremont walked in. She looked directly at him and Rena, frowned, then proceeded to ignore them, taking a seat behind Gogo and Ashley.

Drayco caught the eye of another man seated in the back. Iago Pryce, keeping watch on the proceedings and on Drayco.

No one looked comfortable, despite the unusually soft seat cushions in the pews. Discomfort was what you'd expect from a funeral, ordinarily. Just not the way people were avoiding looking at each other, along with their tense shoulders and awkward whispers. Because it was a murder, perhaps? Or due to the undercurrent of ill will, jealousy, and all the other myriad problems Jerold had with the "mourners"?

Rena said, "Jerold and I actually had a good relationship until his behavior changed at the end. Professional, but friendly. We had our minor disagreements like his annoying habit of humming in meetings. I got back at him by bringing in my favorite Clibo candy."

As Drayco looked at her in confusion, she explained, "I'm addicted to caramel and came across Clibo when I visited Japan. Jerold was one of those 'Made in America only' zealots. Even candy. Wouldn't even touch Belgian chocolate."

"I see," Drayco replied, as he adjusted his legs so his knees didn't bang into the pew in front of him. "Are many of his former TSA co-workers here?"

"Several. I'm sorry Barney Schleissman can't be here. Probably Jerold's best friend at the TSA, but he developed dementia. I hear he's in an assisted-living home somewhere."

Sarg had also uncovered and passed along that tidbit to Drayco earlier. Of all the people at the TSA, Schleissman would be most likely to know if Jerold were knee-deep in gambling or fraud.

Since the TSA had heaped multiple commendations on Jerold, it didn't seem likely his other co-workers knew about Jerold's secret life. Bless Sarg's heart, he'd already contacted many of them using his FBI creds, enough to cross them off the list.

Rena leaned over to be heard above the music. "I loathe funerals. People pretending to care about each other, saying and doing things the deceased would despise. That's why I have a Living Will. The details of my funeral and graveside service are planned down to the second, including the type of flowers."

"Practical," he said while thinking to himself, *a Martha Stewart clone or OCD?*

Drayco took stock of each guest, their various heads floating above an ocean of black and navy, with smatterings of browns and grays. One woman wearing a white pantsuit stood out like a great white shark in the dark sea.

He wasn't learning as much as he'd hoped from this gathering of siblings, supporters, and suspects. The remarks were unremarkable, the eulogies unedifying. Drayco's ear perked up when Edwin walked to the podium.

With the photo of Jerold on an easel sitting atop the casket, it was easy to compare the two brothers. Jerold, five years younger than his brother, had kept most of his dark hair, while Edwin was balding, grayer. Other superficial bits, eye color, nose, mouth, were the same, but it was the weak jawline they shared that fascinated Drayco.

He'd once had a long discussion with a forensic artist on how the cut of someone's jaw told more about their personality than almost anything else, second only to the eyes. As the artist had noted, weak of jaw, weak of character.

Edwin got to an anecdote about the brothers as boys when the woman in the white-shark pantsuit stood up and keeled over. Her companions rushed to her aid as one woman who was fanning the victim said so loudly people in the back could hear, "I told her she shouldn't come to a murderer's funeral."

Edwin paused, uncertainty written all over his face, and the congregation alternated between hushed exchanges and silence. It was Ashley who rose to her feet and helped the woman, now recovering from her faint, out of the sanctuary and through a doorway down front.

Rena whispered to Drayco, "See what I mean?" She started fanning herself, something Drayco understood thanks to the heat turned up higher than the moderate weather warranted.

But when he turned toward her, her face was pale. Thinking he might have another fainter on his hands, he leaned over and whispered, "Need some air?"

When she nodded, he grabbed her elbow and guided her out of the not-quite-sanctuary into the moonlit sky and cooler temps outside. She drank in some of the fresh air, then fished around in her purse for a tissue and dabbed at her eyes. "I haven't been to a funeral in a long time. There was my grandmother's, but she was old, and it was expected. A blessing, really. Before that, it was my mother's. Worst day of my life."

The mother she'd said was murdered, just like Ashley's mother, Ophelia. Had Rena noticed the parallels? Had she tried to reach out to Ashley but was rebuffed as her father's former co-worker? On the other hand, Ashley might have cheered Rena on for filing the claim against him, effectively forcing him into early retirement.

Rena tucked the soggy tissue in her coat pocket. "I doubt I'll go to my father's funeral, whenever that day arrives. He can rot in jail, for all I care."

That thought seemed to cheer her up, and she smiled at him. "Why did you come today? To study the wild animals in their native habitat?"

"Something like that," he said as he walked her to her car.

"Still tilting at windmills? Trying to prove your mother's innocence?"

"Or end up proving her guilt. That's beginning to appear equally likely."

Then she surprised him further by reaching up to kiss him on the cheek. "My hero."

"Glad someone thinks so." As he watched her drive away, he caught a glimpse of Iago Pryce framed in the doorway of the church, staring at Drayco. Since they were becoming such bosom buddies now, Drayco gave Iago a big bow as he left Jerold's piranha party behind.

≈ ≈ ≈

Iago stood back to admire the gleaming white surface of the Gulfstream III, then walked around it for a better look. A nice jet, all in all. Pretty good range, too. Forty-two hundred nautical miles and a service ceiling of forty-five thousand feet.

Fortunately, the drive from the funeral had only taken an hour in post-rush traffic. When he tried to drive west on I-66 most other times, it was a parking lot. Too bad he didn't have a flying car to soar above it all.

A man dressed in a pilot's uniform walked up to him. "If you're looking for a charter flight, we don't do those. Privately owned." He didn't say by whom, but in these parts, you didn't ask. Government, military, business, they all used something like this baby to avoid the pitfalls of commercial travel. And the Manassas hangers were full of them.

Iago replied, "No charters. Just here to check up on that," he nodded over at the Gulfstream 650 on the other end of the hangar. "My plane."

The pilot whistled. "She's a beauty, all right. Been trying to find a gig flying one of those. Don't suppose you're hiring?"

"Not right now. You got a card?" The man handed one over, and Iago thrust it into his pocket. Didn't hurt to keep it, but Alistair was pretty picky about his pilots. With a nod at the other man, Iago headed to the 650 and entered the cabin.

The G3 was nice, all right, but the 650 was better. Not just its range of seven thousand nautical miles that meant it could get to most global cities on a single tank of gas. It had an interior nicer than some hotels—bedroom, convection oven, shower, handcrafted leather recliners, wireless internet, satellite phones. But then, sixty-five million should buy you something nice.

Iago only had to duck an inch or two to walk through the cabin, another plus. He'd only partly lied to the pilot since it was Alistair's jet, not Iago's. It was part of Iago's duties to keep an eye on it, keep it stocked and ready to go on a moment's notice. He checked the food staples, toiletries, first aid supplies, and of course, the bar.

Finally, he flipped open a drawer in the stateroom next to the bed, lifted out the socks and boxers, and eased his hands along the base of the drawer until he fingers found the little switch. After pulling out the false bottom, he pulled out a stack of passports and IDs.

He flipped open one of them, with his photo and the name Jonathan Adams. Quite an impressive list of ports of call ole Jonathan had been to. After making sure "everyone" was accounted for, he replaced the passports and drawer.

When he spied the little red telephone call box toy they'd picked up on their last trip to the UK, he chuckled and laid it next to the small stuffed camel from Dubai. They could keep each other company while he was gone. With one last look around the cockpit to make sure everything seemed copacetic, he headed toward the exit.

After all, he couldn't afford to stay away from tailing Scott Drayco too long. He smiled at that. The kid was good at what he did—if you could call a thirty-six-year old man a kid. But then, what would you expect from Maura's son?

35

Saturday, February 23

There was nothing quite like flying over the Chesapeake Bay as the sun rose, its crimson and orange light reflecting off the water like stained glass. Drayco managed to rent a Cessna at the last minute—thankfully, demand for planes at his usual FBO weren't as high in the winter. The plane handled a lot better in the cooler temps though. It certainly climbed faster. And the lack of thermals meant the air was almost as smooth as the bay below.

He didn't need to travel this particular weekend to see how the renovations on his opera house were progressing. He bit back a groan, knowing he'd never get used to being the owner of such a place. Still, he'd made the decision not to sell it after it was bequeathed to him, so renovate it he must.

He wasn't fooling anybody with his excuse about the reason for his trip, let alone himself. He needed to talk to someone, and it wasn't the woman whose house he was standing in front of right now. He probably shouldn't be here, but word would get out he'd been on the shore. With a sigh, he knocked on the door and juggled the vase of fresh-from-the-florist red roses, purple lavender and something called Stargazer lilies.

Darcie wore a lot more than a bow this time, dressed in her more customary designer duds from Calvin-Donatella-Armani-Prada. She and Lauralee would probably get along beautifully. Darcie broke into a seductive smile when she saw him, grabbed the flowers and put them on a table next to the door.

Then she grabbed his coat and yanked him into the house. "Just can't stay away from me, can you?"

Well, yes, he could. Or should. Or what the hell, he wasn't sure. "It's only the weekend. One night."

"Then we'll have to make that one night count."

He cleared his throat. "Ah, I'm staying at the Lazy Crab, actually. Haven't seen the Jepsons in a while."

Her smile morphed into a pout. "They can't give you what I have to offer."

"Not exactly, no. But I'm overdue, and I owe them a lot."

"Well, then. She unbuttoned his coat and pushed it off his shoulders. "We'll have to make what time we do have count." She clutched his hand in hers and pulled him upstairs after her toward the bedroom.

"You're insatiable, you know that?"

"Takes one to know one." She unwrapped him almost as fast as she had that bow, and after a few hours of not-so-unpleasant-time together, he got dressed and made his excuses and his escape.

First, he made a brief stop by the opera house and peeked into the auditorium. The old chairs were gone, at least temporarily, dispatched to a restoration warehouse. The ripped-up carpet was nowhere in sight, and the curtains from the stage had vanished. He kept tabs on all the work being done via the contractor, but it was still a bit of a shock to see the old girl looking denuded and stark.

He couldn't play the Steinway this time because he'd forgotten it was in its temporary new home being refitted. That is if he could even bring himself to play. He'd hoped the different setting might make it easier for him to try to ease into playing again, but even that opportunity was thwarted.

After turning the lights off, he finally made his way to the Lazy Crab, where the always-bubbly Maida Jepson welcomed him in a much more matronly way. "Scott, we were thrilled to hear you were coming. Wish it were longer, but we'll take what we can get."

"Still hoping to make it over for a week or two soon. But work, life, the usual."

She studied his face. "You sounded a bit off on the phone. And now that I see you in person, you look a bit off, too." She nodded at the kitchen. "You know what's waiting for you, don't you?"

"The Major?"

"Well, him, yes. I was thinking more along the lines of something hot and eighty proof, give or take."

He wasn't about to turn down a should-be-world-famous Maida hot toddy, but as he sat in the kitchen sipping on her latest creation, it didn't feel as satisfying as usual. She must have noticed he was only taking the occasional sip. "Either I'm losing my touch or you really are in a funk. Do I have to sic my better half on you?"

A man's grumbled voice preceded its owner down the hall. "What's all the racket, Maida? Not time for lunch, is it?"

Major Jepson's ponytail and braided beard seemed whiter than the last time, but his eyes were as piercing as ever. He ambled into the kitchen. "Scott, my boy. Forgot you were coming today. You don't look well, son. Got a touch of the flu?"

Drayco relaxed into the chair. He'd only known the Jepsons for a little under a year, and yet they seemed like his idea of what good parents were like. Or would be, if they had children. Maybe being an unofficial "adopted" pseudo-son wasn't such a bad thing.

As he sat there, sipping the toddy, with the two pairs of concerned eyes turned on him, he realized why he'd really come. Brock and Maura felt very far away, in more ways than one.

"I was just going to ask you the same thing, Major. Your voice sounds different. Have you got a cold?"

"Never felt better. Must be early season pollen clouding your ears."

Drayco frowned. He could have sworn the man had a cold. The usual electric-blue wool cotton threads in his tones had morphed into gray steel wool. Major was probably right—just an artifact of the early pollen season.

After Drayco filled them in on the basics of his mother's reappearance and murder case, Maida dropped into the chair beside him with a shake of her head. "I'd have thought Nelia Tyler might have mentioned this. It's been, what, ten days now since it all came to pass?"

Ten days. She was right. Felt a lot longer. Felt eons longer. "Deputy Tyler and Sheriff Sailor had to work a shooting that happened late last night." He'd called Nelia before he arrived, not sure if he should or not. Calling her at the Sheriff's Office seemed safer, although he was disappointed she couldn't join them at the Lazy Crab for dinner.

Maida clucked her tongue. "I'm sorry, Scott. Truly sorry this bombshell landed on you from out of the blue. You don't deserve it. Any of it. Now I can understand why you never mentioned your mother before. I admit I was curious—"

"You were downright nosy," Major piped up. "About ready to do a little private eye-ing on your own."

"Now, Major." She frowned at him. "It wasn't that bad."

Her husband snorted, then got up to grab a plate of something bready with nuts and chocolate and placed it on the table. "What would make a mother do that to her own children, I wonder? And you say even now she won't discuss why she left, where she's been, or why she's back."

"Not to me. Not to anyone."

Maida pushed the plate of pastries closer to Drayco. He spied a ribbon of chocolate inside one, and his stomach rumbled. She shook her head. "You haven't eaten much this morning, I'll bet. You need more than sugar."

She jumped up and started rummaging through the refrigerator. "I'll fix that in short order. I think you're ten pounds thinner than the last time I saw you."

He protested, "I'm not very hungry."

"Yes, you are. Your stomach just said so."

She moved from refrigerator to cupboards in her food quest, but stopped in mid-stride. "You say your mother rented an apartment not all that far from you? Maybe you're looking at this the wrong way. Maybe she wasn't in the area for some shady business deal. Surely she'd know she might be seen, might be recognized. Seems to me she was checking up on you."

"Me? Why now?"

"Maybe not just now. You don't know if this is the first time. She could have passed through off and on, and you'd never know. You only found out now because of the whole murder angle."

Maura did say she knew about the carjacking and his injury. She certainly hadn't seemed surprised when he'd mentioned he'd been employed by the Bureau or that he no longer worked there. If Brock wasn't speaking to her, then there was only one logical conclusion—she *had* been keeping tabs on him.

Major nodded. "What was it she told you? She didn't want you to know the kind of person she was. Love takes many forms, Scott. Sacrifices aren't just for soldiers and firefighters."

Drayco didn't have time to mull over Major's words when Drayco's cellphone rang. He picked it up to check the number, thinking he should turn the bloody thing off. But when he saw the caller's ID, he punched the answer button. He had to pull the phone partly away from his ear due to the decibel level of the man's voice on the other end.

Detective Halabi's gold-colored baritone voice boomed out, "Figured you'd like to know we've arrested Edwin Zamorra, thanks to your efforts, it seems. Since you're making me cancel my weekend plans, thought you might like to come to my office and join us."

It was less of a polite request and more of a command. The Cessna was going to get more of a workout today than Drayco had anticipated.

He sprawled back into his seat and looked out into the garden of mostly dormant plants, except for a few pops of red from spring-blooming camellias. "Well, Maida. Looks like I won't be staying after all."

"Bad tidings?"

He sighed. Bad, good, who knew? One thing was for certain—when this was all over, he was definitely coming over for a week. Maybe two. No, make that a month.

36

Halabi had also called Sarg, who greeted Drayco as he arrived midafternoon at the Arlington PD. The two got checked in and ushered to Halabi's office together. The detective, who'd brought in extra chairs to accommodate both men, pointed to a box of stale donuts on his desk. "Take all you want. I'm chowing down on alphabet soup today. A little bit of FBI, FDA, HHS, FTC."

That fact wasn't a complete surprise to Drayco. After Sarg had called in his favor with the lab techs, he'd phoned Drayco late last night with preliminary results—the meds Drayco obtained from the elderly women were suspect. The real surprise was that Halabi's alphabet soupers hadn't camped out on Drayco's doorstep. Yet.

Halabi thumped a stack of lab reports. "Those pills from Edwin Zamorra's pharmacy were a combo of watered-down meds and counterfeit placebos. When we approached Edwin at home this morning with a search warrant for his pharmacy records, he turned into the proverbial canary."

Sarg asked, "Did he say why he did it, sir? For the money?"

"That part's a bit hazy. Swears he wasn't altering life-saving drugs like chemo or AIDS prescriptions. We'll check into that. If he's telling the truth, guess we have an unethical pharmacist with a 'moral' code."

Drayco eyed the donuts without much enthusiasm. He was supposed to be enjoying one of Maida's restaurant-worthy suppers right about now. Halabi caught him looking at them and said, "No jokes about cops and donuts. My wife runs a bakery, and these are hers. I can't turn them down, can I?"

Drayco found himself wishing Halabi's wife was a coffee barista, instead. "Did Edwin mention a partner or partners in his prescription fraud scheme?"

Halabi put on a pair of reading glasses and peered over the rim at Drayco. "He did not. You're thinking Jerold, right?"

The detective hadn't asked Drayco about Maura and her con-woman past or Iago or Brisbane. So far, so good. He felt Sarg looking at him, asking without asking if they should bring it up. Drayco shook his head a fraction, and Sarg settled back in his chair.

Drayco replied, "Jerold, certainly, or anyone else."

"If Jerold found out and threatened to expose Edwin, that would be a damn good motive for murder, I'll hand it to you." Halabi continued to study Drayco. "Anything else you want to tell me?"

Sarg answered first, "Might check on Jerold's sports gambling habit." And he proceeded to fill Halabi in on the FBI's newly opened investigation into the outfit Gogo had attended.

Drayco added, "You can also check Western Unions to see if anyone matching Jerold's description has cashed money orders. Match them to lottery fraud complaints registered with the FTC or FBI."

Halabi looked from Drayco to Sarg, who shrugged but then gave Drayco a sharp side glance. Drayco gave Sarg a little raise of his hands in a silent apology. He had a lot of explaining to do later.

Halabi continued with a note of exasperation in his voice, "We got a neighbor of Jerold's who says he saw Edwin with Jerold a day before Jerold was murdered. Edwin says it was just a routine visit. He'd never kill his brother. Family is family."

Well now, Edwin had lied when he told Drayco and Sarg he hadn't seen Jerold in two weeks. Drayco shifted around in the too-short chair. "First Ashley, estranged from her father, visits him on the day he was murdered. Then Edwin, also estranged, visits his brother shortly beforehand."

"Yeah. Odd that." Halabi glanced at his notes. "In Ashley's case, it was to return some of her father's possessions. We have a list she gave us. Nothing strange." Halabi flipped over a page. "Oh, before I forget to mention it, we found where your mother was staying."

He nodded his head at Drayco without looking up, "An apartment in a duplex, paid in cash. We found some high-quality fake ID cards we can't trace and the cellphone she used to call Jerold. Someone's been there within the past few days—a potted plant was watered recently."

He took off his glasses. "You wouldn't know anything about that, would you, Drayco?"

Drayco ignored the question and pulled a key out of his pocket sealed in a plastic baggie. "Something else you can check. After Ashley and Edwin allowed us to look through Jerold's condo, I found this inside one of those fake aquarium rocks."

He reached over and tossed it onto Halabi's desk. Halabi picked it up. "Why didn't you give this to me sooner?"

"Slipped my mind."

"Has anything else slipped your mind?" The detective glared at him for several moments, then rubbed his eyes. "This case has me positively knackered. Don't need more pain from you to add to my budding migraine."

Drayco asked, "Knackered? Thought I'd heard microscopic bits of a British accent."

"With a Lebanese-American father and English mother, it was 'Arabish' when I was growing up."

Sarg said, "With the Sargosians, it was Armenian-ish. Getting back to the case, seems to me Edwin's arrest means the charges against Maura McCune aren't as airtight as they seemed."

Halabi frowned. "Let's not get ahead of ourselves."

Sarg explained, "Edwin could have killed his brother over the medication fraud. He hated the TSA—and by extension his brother, perhaps. And he was in love with Jerold's wife, isn't that right, sir?"

"A few people we talked to speculated on that. He admit it to either of you?"

Drayco nodded. "Making it possible Edwin killed his brother—and his brother's wife—out of jealousy."

"Is that why you've been fixated on Ophelia Zamorra's death, Drayco?"

"I wouldn't exactly say fixated. Besides, of the two brothers, I think it more likely Jerold killed his wife."

Halabi fanned his fingers out on his desk. "Hell, if that's true, I'll owe Ashley Zamorra a big apology. Don't think I'm her favorite person right now."

She'd admitted as much to Drayco, but he didn't voice it aloud. Halabi wasn't exactly his favorite person right now, either. "Ashley's closer to her uncle than she was her father."

"Yeah. I got that when we notified her about this latest development. She's coming in later today to make a statement."

Halabi grabbed a donut and started nibbling on it. With his mouth half full, he said, "Your mother's a flight risk. And she's refusing to cooperate with an alibi or account of her recent activity. Until we prove otherwise, she'll remain our top murder suspect and safely in jail. For all I know, she and Edwin were partners in this."

Sarg chimed in, "We'd like to talk to Edwin if the offer is still on the table."

"I said I'd let *you* talk to him, Agent Sargosian." Halabi stared at Drayco. I guess if you'll function as his chaperone, it'll suffice. If you do anything to screw up the case, the interview is over."

So, Halabi would be listening in. Drayco couldn't hold it against Halabi for his anti-Drayco suspicions. If their situations were reversed, he'd feel the same.

What mattered was they were all on the same side, the side of truth, even though their roadmaps getting there didn't agree. *Truth.* Funny how one little word manifested itself in so many different ways—truth could be haven, hope, heaven, or hell.

37

Drayco and Sarg had earlier agreed they'd let Sarg take the lead in questioning Edwin in a move to placate Halabi. The detective, true to his word, hovered in a corner of the interrogation room, watching and listening. Sarg sat across from Edwin at the table while Drayco stood in an opposite corner from Halabi.

They'd learned from Halabi that Edwin didn't have an attorney and hadn't asked for one, despite being read his rights. But as they entered and he saw Drayco, he said, "I was told I could get a court-appointed attorney."

Sarg replied, "I understand you don't have an attorney yourself, sir."

"At six hundred an hour? You kidding? Can't even afford bail."

"You can request a public defender at your arraignment."

Edwin slumped in his seat. "Probably shouldn't talk to you without one. Guess I'm saying that a bit late, aren't I?"

"That depends, Mr. Zamorra. In the face of overwhelming guilt, cooperating can mean the difference between a lighter jail sentence and a harsh one."

Edwin closed his eyes for a moment then sat up straighter. "As I told the detective over there, I never meant to hurt anyone. And I don't think I did. My elderly customers are addicted to those damned pain pills doctors throw at them. A lot easier for the docs, right? Just push the pills, shut them up?"

He pinched the bridge of his nose. "They shouldn't be addicted like that. I was just helping them."

"Didn't it ever occur to you, sir, that some of those same people could die sooner rather than later thanks to your 'intervention'?"

Edwin balled up his fists. "I didn't water down the cancer drugs. Never those."

Sarg stared at him. "Did you sell the extra painkillers on the market?"

In reply, Edwin looked down at the table. That's one question he hadn't answered for Halabi, and apparently, he wasn't about to start implicating himself that deeply. Not that it would matter when Halabi, the FDA, and the FBI tracked all his phone and paper records. If he'd done it, they'd find it.

"Did your brother know about your scheme, sir?"

"Jerold?" Edwin stared at Sarg. "I never told him."

"But he figured it out?"

"He never said so."

Sarg exchanged a glance with Drayco, who knew what he was thinking. Edwin was dancing around in circles to avoid a straight answer.

Time for a different tactic. Drayco piped up, "Edwin, when you told me you loved Ophelia, you never said whether she loved you in return."

Edwin's head whipped up in confusion as he gaped at Drayco. He blinked his eyes as he replied, "She told me she did. And I believed her."

"Why didn't the two of you ever get together?"

"She was Catholic, which meant no divorce. But she was also a free spirit, and I always wondered if that divorce thing was just an excuse. To answer your question, I don't know."

"When I asked you if Jerold requested a paternity test, you said no. But you didn't seem surprised by the question. Is Ashley your daughter?"

Edwin bit his lip. More silence, but in this case, his silence spoke volumes. Maybe he didn't know for certain, but he suspected.

Sarg said, "That must be hard. Watching another man raise your daughter with the woman you love?"

Edwin processed that slowly. Then, his face hardened when he realized Sarg's implication that he hated his own brother enough to murder him. "On second thought, anything else is going to have to wait for that attorney, whoever it is."

As Edwin was led away, Halabi said, "That bit about his daughter. Good motive for murder. And his refusal to answer directly whether Jerold knew about his drug scheme ... intriguing, I'll grant you."

Halabi pointed his next comments at Drayco, "We're grateful for the tip, but we'll take it from here."

Outside the detention facility, Sarg put his hand on Drayco's shoulder. "What was all that about, the Jerold-and-lottery-fraud angle you mentioned to Halabi?"

"Imogen Layford. She said she gave Jerold an envelope from the lottery scam to investigate for her. She never heard back from him—did he really not have time or was he involved in some way? And then there's those framed lottery tickets on his wall. A possible in-joke."

Sarg asked quietly, "You think that was his big scheme? And your mother was his partner?"

"Iago hinted Maura might be partners with Jerold in something not-quite-aboveboard. Maybe she's not a murderer. Maybe she's just a criminal of another stripe."

Edwin's arrest might make it appear to some that Maura was less likely to be Jerold's killer. To Drayco, it seemed more likely. Were his instincts wrong? Was he blinded by his desire to have her punished somehow?

Sarg, ever the mind reader, said, "You know you'll have to spill the beans about Iago Pryce and Alistair Brisbane sooner or later, right?" He left unspoken the warning that Sarg himself might be forced to bring it up. Withholding information like that, even on an unofficial case, wouldn't do Sarg's career any favors.

Drayco slapped him on the back in reply. "I got cheated out of one of Maida's culinary masterpieces. Got any ideas how we can make it up to me?"

"Ever had *bulgogi*?"

"Please don't tell me it's fried bull testicles."

"I've heard about those—they call them Rocky Mountain Oysters out west. But no, just normal Korean barbecue. Add a little *samjang* and some *saengchae* and you'll want to change your name to something like Min-jun."

"And here I was thinking you'd want to try some Chinese fare in honor of Gogo."

"Next time. Come on, my treat."

❦ ❦ ❦

Drayco and his Starfire followed Sarg and his Range Rover to a strip mall in Annandale and a restaurant with a sign that said Life Is Food. As they stood outside the storefront, Drayco pointed at the sign. "Doesn't sound very Korean to me."

"Guess they didn't want to scare off the less adventurous diner with a more exotic name. I mean, 'life is food' and barbecue in the same sentence? Who wouldn't go for that?"

Despite the unassuming hole-in-the-wall exterior, the dining room had clean, modern decor interchangeable with any high-end eatery in the District. Or New York, for that matter. They were promptly seated at a sleek, shiny ebony table and booth, and after taking one look at the menu, Drayco said, "You order."

Sarg rattled off a few dish names to the waiter who nodded and disappeared through a set of windowless double doors. Drayco said, "No bull testicles, right?"

"Better. You'll see."

After they started chowing down on a spicy pork *bulgogi* appetizer, Drayco nodded. "Outstanding."

"Oh, ye of little faith."

Drayco eyed the last piece of bulgogi, which was the odd man out from the seven-piece order. Sarg cut it in half and pushed the plate over. Drayco made quick work of it before asking, "How's the family? I haven't seen Elaine or Tara since dinner at your place last month."

"Didn't I tell you? Tara's got several offers from colleges with forensic science programs. With full scholarships."

Drayco smiled. Hardly surprising, but he was happy to hear the news, all the same.

"Michael isn't happy with his accounting job. Thinking of joining the Army. Maybe gun for the Ranger program." Sarg's face was beaming so brightly that it almost outshone the light from the glass chandelier bouncing off the ebony table.

"And Elaine?"

"She's taken up Russian."

"Learning another language is good. Why Russian?"

"Likes the way it sounds. And she wanted to learn a new alphabet. Cyrillic fills the bill. Maybe you can help her out sometime? If she needs a little nudge in the right direction?"

"My Russian's a little rusty."

"Better than my no Russian."

The waiter brought something that looked like slabs of indistinguishable mystery meat, which Sarg explained was their signature barbecue beef ribs *kalbi*. Drayco took a few tentative bites and sighed happily. *Oh my, where have you been all my life?*

They munched in companionable silence for a few minutes until Sarg spoke up. "You believe Edwin killed his own brother?"

"My first thought is that it's too pat. And that bit about Ashley being his daughter—yeah, he'd be upset, but why strike now?"

"Because Jerold squandered all Ashley's inheritance. And if Edwin felt protective about Ashley, his real daughter, that could do it."

"But why frame Maura?"

"She was handy."

"Not exactly. The mystery 'witness' who disguised his voice, assuming it was the real killer or an accomplice, had to choreograph everything carefully in advance. People don't usually carry around voice disguisers with them. Edwin doesn't strike me as being that detailed a criminal mastermind. If he were, he'd have never scammed so many customers at the same address."

"It's always the quiet ones, right?"

"Of all our suspects, that should put Lauralee at the top."

"Motive?"

"Maybe that sexual harassment thing of Jerold's didn't just extend to Rena. Maybe he tried it on Lauralee."

"Yeah, but would she have stayed in the quartet afterward?"

"She desperately needed the money." Drayco filled Sarg in on Lauralee's violin sales side business he'd discovered after tailing her.

"Maybe Gogo and his knives make more sense. I mean, if he found out Jerold had pushed his unwanted advances on Ashley ..."

Drayco drummed his fingers on the table. "Both Lauralee and Ashley seemed uncomfortable when I brought up the subject. But they didn't have the usual demeanor of women who were sexual assault victims. Not like those I saw at the shelter where Ashley works."

Sarg nodded and chewed on his *kalbi*, deep in thought. "I hate to ask, but what if it was Edwin and Maura who were having an affair and were partners in crime? Then killed Jerold over finding out?"

"Why would Maura stick around while Edwin vamoosed? And let herself be the one found holding the knife?"

"I hadn't had a chance to tell you yet. Got a call from one of my PD sources this morning. Said the forensic techs returned to the scene of the crime. They found minute traces of human blood on the bricks at Jerold's condo."

"Outside?"

"Yep."

Drayco stopped drumming his fingers. "Possibly Jerold's and possibly left by the killer. Certainly bolsters Maura's story. It would make no sense for her to kill Jerold, go outside, then go back inside."

"You know what makes sense?" Sarg signaled the waiter. "Ordering some *hotteok* for dessert."

Drayco took one bite of the nutty pancake topped with caramelized bananas. Every course of the meal had been better than the last. He wolfed it down in record time, which made Sarg grin. "Need to bring you here more often. Fatten you up."

"Why is everyone always trying to fatten me up?"

"Six-four and one-seventy-five. Granted, it's one-seventy-five of mostly muscle and gristle. I doubt you have an ounce of fat. Me, on the other hand," Sarg grabbed the shirt around his middle. "Don't think I'd pass the Ranger physical today."

Drayco seriously doubted that. Just as he was beginning to doubt he'd ever understand his mother. He had another appointment with Brody McGregor later, so maybe he'd get more of his answers. Or maybe Maura was a puzzle he'd never solve.

38

Drayco had no sooner entered his townhome that he realized, yet again, he wasn't alone. Might as well ditch the security system. Not Brock or Darcie this time, but Iago again, sitting in Drayco's den. He'd helped himself to a beer.

"You must tell me which decryption device you're using, Pryce. I think I should buy stock in the company."

Iago just smiled and tipped the beer up in salute. "Congratulations, by the way. Edwin Zamorra, eh? Mean's Maura's getting closer to a release."

Drayco planted himself in front of Iago. "Tell your employer he may be celebrating too soon. Edwin's arrest doesn't mean she wasn't involved in his scheme or with Jerold's murder."

Truth be told, Drayco was close to believing Maura had schemes going with both Zamorra brothers. The thought wasn't helping his mood. Nor was this approach of Iago and Brisbane, using him to play the system.

"Look, Pryce, you were Maura's 'handler' and the one tasked with helping clean up after her. You should know if she's involved with the Zamorra boys or not. Tell me what you know. It will save us all a lot of time, money, and antagonizing innocent people."

"You're right. I'd know if she was working with Edwin Zamorra. She's not."

"But you admit she was Jerold's partner, the same Jerold who's six feet under. Why didn't you tell me about the lottery scam they had going?"

Iago uncrossed his legs and sat up straight. "The police know about that?"

Bingo. Finally, a crack in the wall. "After I told them to look into it, yes. Come on, you knew we'd find out." He paused. "Unless that's the tip of a pyramid buried in layers of dirt."

Iago ran his hand over his face. "You didn't get a chance to know her. It's not her fault she sprang from a rootless family tree. You don't see her when she's laughing at my bad puns, crying at old romance movies, sitting with Alistair during radiation treatments. Her work isn't who she is."

Drayco bit back a retort that confidence games didn't qualify as work. "If you knew about her lottery schemes or other cons, that means Brisbane knew. Why didn't he put a stop to it?"

"Who says he didn't?" The corners of Iago's mouth turned up briefly, which was the closest he'd come to a smile.

Drayco was getting pretty damned tired of the Escher-esque twisted head games from Iago and Brisbane. "Look, I'm going to see this through to the end, even if it means finding out Maura killed Jerold. That won't make you or your employer happy, but I *will* know the truth."

"You mean, you have to punish her for what she did. For abandoning you, is that it?" Iago drained the last of his beer and got up to head toward the door. "You know," he said, with one hand on the door knob, "family is what we make it. You should remember that."

❧ ❧ ❧

Drayco didn't have long to think about Iago or his words because the appointed time had arrived for his video conference with Brody. For a moment, he thought his internet connection was on the fritz, but then he realized he'd shut off the router. He rubbed his eyes and took a few deep breaths, then established the connection.

Brody yawned in greeting, apologized, then grabbed a mug of steaming coffee next to his monitor to take a few swigs. "We gotta stop gaitherin' like this, Scott. Maybe next time, we can schedule our wee dates a bit earlier in my day?"

"Sure thing, Brody. I'll send you a case of hamburgers as penance."

Brody brightened. "You can order those through the post?"

"Not prepared, usually. But I'll see what I can do."

"Make sure they have those little fried onions and tomato ketchup and mustard."

Drayco grinned. The Church of the Golden Arches had claimed another acolyte for its choir. "Deal. What else do you have for me tonight besides brogues and burgers?"

"Brogue? I'll have you know this is the way real people talk. It's you who talks funny, my frien.' But all kidding aside, I might have a bit of good news for you."

"Good is good. What did you find?"

"It's about Dugald Iverson, your mother's ex. Turns out he tweren't no saint. A long record of naughty behavior."

"How naughty?"

"Drunk and disorderly assault, for starters. But that would describe half the male population. No, his little misdeeds went way beyond that. He was charged with a couple cases of violent rape. He liked to burn his victims, leave little 'reminders' of his handiwork. But his uncle was a constable, so surprise, surprise, little Duggie always got off on technicalities."

"The killing may have been self-defense?"

"Regardless of who did it, seems likely, aye. Or the family of one of his victims getting revenge."

"And Maura?"

"As I mentioned last time, a couple of neighbors speculated she was Dugald's killer. But that's only on account they knew the two had been dating. They didn't have any proof, mind you."

"But she disappeared around that same time."

"Aye, there is that. Hardly damning, though. And certainly not proof. If every soul who moved to the States from the Isles were murderers, you'd be in deep trouble, laddie."

Drayco pictured the teenage Maura with nowhere to turn. No one would believe a gypsy of killing a constable's relative in self-defense. The perfect recipe for disappearing. "No one was ever charged with Dugald's death?"

"No, and Uncle Constable died not long after. I did track down one fellow from Dugald's former haunts. An old timer who seemed to have a pretty good memory, all the same. He said, and I quote, ' the world was better off without Dugald in it.' And that he probably deserved his fate."

"Did Alistair Brisbane's name come out in any of this?"

"Now that one is interesting, I must say. It's as if he never existed. Oh, there's a record of his birth, to be sure. But not much else. Don't know if he purposely made himself invisible early on or cleaned up his records after the fact. Either way, he's a bogie. At least, until he reappeared on your side of the Pond."

"He's pretty much a bogie over here, too."

A stack of music CD's next to Drayco's computer caught his eye. He picked one up and turned it over in his hand. "I wonder—with all of Maura's traveling around and dodging the law, how did she learn to play the piano?"

Brody's voice perked up for the first time. "That's an easier one. One of those neighbors of Dugald's knew the vicar in a nearby parish. The vicar's wife took pity on young Maura and gave her lessons when she was in town. Said she was a natural."

Drayco thanked Brody for his sacrifice of losing sleep and made a note to look up hamburger delivery services in Scotland.

So, his mother might have killed a man, and it might have been justifiable homicide. Had lightning struck twice with Jerold? He pushed aside any thoughts of his own self-defense case before the review board. His impartiality was already being pushed to the limit. Maybe Benny was right—his ability to be objective was "manure."

With a sigh, he called Sarg to fill him in on Brody's news, making sure to emphasize the self-defense part. He couldn't keep it a secret much longer, anyway. Not with an ex-Interpol agent knowing the truth.

After hanging up with Sarg, he thought about heading to the piano but didn't. Why bother? He'd just end up using it as a pillow again. Maybe a little boob tube, instead. He settled back on the couch and flipped through the channels, but nothing caught his eye until he stopped on a movie network. *Braveheart.*

He leaned back and started watching. Maybe connecting with his Scottish roots—Hollywood style—would do the trick. But twenty minutes in, the overwhelming curtain of fatigue fell over him, and he gave up.

39

It was a well-known fact Drayco loathed coincidences. And one of the biggest coincidences of this entire case was the fact both a husband and wife were murdered a year apart. It happened on rare occasions, but not usually in such bizarre ways.

None of the alleged facts of Ophelia Zamorra's death made any sense. Thugs carrying around a baseball bat? Nowadays, it was more likely to be a knife or gun. Cramming a debit card down their victim's throat? Then being careful to stay out of the line of sight of the bank's security cameras. The two young men arrested for Ophelia's murder hadn't bothered to hide themselves from the banks when they robbed the other two customers.

Drayco waited until well after noon when the church crowds were out, then navigated his Starfire through several neighborhoods in Fairfax where home values matched those of Ashley's. A few fractions of a mile later he was in a different kind of suburban landscape, with bars across the windows and hardly any "For Sale" signs. The metro D.C. area might be home to seven of the ten highest-income counties in the country, but pockets of poverty were still here hiding in plain sight.

The woman who ushered him into her house was in her mid-sixties and walked with a cane. The yellow sweater she wore contrasted against her dark skin and salt-and-pepper hair like a jonquil opening to the sun. She lived alone now that her grandson, Leon Mecko, was one of the two boys in jail for Ophelia's murder.

The room was spartan, but homey, with rainbow quilts hanging on the walls. The only thing out of place was a stack of hand-painted blocks in one corner labeled with symbols from the periodic table of elements.

Every inch of every surface was spotless. He caught a whiff of something vanilla and smoky and glanced at a table in a corner filled with lighted candles and a little statue of the Madonna.

Rozalia Mecko hadn't seemed too enthused to talk with him when he called her on the phone until he told her the reason for this visit. Now, she made sure he was comfortable on the only recliner in the room. He didn't want to offend by offering to switch seats, but he was pretty sure the recliner was of the lift variety, designed to make it easier for the disabled to stand.

He thanked her and came right to the point. "I want to be upfront with you, Mrs. Mecko. Both your grandson and my mother are in jail for murder, murders I'm not convinced they committed. There's an outside chance the two cases might be related. If I can find the real culprit in my mother's case, I might be able to prove your grandson's innocence."

She smiled at that. "Leon deserves a second chance. My grandbaby made mistakes. Admitted he stole money, but I know my Leon. He'd never kill another soul."

She perched on the arm of the only other chair in the room, grasping the cane in both hands. "I've tried to do my best. Leon never knew who his father was. And his mother, God bless my daughter's soul, OD'd on prescription drugs. Painkillers."

He winced at that bit of irony. She died from too much prescription meds while Edwin's customers could have died from too little.

Mrs. Mecko continued, "He ran with a bad crowd. But he's a smart boy, he's good at math and science. I know he could make something of hisself, given the chance."

Drayco pointed at the blocks in the corner. "Is that Leon's handiwork?"

She beamed. "Did them all by hisself. Cut and sanded the wood and painted 'em up."

"Did Leon or the other boy, Dante DiBiase, own a baseball bat?"

"That's what I tried to tell those police officers. He most certainly did not. Neither did Dante. And the police admitted they wasn't any prints on that bat. Where did those boys get gloves? And why did they go to all that trouble with that poor woman and not the other two robberies?"

He smiled at her. "Those are the same questions I've been asking."

She leaned over to rest her head on her hands that still gripped the cane. "Like I said, even though he made some bad choices, Leon was smart. Too smart to do one robbery then go back an hour later to the same bank to rob some other poor soul."

"Did the police tell you the victim's debit card was placed in her throat after she was beaten?"

Mrs. Mecko straightened up and shivered. "A horrible, evil thing. That's what makes me know for sure Leon didn't do nothing like that. He has a good heart, don't even like to kill bugs."

She shook her head. "I try and put myself in the place of that killer. It was dark, I'll grant you. But why take time to do a thing like that with the card? Seems to be me they'd run off straight away, less chance of getting caught."

Drayco added, "With the gloves and the bat, it seems carefully planned."

"You see? That's what I've been trying to tell those officers. But they like to close cases, get them off the books, go on to the next crime."

With a heavy sigh, she added, "They was rushing to convict somebody. And my Leon was the scapegoat. That prosecutor, he's working to get him tried as an adult."

"You never heard Leon mention the names Ophelia Zamorra, Jerold Zamorra, or Maura McCune before?"

"Leon and me, we talked about a lot of things. We was close, and I felt he trusted me. Leon didn't mention those people. He didn't even own a car. It was Dante's brother's car they used for those two robberies. I had Leon on a curfew. He had to be back by ten."

"Did he ever miss curfew?"

"Not once."

Drayco stood up, not wanting to hog the recliner any longer. "You were very gracious to see me, Mrs. Mecko. I can't promise anything, but I'll do my best."

She started to rise off the arm of her chair, and he reached over to hold her arm and steady her while she stood. She searched his face and nodded. "You said your mother was also in jail for something she didn't do. I shore hope you can help her too. She's lucky to have you."

Drayco wasn't entirely sure Maura would agree, but he thanked Mrs. Mecko and headed to his car. His car wasn't alone.

It was hard to miss the man leaned against it, his arms folded across his chest. Bald, at least six-six, an African-American clone of Iago. The stranger stared at Drayco, then said, "Hear you're trying to help out Leon."

"I believe in justice. And putting an innocent young man behind bars isn't justice."

"Leon's a good kid. Sees a lot of people on TV having nice things. Sees the Jaguars and the BMWs driving around, and a bag boy job sure don't buy that." He turned around and ran his hand along the top of the Starfire. "Sure wouldn't buy this."

"That was a gift."

"A gift, huh? From a rich relative?"

"For helping someone."

"Well, Mrs. Mecko in there don't have nothing to give you for helping."

"I don't expect anything in return. Except maybe seeing Leon graduate from a place like MIT or Harvard."

The other man tilted his head. "You think he could do something like that?"

"If he's as good at science as his grandmother thinks, why not?" Drayco added, "I don't think I caught your name ..."

"Washington Gaines. But everybody calls me Wash."

"You're a friend of the family?"

"I help out now and then. Odd jobs, mostly."

"They must be grateful."

"I owe 'em. Mrs. Mecko, she let me stay here when I got booted from my hotel job—one of those big chains bought up the place and changed out all the staff. Took me three months to find another gig."

"So you got to know Leon pretty well."

"Kinda like a kid brother to me. And I owe him, too."

"How so?"

"That's how I know Leon didn't whack that woman."

"What do you mean?"

Wash looked around and lowered his voice. "I got in over my head with some dealers. Percs, Oxy, Dillies. Leon knew I was taking some heat. And between jobs, ya know? How was I gonna pay?"

Drayco connected the dots. "The bank ATM robberies? He gave you some of the money?"

"He gave me all the money. Not only that, he came straight to me after he'd knocked off the bank that night. No way he coulda killed anybody."

"You were afraid to go to the police?"

Wash snorted. "Think they'd believe me?"

"Then why are you telling me all this?"

"You're not a cop. And I can't let Leon take the rap for something he didn't do. You told Mrs. Mecko you were goin' to help. You a man of your word?"

"Always."

Leon held out his hand, and Drayco shook it. "Mrs. Mecko told me earlier your name was Mr. Drayco, that right? Well, Mr. Drayco, you play poker?"

Drayco nodded.

"Just make sure you wind up with a royal flush. Otherwise, Leon's out of the game. For good."

40

Following his chat with Mrs. Mecko, Drayco had considered doing some flying as a consolation prize for being denied his relaxing weekend. To get above it all, just him, the plane, and the sky, had seemed so blissfully ideal.

Instead, he'd spent the rest of Sunday making calls, trying to put more of the picture together of his mother and her case. He didn't touch the piano. Not once. Maybe that's why he woke up this morning with a headache—piano withdrawal. More likely, it was the first two meetings lined up on his schedule.

After stumbling into the bathroom, he looked at his blood-shot eyes in the mirror. Worse than Nelia's. "You look like you've been on a bender for a week." His reflection stayed silent.

He forced down coffee and fluffernutter toast—flipping Sarg a mental bird—then got dressed and headed to an office he hadn't visited in a while, partly out of avoidance, partly out of necessity. Both of those partlys helped keep his blood pressure down, for the silver-haired man who greeted Drayco was better than caffeine for a systolic boost.

Brock was uncharacteristically wired and even greeted Drayco with a big grin. Too bad it didn't last long. "Heard the news about Edwin Zamorra, Scott. Great work on your part. You bagged a lowlife scumbag. And may have nailed Maura's partner in the process."

"Aren't you celebrating a little too soon?" Not that Brock was the celebratory type since here he was working on President's Day.

"I need to move on, you need to move on. Bet you haven't taken on any new clients since this whole thing started."

"Was Halabi the one who called you about Edwin's arrest?"

"What? Oh, no, it was Agent Sargosian. He phoned me this morning."

There went the systolic with a diastolic chaser. Drayco was accustomed to Brock going behind his back, but Sarg?

Brock didn't seem to notice the gathering clouds on Drayco's face, adding insult to injury, "Sargosian also told me about that Iago Pryce fellow. I've put some feelers out on him."

Still stung by Sarg's apparent breach of trust, it took a moment for Drayco to process Brock's words enough to reply. "Pryce is Maura's bodyguard. He may be heavy-handed when it comes to taking his duties seriously, but he's not the main player."

Brock turned away to look through the window blinds. "Oh? And who would that be?"

"Alistair Brisbane. A high-powered shadow man who happens to be Maura's twin brother."

Brock's ability to hide his reactions had helped make him a successful FBI agent then consultant. But through the years, Drayco had learned to tell when Brock lied by the almost-imperceptible twitch on the left side of his jaw.

"Brisbane? Don't think I've heard of him." The jaw twitch was as quick as a Nolan Ryan fastball. Blink and you'd miss it.

The extent of Brock's duplicity enveloped Drayco in a heavy blanket of bitterness—the note from Maura after she was declared legally dead and now this. His father's tangled web of deception had a lot of threads.

Two quick strides took him face to face with Brock. "When did you find out about Brisbane and Maura and her shady past? Before or after you married her?"

A rare flicker of guilt passed across his father's face. "I told you the truth when I said I didn't look into her disappearance. But I did research her background. Anger, curiosity, pride, don't remember now. Regardless, I couldn't dwell on it. Not with two small children I suddenly had to raise on my own."

"Then you knew all along about the note found on her, with BRISBANE on it."

Brock nodded.

"Why didn't you tell me all this?"

"Would it have mattered? Would you really have wanted to destroy any positive memories you had of your mother?"

"Was this about destroying my memories of her or protecting my memories of you?"

Brock looked briefly at Drayco, then out the window again. "I don't expect you to understand."

Drayco pushed further, "Do you know I didn't even recall she had a scar on her neck? Did she have it when you met her?"

Brock's shoulders barely nudged an inch, but Drayco took that as a yes. Well, this was getting him nowhere. One way to change that. "I spoke with Alistair Brisbane."

Brock's head swung around and his eyes bored into Drayco's. "When? What did he say?"

"That Maura didn't kill Jerold Zamorra. And that he was counting on me to prove it."

"And that's all?"

"Pretty much, yeah. It was over the phone, not face to face."

"I'm not surprised he'd think his sister was innocent. Or that he'd try to cover up for her."

"I wasn't sure I believed him then. I believe him now."

Brock scanned his son's face. What was he looking for, signs of deception? *Takes one to know one, Brock?*

Brock said, "This man Brisbane. He's more powerful than a senator and twice as dishonest. His connections are fiercely loyal or fiercely afraid. He's a master at self-preservation and won't hesitate to toss you under the bus and happily roll right over you, son."

"Does he have ties to organized crime?"

"Too independent. He's an entity unto himself and doesn't like to be tied down."

"You should have told me. About him and her both. I had a right to know."

"Truth works both ways. When exactly were you going to tell me about Pryce and Brisbane if Sarg hadn't beaten you to it?"

Brock had him, there. Perhaps it was partial payback for Brock hiding the truth about Maura's "death."

It was Brock's turn to sigh. "You know, the main reason I wanted you to drop by today wasn't to argue. It was to apologize. For my drunken rant the other night. Didn't want you to see me like that."

"Maybe if you'd let me see that side of you more often, the ocean between us wouldn't be so wide."

Brock's clenched jaw loosened a fraction. "I think I should have encouraged your piano thing more."

"Why is that?"

"Angry conductors and audience members are a lot safer than the Brisbanes of this world."

In his own camouflaged way that was the closest Brock came to admitting he was worried about his son. That he cared.

"I have to see this thing through. You know that."

"Yeah. You're as stubborn as ..." Brock shook his head. "I was going to say you're as stubborn as your mother. But I think you got the stubborn gene from me."

"Could have been worse. At least, it wasn't your love for karaoke."

A sliver of a smile returned to Brock's face. "Agent Sargosian's a good man. He's got your back. But if you're right and Maura and Edwin aren't behind Jerold Zamorra's murder, the killer is still out there. Keep me in the loop."

Drayco nodded. He could do phone calls. Iago's words rang in his head, "Family is what we make it. Maybe you should remember that."

41

An hour later, Drayco was plunged into his second dreaded meeting of the day, a luncheon. He hated luncheons. Lame jokes from clueless speakers, presentations that looked as if they were crafted by a second-grader—no, a second-grader could probably do better. And everyone was always so afraid to offend anyone else, even handshakes were tactical.

He'd wanted to talk with Rena Quentin again, so she'd arranged this particular time and place. What she neglected to tell him was that she was an honored guest at this soirée, seated upfront, and that she was using him as her "date."

The male half of the couple who was supposed to join them at their table was a doctor called away to an emergency and neither the doctor nor wife were present. It was just Drayco and Rena. He looked at the place card in front of him. It read "Mr. Quentin."

Rena patted her hair, pulled up into a chignon. "People will call me a cougar. I love it."

She did remind Drayco of a cougar and not in a good way. He felt a little like growling, himself.

With a smile, she added, "They'll think I've gone to the other end of the spectrum, since my late husband was twenty years older than I. God bless him. And his generous divorce settlement, of course."

Drayco pulled out his wallet and opened it to show the lack of big bills. "I doubt I'd make a tasty meal for a rich cougar."

She put her hand on his arm. "Ah, but there are other ways in which I think I'd find you quite tasty."

Before he could change the subject, and he *really* wanted to change the subject, she added, "You know, I underestimated you. Thought you were just another one of those dumb cop types. And believe me I've worked with a lot of them. Of course, some dicks are better than others."

Subject change, commencing now. "Edwin Zamorra was arrested yesterday. He ran a drug-tampering scheme. Watered-down drugs or used counterfeits, then pocketed the difference."

He'd waited to tell her in person rather than over the phone, because he wanted to see her reaction. He was surprised. After an initial look of shock, she laughed and shook her head.

"I'm glad you find the news amusing."

"It's just I never imagined Edwin could do such a thing. Always strait-laced and dull. As I mentioned before, a prude."

"You saw no signs whatsoever?"

"Not a one." Rena re-arranged the salt and pepper shakers on the table until they were perfectly parallel. "Poverty can do funny things to people. I saw it first-hand—I was raised in poverty by my grandmother, and I like to think that's why she beat me. Some say poverty is society's cancer, but I say it's more like an ugly birthmark you want to keep covered up."

"Edwin wasn't exactly rich, but he wasn't poor, either."

Rena frowned. "How horrible this must be for Ashley. Her mother and father dead, her uncle in jail. I *would* say I'm glad she has that young Asian boyfriend of hers ..."

"You don't like Gogo Cheng, I take it?"

"I got a funny feeling about him the one time I met him. Guess it comes from my years of being a suspicious TSA sort. I'm probably just being paranoid." She hesitated. "He reminds me of a guy we put on our watchlist."

Rena wasn't exactly batting her lashes, but she switched easily into her cougar role, scanning his body with her eyes. "You clean up real nice, Scott Drayco. That blue-violet shirt matches your amazing eyes."

Nelia Tyler said something similar to him once when he wore the same shirt. He made a mental note to stop wearing it. "You didn't see any signs of Edwin's crimes. And you also didn't know about Jerold's gambling. What about a lottery scam aimed at elderly women?"

"Like brother, like brother? Well that's disappointing, I must say. Despite my differences with Jerold, I can't imagine the circumstances that would lead him to get involved in something so mean-spirited."

"It's possible they were in on it together."

"And your mother? What was her role?"

"She may have been right in the middle. We don't know yet."

Rena picked at her fish and turned it over, wrinkling her nose in disgust at the silvery skin on the bottom. "If I were in charge of this shindig, there'd be no fish. Chicken is neater. And who in their right mind would pair yellow squash with pearl onions?"

She took a dainty sip of her coffee. "I hope they have crème brulée for dessert. Or *something* caramel."

"Did you know Edwin and Ophelia had an affair?"

Rena looked at him over her coffee cup. "You don't pull any punches, do you? Next you'll be telling me Ashley is Edwin's love child."

When he didn't respond, she slowly put her cup down. "You aren't serious?"

"We're a little short on proof—for that and for other odd behavior from the Zamorra clan."

"Like that lottery thing you were telling me about?"

He nodded.

"You don't suppose the entire Zamorra family was involved in this? Ashley and Gogo included?"

That was pretty much the same comment Sarg had made about a "scamily." Drayco replied, "That would make Ophelia the wild card."

"Oh, what a noble mind is here o'erthrown." Rena twirled her fork on her plate, then put it down, giving up on the fish.

"Shakespeare's *Hamlet*?"

She smiled. "The poor, mad Ophelia."

"Some Shakespeare scholars claim Ophelia was murdered. That Hamlet's mother Gertrude witnessed Ophelia fall into the brook and did nothing to save her. Or even helped break the branch Ophelia was standing on when she fell and drowned."

"Of course you would know that." She laughed briefly. "Although it's funny you should mention it."

"Why?"

"Because I had a similar conversation with Jerold once. Before his wife was killed. And he said pretty much the same thing."

"I didn't know Jerold was a Shakespeare expert."

"He wasn't. His idea of a good read was Zane Grey. But he knew a lot about Hamlet and Ophelia."

The waiters in their white shirts, gold ties, and maroon vests buzzed around the various tables like a hive of bees in Washington Redskin uniforms, with plates appearing and disappearing at a quietly frantic pace. As the remains of the ill-fated salmon were whisked away, Rena's eyes lit up when a ramekin of golden crème brulée took its place.

The top of the dessert reminded Drayco of burned skin. That thought segued to his evidentiary hearing and the reason for it. He pushed his untouched crème brulée over to Rena. "Why would Jerold compare his wife Ophelia to the character in Hamlet? Both were doomed loves? Or both were collateral damage?"

Rena finished the second crème brulée in record time and licked the spoon clean. "Maybe it was that affair you alluded to. Between Ophelia and Edwin. It's also possible she started showing signs of mental illness, but Jerold never mentioned it other than the Shakespeare thing—the mad Ophelia and all. Does it matter now?"

That was the question. Everyone had written off Ophelia's death as a random act of violence, being in the wrong place at the wrong time. Maybe Ashley was right and Jerold did kill her mother, yet another love triangle gone awry. Nothing to do with Jerold, Edwin, Maura, or any fraud scheme.

But one detail kept hammering Drayco over and over, the thing that made the least sense. Why was that ATM card crammed down Ophelia's throat?

42

Sarg greeted Drayco with crossed arms and a scowl outside the entrance to the Sackler Gallery. As Drayco approached, Sarg drained the last liquid from a cup in his hands and hurled it into the trash.

Drayco checked his watch. "I'm five minutes early. You been here a while?"

"Got a call from Halabi a half hour ago. After listening to him rant for five minutes, I think it's safe to say we won't be invited to the police ball anytime soon. At least, *you* won't. Or Brock."

"What did he say?"

"Oh, just a little conversation he had with Brock about your mother and that letter she sent to him after she was declared legally dead. Brock neglected to mention it when he was first interviewed by the PD."

Drayco stared at Sarg, hardly blinking. "Looks like you can add yourself to the forgot-to-mention club. Brock told me you called him. About Iago and Brisbane."

Sarg leaned against a tall trash can beside him. "And I'm not going to apologize for it. You've already got one sword of Damocles hanging over your head. And I have a feeling Brisbane could nail you if he wants, uncle or no."

Drayco glanced over at the multi-colored banners hanging on the front of the Sackler. The lettering touted an exhibition on ancestor veneration in Asian cultures, with objects from family shrines. He wasn't feeling the veneration love right now. "Did Brock tell you he knew about the existence of Brisbane already?"

"No, he didn't." Sarg frowned. "Exactly how long had he known about Maura's notorious twin?"

"Long enough. I don't know which of the two has lied to me more, Maura or Brock."

"You know what my sweet little college-senior Tara told me? That lies are at the heart of all relationships."

"They teach her that in Philosophy 101?"

"Money well spent, don't ya think?"

Drayco frowned, prompted Sarg to add, "I was kidding."

Drayco replied, "Do you have a cold?"

Sarg gaped at him. "Never felt better. Why?"

"Oh, it's nothing. Your voice just sounded different." Everyone's voice had started sounding different to him, their usual colors, shapes, and textures off-center. And it wasn't just voices, it was all sounds, something that hadn't happened to him since the stress following the Cadden twins tragedy. Without his normal palette of 3D sound, the world was a less interesting place, more like gruel than a five-course meal.

It was Sarg's turn to look at his watch. "We better go meet Agent Hanlon, or we'll be late."

After presenting their credentials to the gallery receptionist, she pointed them through the long hallway, past ancient statues made of travertine and limestone from Persia, Yemen and Syria, and down the stairs to one of the smaller galleries.

Sarg had met other members of the FBI's art fraud division, but Hanlon was new. They'd been told to look for a blonde woman in brown leather boots, but it was moot, since she was the only person in the room.

When she turned to greet them, Drayco could feel Sarg's posture stiffen and guessed he was trying as hard as Drayco not to stare at the woman's face. Unlike most people following major facial cancer surgery, Agent Holly Hanlon didn't try to hide her scars behind heavy makeup. From the looks of the slightly sunken cheek and missing right nostril, he guessed more plastic surgery was in her future.

She shook their hands and got down to business right away. "I checked our art theft database after you contacted me. The art broker you mentioned, Giovanni Nardello, did pass away recently as you were told by Faust Marchand." She shook her head. "We've had our eye on Marchand for a while, but Nardello was clean. Near as we could tell."

Sarg said, "I don't suppose there's any chance we could get our hands on Nardello's ledgers?"

The facial scars made it difficult for Hanlon to smile, but she flashed some teeth as she reached into the large portfolio case slung over her shoulder and pulled out a cloth-bound book. "Nardello was the old-fashioned kind. No computers."

Drayco exchanged a hopeful glance with Sarg and tried to contain his excitement as Hanlon continued, "The painting you described—that Chinese calligraphy. It was sold on February tenth."

Two days before Jerold's murder. "Did Nardello note the buyer's name?"

"He used a number, not a name."

At Drayco's disappointed look, she flashed more teeth again. "But after talking to Nardello's daughter, we learned he kept a separate unlabeled log in a wall safe, with numbers linked to buyer names. His way of protecting the privacy of rich clients."

She pulled a second, smaller book out of the portfolio and opened it to a bookmarked page, pointing at one entry. "The painting was bought in the name of an LLC."

She put the book down and walked them over to a nearby gallery with an exhibit of Chinese calligraphy paintings, nodding at one in particular. "Is this similar to your painting?"

Drayco examined it. "All I know is our missing piece is Song Dynasty."

"So is this one, from around AD ten eighty-two. They should share characteristics, in case you come across it, yourself."

She stood next to the painting and pointed out the brush strokes of the thin, elegant script. "Calligraphy is like a mirror for each artist, a silent reflection of the soul. Each artist had his own technique."

"Enhancing its value," Drayco said.

She nodded. "I couldn't find info your piece was sold to a museum yet, but we've tagged it in the database in case it is. Whether the buyer knew it was stolen or not, there's still a crime involved. That is, if your young art owner wants to press charges. His word is the only proof we have it was stolen in the first place."

Sarg asked, "What's your recovery rate of stolen artworks?"

"Still only about a third. And we get new reports of missing pieces all the time. The elderly are particularly vulnerable, especially once dementia kicks in."

They thanked Hanlon for her time and snaked their way through the maze of rooms to the first floor. Drayco paused at a case that was part of the ancestor exhibit to look at the row of small statues, reading the description.

In certain Chinese cultures, it was believed offerings for the deceased provided for their welfare in the afterlife, and in turn, the dead influenced the fortunes of the living. What would Jerold Zamorra have to say to him right now? Or to Ashley or Edwin?

Once Sarg and Drayco were back outside the gallery, Drayco felt drawn to those banners and couldn't stop looking at them. "Did you see the name of that LLC?"

"Yeah, why?"

"Same one Brisbane used to buy his island home."

Sarg whistled. "I guess it's possible Jerold had more than one fraud scheme going. Not just a scam lottery but a stolen artwork ring. Maybe he teamed up with Gogo and got cut out of the deal."

"And Maura was involved, so Brisbane covered up the scheme."

"Hell, maybe Ashley was part of it, too."

Drayco added, "Like you said, a circle of theft and fraud. All of our suspects in one, giant theft ring. A family of con artists, like my own."

Sarg put his hands on his hips. "I gather you don't think that's a possibility."

"Why?"

"Because you have that little twitch thing going on."

"Twitch?"

"When you don't buy an idea. You get this little twitch on the right side of your face."

Drayco stared at him. "Are you making that up?"

"Nope. Never said anything because me knowing and you not knowing came in handy at times. But in the interest of our newfound openness and honesty," he tilted his head up at Drayco, "I thought I'd share."

Drayco rubbed a hand through his hair. He'd never thought he was like his father in any way. Before he could dwell on that little tidbit of unwelcome insight, Sarg added, "I contacted the TSA chief. That former friend of Jerold's you told me about, Barney Schleissman? Found out the address of the home he's in. You interested?"

Having taken a taxi to the Sackler, Drayco only hesitated briefly before accepting Sarg's offer of a ride. Their recent case together a few months ago had gone a long way toward bridging the chasm that opened up after Drayco took the fall for Sarg on a case and left the Bureau. But any bridge can develop cracks.

He didn't doubt Sarg had his best interests at heart. But practically everyone close to him had lied. Drayco was beginning to think that whole not-trusting-thing Maura had going on wasn't such a bad philosophy to have.

43

The assisted-living "home," with its mangy gray-and-white wallpaper and antiquated alarm system, looked like a cross between a rabid raccoon and an aging guard dog. The staff were about as friendly. Despite Drayco having the okay from Barney Schleissman's family and Sarg holding out his FBI bona-fides, it took one receptionist, two nurses, and one administrator before Drayco and Sarg were led to Schleissman's room.

They'd expected to see a man similar to the other shuffling, empty-eyed residents they'd passed in the hallways, but in the middle of the studio-sized space sat a surprise. Schleissman had on a full three-piece suit, was perched in a chair where he could watch a documentary on aircraft carriers, and pinched the nurse's rump as she turned to leave.

He greeted them as if they were old friends. "My son said you were coming to chat about Jerold, the poor chap. Always thought he'd outlive me and make it to the century mark. Sorry I couldn't make the funeral. They won't let me drive anymore." He leaned over with a conspiratorial whisper, "But I took the groundskeeper's golf cart for a spin last month."

It was hard not to like this man. Had his family cast him into the facility because he cramped their lifestyle—or, perhaps, to get their hands on his estate? "Mr. Schleissman—"

"Call me Barney."

Drayco smiled. "Barney, it is. We hoped you could tell us more about Jerold. And his co-workers or any reason he might be a target for murder."

"Went to one of Jerry's recitals a while ago, that music group of his. I recall that young Chinese who's engaged to Ashley. What was his name? Something like hurry-up, hurry-up. And that young woman, that mulatto, she was a chatty one. Asked me about Rena. Reminds me a bit of her, too."

Drayco winced at the "mulatto" term, maybe a hint of Schleissman's era or mental slips. "By Rena, you mean Rena Quentin?"

"Who else? That Rena thrived on taking control of any project and whipping it into shape. Kind of a control freak. Real OCD. Liked showing she could play right up there with the Big Boys. Must have made it harder with that sexual harassment thing. Took us all by surprise. Seemed so out of character for both."

"He never discussed it?"

"Jerry kept his cards so close to his vest, they kinda merged with his DNA."

"That's why he left the TSA, wasn't it, the harassment charge?"

"If you listen to the rumor vine. But he seemed kinda happy about it, almost giddy. Like he'd been waiting for an excuse to leave."

"And he never talked about threats or stalkers?"

"*Au contraire, mon frère.*" Schleissman winked. "That's French. Means no, bro."

Drayco and Sarg had both stayed standing due to the lack of chairs, but now chose to sit on the bed. Sarg spoke up from the corner where he'd wedged himself. "What about his wife Ophelia, Mr. Schleissman? She was murdered a year after they got divorced. Must have been hard on Jerold."

"Sad, very sad. Didn't see it coming. The murder, that is. The divorce, well, that was a long time in the making. That Ophelia, she was a gold digger. His daughter, too. That's women for you. Always wanting equal rights while holding their hands out for money."

"Ashley believes Jerold killed her mother, Mr. Schleissman. Do you agree?"

"Seems unlikely. Guess I was a little too hard on Ashley just now. Don't want to speak ill of the dead, but living with those two hot-tempered parents of hers couldn't have been easy. They were like that. Passionate about life, just not each other. Jerry was the weaker of the two, mind you, which is why I can't see him killing her. Ophelia walked all over him. But she was sexy and beautiful. He always did say he liked his women pretty and domineering."

Schleissman winked at them. "Always wondered if he was into that M&M stuff, you know, the leather and whips."

"Mr. Schleissman, did Jerold mention the name Maura McCune?"

"Can't say I recall it."

"Or possibly Iago Pryce or Alistair Brisbane?"

"Sorry. They friends of Jerry's, too?"

"Possibly. Did you see signs of a gambling habit? Or a side business?"

"Gambling? We had office pools and bet on golf games. He lost most of 'em. Maybe he played the ponies, I suppose. I didn't go with him if he did."

Schleissman frowned. "Now that you mention it, right before he left, he was making a lot of phone calls. More than usual. He hadn't stepped outside the office for one second before he was glued to the phone. Sometimes, he'd excuse himself for a private chat."

He rubbed his chin. "Maybe he was just setting up his retirement portfolio. Maybe it was that side business you mentioned. We kinda lost touch after he left. I called him a few times. He was always busy, he said."

The elderly man had gradually slumped lower in his chair and was looking a lot less energetic than when they'd arrived. "Now where is that nurse? She was here a second ago."

Drayco looked at Sarg and nodded toward the door. Drayco smiled at Schleissman. "Thanks for speaking with us, Barney. Don't go stealing any more golf carts."

Schleissman smiled up at him. "Golf carts? I haven't been on one of those in years. Do tell Jerold and his lovely wife Ophelia I said 'hi' when you see them."

Sarg looked as grateful as Drayco to escape the life-sucking claustrophobic air of the facility. They sat on a bench outside, and Sarg said, "Guess you don't want to think about your mother and all that 'M&M' business. But you can't discount it."

Drayco drummed his fingers on the arm rest of the bench, half-listening to Sarg.

"Okay, junior, what's eating you?"

"Hmm?" Drayco focused on Sarg's searching eyes.

"I know that look. You've got one of your crazy theories percolating in the puzzle-cortex part of your brain."

"Do I?" Drayco gave Sarg his best cryptic smile. "It might have to do with a few phone calls I made to some coroners' offices this morning. Or, as you say, I'm just trying to push Maura 'M&M' images out of my head."

Sarg didn't smile back. "Goddamn you, junior. You're not withholding on me again, are you? Payback for me telling Brock about Iago and Brisbane?"

Drayco hopped up and held out his hand to Sarg. "Withholding? You make it sound like I'm the IRS."

Sarg hesitated before taking Drayco's outstretched hand and allowing himself to be hoisted to his feet. "You know what they say—the only two certainties are death and taxes. This case has given us the death part, but I doubt Jerold paid taxes on his fraud income. Nor his partner if you still think he had one."

"Oh, I'm convinced he had a partner, all right."

"Really?" Sarg raised both eyebrows practically to his hairline. "Based on what? The word of Maura and Iago? Not exactly solid sources."

"You said it. The puzzle-cortex."

Sarg snorted. "Is that where the synesthesia comes from?"

"That would be the freak-cortex."

"Ah, that one. Think I remember it from psych class."

They both turned at the sound of giggling behind them. An elderly man who'd managed to slip through the front doors was being herded inside by two linebacker-sized orderlies. Sarg shook his head. "You know everything Schleissman said is suspect, don't you?"

"Even on cloudy days, a few rays of sunlight can shine through."

Sarg put his hand lightly on Drayco's arm. "Look, junior. You gonna be fine on your own tomorrow? Onweller is pushing me to wrap up my work on that kidnapping case."

"Kidnapping? I didn't know that was your current project."

"The Iowa PD found the guy, but we're trying to tie him to a couple of other older abductions." Sarg added, "I hate kidnapping cases."

He didn't have to say why. Sarg's physical wounds had healed from that three-year-old disastrous kidnapping case of theirs, but the bleeding from the emotional cuts hadn't stopped. With him or with Drayco.

"I meant what I said. About that Pryce guy. And if Brisbane is worse, watch your back. Or wait until day after next, and we'll work on this together, 'kay?"

"You're in more danger driving home through the mixing bowl and down I-95."

Sarg slapped his forehead. "That reminds me. Elaine wants *Crêpes Suzettes* for dinner. I gotta pick up some brandy. What you havin'? Something on a bun just for a change?"

"I'm meeting someone. Although there may be buns involved."

Sarg gave him a sharp look. "Anyone I know?"

"Yes."

Sarg took the hint and headed to his car. If Drayco hurried, he'd just make it in time.

44

Drayco wasn't used to seeing Nelia Tyler the law student as opposed to Nelia Tyler the deputy, but he liked it. Even though she had the day off from law school due to the holiday, she couldn't quite put her conservative-professional attire out to pasture. Above her black slacks she wore a soft gray V-necked sweater and sported dangly earrings shaped like mini-Derringers.

He pointed to the earrings. "Gift from Sheriff Sailor?"

"Mail order. Couldn't resist. Gary thinks I need a knitted gun cozy to complete the ensemble."

"That whole roommate thing working out for you?"

"Gary helps keep me sane. And he makes a great study partner."

"Good, that's good." Drayco didn't tell her he'd done a little background check on Gary, just to make sure he didn't have a record. "How was your weekend? The usual murder, menace, and mayhem in lovely Cape Unity?"

"It was pretty quiet, actually. Even got in some study time at my desk." She looked around the Columbia Island marina set on the Pentagon Lagoon. "It's lovely here."

Since it was out of season, only a third of the slips were occupied by boats. The marina cafe was just shy of closing time, but the staff packed a takeout order for them, and Drayco guided Nelia to the picnic tables.

He pointed out a reddish stone monolith a short distance across a footbridge. "Lady Bird Johnson liked this view of D.C. so much, she hand-picked the Grove for the President's memorial. It's one of the most relaxing spots around. Off-peak it's practically empty." He'd forgotten how well you see Hains Point from here, the place he'd met Rena after her tennis lesson.

Nelia took in the pink and crimson reflections on the water from the approaching sunset as a slight breeze ruffled the bangs on her forehead. "You always take me to the nicest places."

"You aren't disappointed it's not a fancy restaurant?"

"Can't beat the view. Besides, it's the company that matters." She finished the last of her fried catfish sandwich and licked her fingers. "This must be gourmet fare for you."

"Why?"

"Benny filled me in on your unorthodox food combinations and inability to cook."

"Ah. Are you a gourmet cook like Sarg?"

"No, but I make a pretty mean beer omelet. I'd love to cook for you sometime." Her cheeks turned pink, and she looked away.

Nelia's husband wouldn't welcome him as a guest, for sure. And she certainly wouldn't be coming over to Drayco's place to cook for him anytime soon. "Perhaps you could cook for me and Benny. And Benny's wife."

She beamed at that. Safe, neutral territory. Dinner in the relationship equivalent of Switzerland. "Fill me in on how the case is going. Benny's told me whatever you passed on to him. But I'm more interested in what you *haven't* told him."

He grinned at that. "Apparently, I come from a family of con artists." He filled her in on Pryce, Maura and her family, even Alistair Brisbane. It seemed so easy to talk to her, to blurt out everything. She listened intently, concentrating on every word.

"Wow. I didn't know you had such powerful relatives. Your Uncle Alistair sounds fascinating. In a criminal sort of way."

"Still can't get used to the 'uncle' part."

"How does Gogo's painting play into it? You don't agree with Sarg that this is some big fraud cabal, do you?"

"Seems pretty implausible, but it gives me an idea of the extent of my uncle's reach."

They finished their sandwiches at the same time, then tossed the trash and headed for a walk around the LBJ memorial. Drayco loved this time of day, from the ground or better yet, from a plane.

He stretched his arms out to his sides and breathed deeply, taking in the soul-cleansing crisp night air. "Benny's going with me to visit my mother tomorrow. I'll update him then."

"You can probably leave out that bit about the dominatrix S&M part. Sorry, M&M." She laughed. "I've never been into that sort of thing. Tim brought it up once since I carry a gun and handcuffs."

Drayco coughed, then cleared his throat. He wished she wouldn't talk about sex with her husband. Not that it mattered. Well, it did matter, but suddenly the night air didn't feel cool anymore.

"You're kinda cute when you squirm."

"You're not helping."

Her laugh echoed out into the twilight, skimming off the wind-driven ripples in the lagoon and beyond. He swore he could almost hear it ricochet off the Washington Monument in the distance.

They strolled around the Grove circle in companionable silence punctuated only by the occasional splash of a fish or the rustling of brown leaf husks on the dormant oaks. In Drayco's audio-centric world—where every sound, every voice, every note washed over him with tactile tides of color—the relative stillness of the night was like watching a black-and-white movie.

On more than one occasion, Nelia had exhibited an almost uncanny ability to read his thoughts. Sarg did, too, but they'd been partners for a long time. She asked, "What are you hearing?"

"Not much."

"You once told me you always had music running through your head. Like a soundtrack for your life. Even dreams."

"Would you believe me if said I'd been 'listening' to Queen?"

She smiled. "Freddy Mercury or Queen of the Night by Mozart?"

"Oh, now you've done it. That Mozart aria will haunt me for days."

It had already started up, and that bothered him. Not because of the music itself though he wasn't an opera fan. There was something else trying to worm its way into his conscious brain. But when Nelia looked up at him, her warm brown eyes twinkling, he gave up.

They stood against the railing on the pier and he turned to her, suddenly drawn to those eyes and those soft, red lips. He bent his head closer to hers, and as his lips brushed against hers, she pulled her head back. She looked as stunned as he felt. Had he just committed the most unwelcome and unethical act of his life?

She looked at the ground as she said in a soft voice, "I wish I'd met you five years ago." Then she added, in a tone that sounded part-defiant, part guilty, "I guess that sounds—"

"I know. It's complicated."

She nodded. Maybe not so unwelcome after all. Which meant he was in a lot more trouble around her than he'd thought.

45

After dropping Nelia off at her apartment, Drayco didn't drive off right away. He pulled out his cellphone and stared at it before pressing the screen to dial a number he'd added to his contacts. It was a number he'd tried to trace but determined was a burner phone and likely encrypted.

He didn't expect anyone to pick up. But the same voice as last time, with its smooth rolling burgundy tones, answered on the third ring. "Greetings, dear nephew. I wondered if I'd be hearing from you again."

"I'd almost think you were expecting me to call. Is that why you didn't get rid of this phone?"

"I trusted you not to hand over the number to anyone. Being able to read people is the main tool of my trade."

Not knowing how long Brisbane would be willing to chat, Drayco cut right to the chase. "Why did you buy Gogo Cheng's Chinese calligraphy painting from Giovanni Nardello?"

"I like the arts, music in particular. Runs in the family. I'm a big supporter."

Now Brisbane wanted to play happy families. Well, good for him. "Did you know that calligraphy painting was stolen by Jerold Zamorra?"

"In all honesty, I didn't know officially it was stolen until right this moment."

Officially, no. Unofficially, you betcha. "All right, you didn't know *officially* it was stolen. But I doubt you bought this painting just because you like Chinese antiquities."

"I like this one. It's from the Song Dynasty. The calligraphy is a poem about water and the moon. One flows on but never goes anywhere, the other waxes and wanes yet never diminishes or grows."

"Gogo said it was worth around fifty grand."

Brisbane chuckled. "I paid twice that for it. And Nardello wasn't as up on his Chinese art as he thought. At auction, this rare piece could sell for close to a million."

"You seem to know a lot about art."

"I know a lot about a great many things. But you want to know if this ties in with Maura."

Brisbane sighed. "I've kept tabs on my sister and her 'projects,' including Jerold. I found out about Jerold's gambling, debts, and his other little habits and had him tracked. I bought Mr. Cheng's painting to clean up one of Jerold's messes and therefore Maura's. I've spent most of my life cleaning up the messes of family, friends, and others I'm not at liberty to name."

"You're a regular Mr. Clean. How many of those messes did you participate in?"

"I believe you've gotten the wrong impression of me, Scott. I'm not your enemy. I can help you."

"You can give me the names of everyone Maura and Jerold were seen with before his death. If Iago is as good as you think he is, you must have a detailed list."

Brisbane didn't reply for several moments, but it didn't sound like he'd hung up. Then Drayco felt his phone vibrate in his hand.

"I've sent you a list of names, dates, and times. I'll forward along some surveillance photos later. Although I'm not sure it will be useful. I've been over it all quite thoroughly and didn't find any possibles."

"I don't suppose you had Jerold followed even when he wasn't with your sister."

"A few times. Those names are on your list."

Drayco checked the text message and opened the attachment. Some of the names he didn't recognize, some he did—Gogo, Lauralee, Rena, even Ashley, who was allegedly estranged and hadn't seen him except to drop off the box of his belongings.

Halabi would salivate at the notion of getting his hands on the list. Drayco wasn't sure he was ready to pass it along, and that thought made him stop short. Ordinarily, he'd turn it over to the police without blinking. First Jerold's condo key, now this.

But there was nothing normal about this case or about Brisbane, and that made Drayco irritated. He'd learned to read others like he read music—with voice colors and timbres, the twitch of an eye, the way someone held their hands, all standing in for musical notes. Put them together and out came a personality composition. But Brisbane was more a case of personality macular degeneration, with the center image fuzzed out and only the edges showing.

As if to punctuate Drayco's thoughts, Brisbane took pains to show he was keeping tabs on Drayco, too. "I like that lovely deputy from the Eastern Shore, Nelia Tyler. Her husband's situation is unfortunate, of course. I'm sure things will work out for the best."

"Is that a threat?"

"If I were threatening you, Scott, you'd know it. When I said I spend most of my time cleaning up messes, especially family messes, you are an exception. Then, in your line of work, it's probably best we not cross paths too often. It could get rather ... awkward."

He rang off, and Drayco tossed the phone onto the passenger seat. In his recent case with Sarg, he'd been used as a pawn in a deadly game of music codes. He'd sworn to himself he'd never get in that position again, but with Brisbane, it was déjà vu, even if Brisbane was telling the truth and trying to help. Feeling the weight of the long day sapping his strength, Drayco headed for home, hoping he wouldn't have any uninvited visitors waiting for him, for once.

❧ ❧ ❧

After determining he was indeed alone, Drayco was almost sorry Iago hadn't broken into his townhome again. He'd love to ask Iago about some of the names on the list Brisbane had passed along, but had to make do with old-fashioned calls and a little computer research.

Drayco turned off the lights in the front hallway and peered out the window. An unfamiliar black sedan sat parked across the street.

Drayco couldn't make out the driver of the car since the sedan was out of the range of streetlights. Conveniently out of range.

Should he feel safer, thanks to new bodyguard, maybe even invite him in for a cozy cup of tea? Or should he call the cops?

He did neither, first checking the back door to see if there were any signs of the stray cat. He hadn't seen the little silver tabby in two days. Had she found a good home? Or some other not-so-happy ending? He missed the tiny furball. Just in case, he refilled the cat bowl with some dry food, hoping the squirrels didn't eat it all first.

He grabbed a Manhattan Special soda from the refrigerator and headed for the piano where he'd spread out several sheets of printed data on top of the closed lid and added the new printout with the info from Brisbane to the collection. He bent over to read them again for the third time, scanning the lists of names, bios, dates, locations.

He was looking for anomalies, outliers, anything that would tie someone other than Maura to Jerold's murder. So far, he'd only seen one item of interest, thanks to Brisbane following through on his promise to send along surveillance photos of Jerold. And even that item would have to wait until he got some follow-up intel from Sarg, coroners' reports, and police databases.

Suddenly realizing how much his neck and head hurt, Drayco straightened up and swept the papers onto the floor with his right hand, which was also throbbing. He massaged it for a few minutes before gingerly easing into a Bach prelude and fugue. He stumbled at first, but his fingers soon picked up the lines as if he hadn't been away, as a rainbow of colors and textures exploded around him.

He reveled in the return of the 3D world of sound and the way it fired all regions of his brain. It was easiest to think while playing Bach. The counterpoint focused scattered thoughts in his brain like a laser beam focused photons onto a single point. The music was always a revelation, in more ways than one.

Maybe he'd forgive his mother some day or maybe he'd never find peace where his mother was concerned. But he'd be forever grateful for the day she'd first placed his small hands on a piano keyboard.

He played for the better part of an hour, losing himself in time and space as he always did. So, when a loud knock thumped at the front door, he was as startled as if a gun had gone off.

He couldn't see anyone through the one-way glass, so he opened the door and looked across the street. There was no one around, except for a young couple waiting for a bus who were spending the time getting to know each other's lips better. And the black sedan was gone.

Then he noticed the tall object wrapped in brown paper to the left of the door. He studied it and looked for messages or printing, but finding none, hauled the object inside.

He was pretty sure he knew what it was. He got some scissors to cut the tape holding the brown paper together, then peeled it away to reveal a painting with Chinese calligraphy. Alistair Brisbane had sent it along as what—a clue? A gesture of good faith designed to appease Drayco's suspicions?

With the painting propped up against a chair, he sat across from it and studied the lettering. What had Brisbane said? It was a poem about water that flows on but never goes anywhere and the moon that waxes and wanes but never diminishes or grows. If only relationships were like that. Steady, dependable, predictable.

He grabbed the remote and turned on the TV, flipping through the channels. No *Braveheart* this time. Stopping on a channel showing *October Sky*, he watched for a bit. But the father and son's strained relationship was hitting a little too close to home. Foregoing the TV, he put in a CD of piano elegies, and as Rachmaninoff's Élégie in E-flat minor began playing, he stretched out on the sofa and closed his eyes.

46

He managed to catch a few hours of sleep on the couch before a knock on his door roused him. Nelia had stopped by to see how he was doing. After the almost-kiss last night, he wasn't sure it was a good idea to invite her in when he was alone. But going out in his rumpled state wasn't an option, so he had her wait on the couch while he threw on some clean clothes and set a new record for shaving.

They hopped into his car and headed for the same Northside Social coffee bar where he and Sarg took Lauralee after rescuing her from jail. His discomfort increased when he noted how subdued Nelia seemed. "Something wrong?"

As they climbed back into the car, coffee in hand, he knew by her stalling tactic he wasn't going to like what she had to say. "Tim and I had an argument. I thought he'd be happy I was pursuing my law school dream."

"He's not?"

She gulped down some of the coffee. "It takes me away from him more. I guess I can understand his side."

"Is that the only reason?"

Nelia stopped smoking years ago. But as she saw a smoker outside who was puffing away, she licked her lips. She'd once told him smoking had been more of a nervous habit, and right now her nerves seemed as raw as steak tartare. "He accused me of doing this whole law thing as an excuse to come to D.C. more often."

She didn't have to voice the rest of it—as an excuse to come to D.C. to see Drayco. Then, she had dropped by this morning, hadn't she? If that had been a surprise, her next comment was a complete shock. "I talked with Benny about divorce proceedings. I know I've always said how important my vows were to me, especially the whole 'in sickness and in health' part."

"Is Tim getting worse?"

"No, he's stable." She'd finished her coffee in record time and was giving his coffee a wistful look, so he handed it over. She took a sip and wrinkled her nose. "I forgot you put salt in it." She took another sip. "It's not so bad when you get used to it."

"Are you serious? About the divorce?"

She sighed. "Maybe. Maybe not. Just an informal conversation with Benny. Nothing official."

Not knowing what to say, he changed the subject. "Feel like playing delivery girl?"

She managed a small smile which he took as a yes. He'd already made a mental map of the route he needed to take to an area he'd never visited before, near Holmes stream in Annandale. It was close to one of the many parklands throughout metro D.C. that made flying over it look like an aerial view of a rainforest.

The house they found was worlds away from the wall-to-wall brick colonials in northern Virginia. It looked like it dated from around 1950, with lots of wood and glass and hints of Frank Lloyd Wright's Usonian architecture.

Drayco rang the bell. Gogo Cheng answered, dressed in a purple embroidered silk tunic that was a far cry from his customary martial arts uniform. He frowned when he saw Drayco. "Mr. Drayco. I was expecting someone else."

"Sorry if I caught you at a bad time. When I called your studio, they said you came in late on Tuesday mornings."

"It's my parents. I asked them to come over—time to face the music. I've decided to tell them the truth about the painting."

"Perhaps this will help." Drayco gestured behind him, and Nelia joined him in the doorway, holding the re-wrapped painting. She handed it to Gogo, who looked from one to the other in shock, then motioned for them to follow him as he headed inside. Gogo carefully peeled off the paper and stared at it, a smile slowly spreading across his face. "Where did you find this?"

"I tracked it down with a little help from Nelia here." That, and a lot of help from a shadowy uncle.

"This will make it easier to tell my parents I've asked Ashley to marry me."

As if on cue, Ashley Zamorra walked in from the back. She'd ditched her usual jeans in favor of an emerald green dress and earrings that set off the chestnut highlights in her updo. It made her look like a Hollywood starlet of the same era as the house.

Gogo thrust out the painting to her, and she beamed at him—obviously, he'd decided to tell her about it, after all. Taking it from him, she gingerly hung it on the empty hook on the wall. Then Gogo wrapped his arm around her waist as the two stood admiring the painting.

Ashley turned around to address Drayco, her expression turning more serious. "I went to the jail to talk with Uncle Edwin. He's sorry for what he's done. Turns out, he made some bad investments also on tips from Dad but was too embarrassed to tell anyone. My father was a regular Bernie Madoff."

She slumped on the arm of a chair nearby, with Gogo's arm still around her. "I've been thinking about my father more since Uncle Edwin's arrest. I'm still angry with him. But I'm even angrier I won't have the chance to hear *him* say he's sorry."

Her wide, brown eyes looked off into the distance. "If I've learned one thing working at the women's shelter, it's that how we're treated as kids makes a big difference in how we deal with the world. Time to stop avoiding my grandparents and talk to them. Maybe they can help me understand my father."

Drayco studied her wrinkled brow and clenched jaw, knowing the path to that understanding was going to be bumpy. "You told me you only saw your father once recently, when you took items to his condo. Was that the only time?"

She wiped a hand across her forehead. "What? Oh, you must mean that time I ran into him outside an ice cream shop in Clarendon. We exchanged some words. Not very kind ones, I'm afraid."

Drayco heard a car's engine shutting off in front of the house and nodded to Nelia so the two of them could make their exit. As they left, an elderly Chinese couple stopped and bowed to them.

Nelia slid into Drayco's car. "You didn't treat Ashley and Gogo like they were still murder suspects."

"We can talk about that on the way."

"On the way?"

"This is going to sound like a cheesy joke, but I'm taking you to meet my mother. Of course, when most people say that, they're not referring to jail."

"Will Benny be there?"

"All four-foot-nine of him."

Whether his mother wanted to see him or not, Drayco didn't really care. He'd lived most of his life without her approval, and he wasn't going to start now. Sarg's words echoed back to him, about Drayco feeling like he didn't need anyone. He cast a sideways glance at Nelia who shot him a wicked smile as she fiddled with the radio and found a radio station playing KISS.

47

To Drayco's surprise, Halabi agreed with Benny's request to allow both Drayco and Nelia to join the attorney in an interview room at the detention facility. No sitting across glass windows, this time. He'd half-expected Maura to refuse the meeting, but she hadn't.

Halabi himself ushered them in, then hovered close by outside. Drayco hoped the detective was as trustworthy as he seemed and wasn't "accidentally" listening in via a monitor. It would be tempting, considering this was the first time Maura said she was willing to offer up more details.

Benny introduced Nelia as his assistant, but when Nelia sat next to Drayco, Maura focused a microscope gaze on the deputy. Nelia stared back, the two assessing each other. With a slight nod, Maura turned her attention back to her son. "You are persistent. Definitely take after your grandfather. His eyes, his temperament."

"Is he still alive, this grandfather of mine?"

Shadows crossed Maura's face at the accusation in Drayco's voice. She shook her head. "He died ten years ago."

"Is he the one who taught you how to run cons like the lottery fraud you and Jerold Zamorra cooked up?"

She exhaled softly. "I worked as a psychic reader for a while. Mostly rich widows. Didn't see the harm in it. Just cold readings, telling them what they wanted to hear, making them feel better. It's a form of therapy—maybe it's fake, but so are placebos, and they work, too."

She looked at Drayco briefly, then back down at the table. "One day, I did a reading for Imogen Layford, and she told me about the lottery. I saw an envelope she'd addressed for that purpose with a mail drop in the District. I can't explain why, but I haunted the address for a few days and waited until I saw Jerold walking out with that envelope. I confronted him, but after we got to talking, we ended up partners."

She'd mentioned pieces of this story to Drayco briefly on his second visit, but from her glance over at Benny, then Nelia, he guessed she was mentioning it for their benefit. Still, a mail drop in the District? That could be traceable—a Canadian account would have been much safer. But then, this was from the same man who'd filed his passwords under "P" in his Rolodex.

He asked, "How did you run the scam?"

"We'd tell seniors they'd just won a huge lottery cash prize but needed to send in a money order to free it up from customs. Just a few thousand here and there. Not enough to draw suspicion or drain anyone's account. I didn't want to hurt anyone. As I said, I targeted only rich seniors."

"And Edwin?"

"Edwin? Oh, aye, the police asked me about that. He was defrauding his pharmacy customers, wasn't he? Funny thing, I don't think either Jerold or Edwin knew about each other's little projects. I certainly had no clue about Edwin."

"How did you get the names of your victims?"

She winced at the use of the word. "Jerold started with some of the women at the condo. The rest is easy enough. The internet is full of sucker lists. Once someone takes the bait for one scam, those thieves sell the names, addresses, and phone numbers. But as I said, I filtered out most names and picked the wealthy ones."

Drayco didn't dwell on the irony of both Zamorra brothers scamming the same woman and not even knowing it. "Why didn't you tell any of this to the police?"

"I had my reasons."

"Alistair Brisbane?"

She pulled her clenched hands on the table closer to her. "I needed to protect Alistair. But not just him. My family's been on the run in Europe for so long now, hiding from the law. I've vowed to protect them. So has Alistair."

"They're still on the run?"

"Not so much now, but a few are. And some of the marks have long memories and are still angry. Violently angry."

"Is that why you and Alistair left Europe all those years ago?"

"I wanted to make a clean break, start a new life. I tried, you know, as a music teacher in Fredericksburg. That's where I met your father. But my brother was, still is, very powerful and clever. And when necessary, he can be ruthless."

He waited for her to talk about Dugald Iverson, her dead ex-boyfriend from years ago. He hadn't told anyone but Sarg, swearing his former partner to secrecy unless and until it became absolutely necessary to bring up the cold case. But apparently, even now she wanted it to stay forgotten.

"You said you protect each other, you and Alistair."

"When Alistair followed me to the States, I was furious. But he was a reminder of who I was pretending to be versus who I really was. That's why I kept that piece of paper with the word 'Brisbane' with me. I don't want to forget who I am."

"People change. All the time."

"We're the sum of all we've been, don't they say? Every fraction of our life adds up to make the whole of us. The fraction of me that was the perfect telly housewife was too small. It didn't weigh enough inside my soul."

He was trying to understand. Trying to override the five-year-old voice in his head screaming "Mommy, don't leave me!"

Maura opened her clenched hands. "You asked me last time you were here why I married your father. Fact is, I was in love. Maybe I still am. Must have been madly in love for someone with my background, someone who had so much to lose, to marry an FBI agent. Temporary insanity, the kind only love can cause."

He glanced at Nelia out of the corner of his eye, but her head was down, focused on the pad of paper as she scribbled some notes.

"Let's get back to Jerold. You had this exclusive partnership, or so you thought. But you found out he had another partner, and in your words, double-crossed you. How did you discover this mystery partner in the first place?"

"I overheard Jerold's end of a phone conversation. Jerold had been canny, I'll grant you. But it's hard to fool an old conner like me."

"When was this in relation to the murder?"

"The day before. So, I decided to confront him. Look, I was furious with Jerold for betraying my trust. And yes I did stick a knife in him once when he was already dead. But in a way, I was stabbing myself. Jerold represented my life, my choices, my folly."

Her hazel eyes tried to pierce a hole in his soul. For some reason that knocked him off-kilter in a way he couldn't articulate. "When I first spoke with you, you said Jerold wanted you to come over to discuss that trip to Nevada. Have you thought more about what he meant, other than you've always wanted to go to Reno?"

She hesitated. "Jerold actually said something even odder after that. It seemed so out of character, I put it down to stress. Or he was half-way to being sloshed. He said it would just be us two 'twin guns' out on the town having a blast."

"Twin guns? Did Jerold have a gun that you recall?"

"Kept one in his condo. Hidden under the carpet and floorboards. I didn't like it. I hate guns."

Drayco thought back to the list of items from Jerold's apartment Benny had gotten from Halabi. There was no entry for a gun or ammo. Nor had Ashley or Edwin mentioned Jerold having one. Was it taken by the killer?

Maura could be lying, but there was no reason, since a gun wasn't used in the murder. Halabi had promised to provide Benny with a list of the items Ashley delivered to Jerold in a box on the day of his murder, but he hadn't followed through yet. Maybe there'd be a gun there.

"Did he know you and Alistair were twins? Could he have been referring to that?"

She frowned. "Absolutely not. I knew you'd think Alistair had something to do with this. Which is exactly why I didn't tell the police."

Benny had stayed silent, checking a timer on his watch occasionally to keep track of their time limit. But as he held up three fingers to Nelia and Drayco to show they only had three minutes left, Drayco asked,

"Knowing the knife was likely the murder weapon, why did you wash it before you used it on Jerold after he was dead?"

"I admit I wasn't playing genius at the time, but I didn't do that. Why would I? I just picked it up off the table."

"It was lying there on the table, not on the floor? All nice and clean?"

"Aye. I didn't think about it being clean. Or it possibly being what killed Jerold. It was handy, and I just picked it up."

Halabi opened the door promptly on the thirty-minute mark, and the trio left Maura to be escorted back to her cell. Halabi handed a list to Benny, which Drayco peeked at over his shoulder. It was the list of Jerold's belongings Ashley took to him the day of his murder. Ask and ye shall receive.

Halabi then looked at each of the three in turn, but directed his pointed comment to Drayco. "We still have no proof to tie anyone other than Maura McCune to Jerold Zamorra's murder, his brother notwithstanding."

"Maybe tomorrow, detective. Maybe tomorrow. Oh, and you might want to search Jerold's condo again for a hidden compartment under some floorboards beneath the carpet. I'm guessing the bedroom. Where a gun might have been stashed."

"For your information, we found that compartment already. It was empty. But what's this about a gun?" Halabi scowled, but Drayco just waved and followed Benny and Nelia out the door.

Outside, Drayco asked the attorney if he could take Nelia back to his townhome to pick up her car.

"Hot date?" Benny was never the model of tact.

"I have an appointment."

Benny handed Drayco the list Halabi had given him. "Well I hope it's not with the murderer, because you've done that Lone Ranger thing of yours too many times. You'll give me a heart attack some day."

The look Nelia gave him was what she herself had once dubbed "worriosity," but he waved them both off with an "I'll be fine." Sitting in his car, he gave a quick glance over the list from Halabi and made a comparison with his mental note of items in Jerold's condo. No gun.

The two lists seemed to gibe, except for one oddly missing item. But it was that one item that sealed the deal in his mind. After all, an addiction was an addiction, no matter how unusual.

48

Wax museums. Ugh. He'd rather go to an art gallery and see paintings of famous people than these monstrosities that looked like Halloween candy for giant ogres, like the wax lips of his youth. He'd promised the docent he was meeting he'd buy a ticket to D.C.'s Madame Tussauds and schedule a private tour at the front desk. The docent, none other than Lauralee Fremont, greeted him in her uniform, and they started walking through the exhibits.

"If it hadn't been for a friend of mine who got me this job after I got fired from my last one, not sure what I would have done. McDonald's, maybe. If they'd take someone with shoplifting on their record."

"What about the quartet gig?"

"A pittance. Split four ways. I also fill in with local symphonies. I've got a concert tonight after I get off work here."

They stopped at the wax likeness of J. Edgar Hoover. She didn't seem to notice the irony and grabbed the ever-present little tube of coconut lip balm from her pocket. Her hair was in a very familiar style, a chignon, that he'd seen on another female recently.

Women's fashions were a bit of a mystery, but he really should try to learn the fine art thereof. If he were more of an expert, he'd have noticed sooner that Lauralee copied the look, down to the same designers, as Rena Quentin. And the same jewelry, like a certain stolen pink-gold watch.

He asked, "Did you find out Rena Quentin was your mother before or after you went to work at that adoption agency?"

Her jaw dropped. "How the hell did you find that out?"

"More importantly, how did you manage to worm her identity out of the agency? They don't usually give out that info."

"I might have bribed someone there, okay? But I'm not going to tell you who. Don't want them to get into trouble."

"Why do you keep Rena being your mother a secret?"

She folded her arms across her chest. "As I said, my adoptive parents are very strict, very religious. They'd be angry with me for tracking Rena down."

"But you're an adult now. What you do with your time is your own business."

"A near-penniless adult. One whose parents still give her money."

But Rena wasn't penniless. Polo, tennis, all paid for by the money from her ex-husband. A ready-made bank for Lauralee. "Have you contacted Rena? Does she know who you are and where you are?"

Lauralee scrunched her eyes tightly for a brief moment. "I was afraid. Afraid she abandoned me because I was not just a bastard but a half-breed bastard."

"But you did follow Rena. You dress like her. You must feel connected to her on some level."

"I guess."

When he raised an eyebrow and just stared at her, she added, "Fine, so I got a little obsessed. But I pulled back once I found out about her father, my grandfather, and him killing my grandmother."

"That it's genetic, you mean?"

"I learned he's out of jail. And now I'm afraid he'll find out about me and maybe target me, too."

Out of jail? Drayco mentally kicked himself for not checking out that line of inquiry. Just went to show how much his timing, his thought processes were off. He forced his thoughts back to Lauralee and Rena. "When did you really find out about Rena's sexual harassment claims against Jerold?"

"He mentioned it once, and only once, when the four us went out and had some beers after a concert."

"The police could point to that and say you killed Jerold Zamorra on your mother's behalf. Maybe as a strange way of showing her how much you would do for her."

"They would be wrong. I am not a killer." Her raised voice and creased face made one of Lauralee's fellow docents glare at Drayco.

"You'd met with Jerold several times recently. Outside of rehearsals or concerts. Was that about the instruments he gave you for safekeeping?" Brisbane's photos had indicated at least three such meetings.

"There was that, yes. I also do some painting on the side. Mostly watercolors. Jerold told me I'm pretty good. We were discussing setting up a gallery exhibit somewhere, and he was even going to help finance it. He seemed interested. That is, until ..."

"Until he found out you were in love with Ashley?"

She froze in place, her eyes wide and unblinking. "God, are you psychic?"

"Does Ashley know about your feelings?"

"Would it matter if she did?" Lauralee's voice dwindled to a whisper. "She's marrying Gogo."

Drayco gave her a moment to collect herself. "How do your parents feel about gambling, Lauralee?"

"You kidding? That's right up there with murder."

"And you?"

"I'm too poor to gamble. I mean, it's easy to make money if you have money, right? What's a few thousand to rich people."

"What if I told you both Jerold Zamorra and his brother Edwin were involved with criminal gambling and fraud?"

"What?" She blinked at him as the meaning of his words slowly dawned on her. "Oh God, I'm in so much trouble. A poor girl who must be in cahoots with thieves and murdered one of them out of revenge."

"I didn't say that."

"That's probably what you're thinking. The police, too. I'll never be able to afford a lawyer. And I can't tell my parents. What the hell am I going to do?"

"Nothing."

She looked at him with her mouth agape. "What?"

He said, "Finish your shift, go to your concert, and make music to the best of your ability. Let me deal with the rest."

She shook her head, doubtful.

"What are you playing tonight?"

"Haydn's Miracle Symphony."

"There, you see? It's ordained."

As they parted ways, a slow smile spread across her face. It was the first time he'd seen an actual smile from Lauralee. It made her look a lot like Rena Quentin.

49

Drayco stopped by Union Station long enough to pick up Sarg, who'd hopped the train into town from Quantico. "We could have taken your car," Drayco said.

"Nah, I think the train and I have developed something of a relationship. When my beastie was in the shop last fall, and I started 'train-ing,' I found I liked it. Beats the hell out of I-95 parking lots. And at afternoon rush, I guarantee you it'd be a parking lot."

Sarg stretched out his legs. "When you called earlier and told me about Maura saying Jerold had a gun, I dug around. He bought a gun in Fairfax. Went through the national background check system a couple years ago."

Drayco pointed the car toward the Beltway and eventually into Forestville, Maryland. "At least, Maura wasn't lying about one thing. But the gun disappeared from Jerold's condo at some point. And if the killer took it, why not use it on Jerold instead of a knife? Just because it's quieter?"

"Maybe the killer didn't know how to use a gun. Or has a gun-o-phobia."

"Hoplophobia."

"There's a name for it?"

"There's a name for every phobia, near as I can tell. Even phobophobia."

"What's that?"

"A fear of phobias." Drayco envied Sarg stretching his legs. One day he was going to have to get a bigger car. "Were you able to get copies of the police records I wanted?"

Sarg tapped the black briefcase he'd brought with him. "In here. Haven't had time to look at them yet."

"I'm not surprised. I know how busy you are. I *am* surprised Onweller is supportive."

"You kidding? The dear director owes both of us big time. Especially after he pulled that warrant arrest stunt last fall, *and* you showed him up for being an ass and protecting a killer, even if innocently. Still think he's expecting you to come back to the Bureau."

Drayco shook his head. "That career ship has long since sailed."

"Sure would be nice to have you back."

Drayco gave Sarg a quick glance. "Thought you were considering leaving, yourself?"

"Haven't ruled it out. Guess I like this," Sarg pointed at the road, "much, much better. Action that doesn't involve using a pencil sharpener."

"Oh, I don't know. Wood splinters can be pretty dangerous."

Sarg punched him in the arm. "Anyway, junior, tell me more about this Rocky Quentin fellow, Rena's father. Ex-cop, right?"

"He just got out on parole after forty-five years."

"That's a long time. Don't see how he could have ties to Jerold's case."

"When Rena told me her father had killed her mother, I didn't think much about it since it was years ago. But then Ashley mentioned he was out of jail. I did a little research about him and his case and discovered he was paroled a year ago. A day before Ophelia Zamorra was murdered outside the bank."

"Do tell. The M.O.'s the same?"

"In one important way. Rena's mother, Lilian, was pushed down a flight of stairs, and Ophelia was hit on the head with a baseball bat. But they both had cards crammed down their throats. It was a credit card in Lilian's case and the debit card with Ophelia."

"But why would he kill Ophelia?"

"That's what we're going to find out."

Using the GPS, Drayco wove his car in and out of Prince Georges County through a labyrinth of neighborhood streets. They finally pulled up to a single story home the size of a cargo container, with mildewed siding that was once white. The fence around the yard was more a suggestion, with several links missing. A forlorn-looking plastic reindeer sat in one corner, and a netless basketball hoop perched on a leaning pole threatening to fall into the street.

Sarg mumbled under his breath, "This is the kind of place even a foot of snow can't gussy up."

They picked their way around several empty trash cans and rang the doorbell. A man with a white beard and three thin strands of comb-over white hair greeted them with "What do you want?"

Sarg flashed his FBI badge. "Just a few questions, sir."

Rocky Quentin's eyes widened, and he looked like he was ready to slam the door in their faces. But after a moment of paralysis, he opened the door and let them in. "Look, I'm clean. I hardly ever go out, just ask the neighbors."

"This goes back a lot further than that, sir. It's about your wife, Lilian."

Quentin eased himself onto a sofa with purple stains that looked like Rorschach tests. He shook his head. "That was decades ago. And I did my time."

"We're aware of that, sir."

"Then why the hell are you here now?"

Drayco sat across from the man to get a better look at the man's face. "Can you tell us a little more about what happened that day?"

"I killed her, that's what happened." He rubbed his eyes. "Being an undercover cop takes a toll, you know? Went too deep, got swallowed up by the alcohol and the drugs. I loved her though. Loved my wife. We had our arguments, but show me a couple that doesn't."

"Rocky, the police report states you put a credit card down her throat. Why?"

"My wife always had big tastes. Wanted to be a socialite with the big house and the fancy clothes and the parties with your pinkie out and all. She maxed out all out credit cards. It was a big blur at the time, and it's an even bigger blur now. But I guess that's why I did it. Drunk people aren't smart people."

"Have you seen your daughter Rena since you were released?"

"Haven't seen my daughter since I went to jail. Can't blame her, I suppose. Don't know where she is. Or whether she changed her name or got married. Or if I have grandkids. Don't even know where she works."

"Until recently, she worked for the Transportation Safety Administration."

"Really? Guess she followed in my footsteps."

Sarg had stayed standing this time and towered over the frail, older man. "Can you tell us where you were on the night of January fifteenth of last year?"

"What? Don't know why that matters, but you can ask my probation officer. He can probably tell you if I was taking a dump or whatever since he's practically my owner."

"You weren't anywhere near Falls Church, Virginia?"

"Would have been kinda hard, me with no money and no car and all."

"And you've never heard the name of Ophelia Zamorra?"

He slowly sounded out the name. "Oh feel ee ya zam ora. Can't say I have."

"The day after you got out of jail, a woman by that name was murdered in Falls Church and a credit card was placed down her throat."

Quentin sank back into the sofa, almost disappearing into it. "You're not going to pin that on me. I was nowhere near there. And why in hell would I want to go right back into the slammer when I just got out?"

"Well, sir, there have been many parolees who didn't know how to live on the outside and found ways to go right back in."

Quentin's laugh sounded like an out-of-tune clarinet. "Yeah, I knew a few. But not me." He waved his hand around the house. "This ain't no palace, but after four concrete walls, it sure looks it to me. And I can eat whatever and whenever I want. There's no way I'd ever go back."

Drayco noted the man's shaking hands, the way his head kept turning, and his eyes blinking. Parkinson's. Drayco nodded at Sarg, "I think that's all the questions we have for you, Rocky. We appreciate your time."

They let themselves out and headed to the car. With Drayco driving, Sarg made some calls and got the name of Rocky's probation officer, who rang off long enough to check his files before calling Sarg back. Sarg replied, "Uh huh. Right. Thanks for the info."

He hung up and turned to Drayco. "Rocky was not just under his probation officer's thumb at the time of Ophelia's murder. He was in a meeting with the officer, give or take a few minutes. Would have been impossible for him to drive to the murder site in time."

Drayco sighed. "Kind of what I figured. But we had to check it out, just in case."

"Kind of what you figured?"

Drayco glanced at the dashboard clock. "You up for a little visit to Jerold Zamorra's old neighborhood? There's someone I think we should meet."

"Sure, why not? Love making new friends."

50

Drayco's cellphone chimed out a Prokofiev ringtone, and the screen showed it was Benny Baskin's number. Drayco almost didn't answer at first. "Yeah, Benny, what you got?"

"Just giving you a chance to make some party plans tonight. Floozies, booze, whatever. We got a dismissal."

"Of Maura's murder charges?"

"Of your case in front of the board, dumbass. Or have you completely forgotten about that? Your record and reputation are back to Def Con 5. You can relax. Well, there's the teensy bit about being on probation for six months. But as Carlotta Peggs told me in confidence, it was the only way to get Saul Bobeck on board. And Mayor Kozell will likely be ex-Mayor Kozell by then."

"Oh, well, that's good news, Benny. Thanks."

"Your enthusiasm underwhelms. Thought you'd be thrilled. You want me to go back and tell 'em you're really a serial killer?"

"Just a little distracted. Can you be ready to spring Maura if I find the real killer?"

"Since she hasn't been charged with anything else like corpse desecration nor fraud, easy peasy."

"I'll get back to you, Benny."

Drayco hung up and turned to Sarg, still seated in the passenger's seat of Drayco's car as they parked under a streetlight near Jerold's old condo. "Looks like I don't have to worry about working sans license."

Sarg grunted. "Oh, I don't know, it was fun thinking of you going rogue."

"Maybe that would be more fitting. I've spent my career fighting crime and turns out I come from a long line of criminals. Think that evens the score on some cosmic balance sheet?"

"At least your family is more interesting than my lineage of car salesmen."

Drayco glanced at the list of items in Jerold's condo that Halabi passed along, then said, "I'm still worried about that missing gun."

"Still not seeing why that's important."

"Maura said Jerold sounded very tense over the phone when he called her. I think it's possible he already had a visitor, someone who knew him, knew Jerold had a gun and where it was. Then the visitor pulled it on Jerold to force him to call Maura to come over."

"And thus frame her for the murder."

"Jerold told Maura something cryptic about the two of them being 'twin guns' heading off for a trip to Nevada. The Nevada reference could be about gambling. Add in the 'twin guns' part, and it might have been him using a coded message to let her know what was going on."

Drayco flipped the papers over to a different page. "The PD's interviews with neighbors show one man thought he saw a car that night but didn't have a description since it was dark and raining. They blew him off because they didn't think it was related. Might be a long shot."

"My favorite kind of shot. After Tequila shots. Where do we find him?"

They found the neighbor-witness, Vito Armas, at an apartment in the more rundown building across the street from Jerold's. When he answered the door, he seemed reluctant to let them in for a chat. The belt Armas wore was fighting a losing battle to keep his pants up, and his shirt looked like a skeleton's idea of what a human would wear at a costume party.

Drayco pointed to a mobile taco truck a block down the street. "Hungry?"

The man hesitated, then followed Drayco and Sarg, and they ordered burritos with habañero salsa. When Drayco asked the female server if they had any pineapple he could add to his, she wrinkled her nose and mimicked sticking a finger down her throat, making both Armas and Sarg laugh.

Armas wolfed his burrito down in only three bites and licked his fingers. Drayco looked at his foil-wrapped meal and handed it over. Armas didn't hesitate this time. He grabbed the offering and peeled away the foil slowly as if it contained a rare treasure.

His Spanglish was better than Drayco's Spanglish, so Drayco asked him in English, "We know the police talked to you about the night Jerold Zamorra was murdered. But we're not the police. We're just trying to make sure an innocent woman doesn't hang instead of the real sinner."

Armas washed down the last of his burrito with a Mexican coke and nodded.

"You said you thought you saw a strange car that night but don't remember anything about it." At least, Armas told the police he didn't recall anything. More likely, didn't want to recall anything, better to stay out of trouble.

Armas nodded.

Drayco continued, "But maybe there's something you didn't think was important. Or some little detail that may have stood out to you."

Armas looked at the ground, and Drayco thought he was going to refuse to talk to them. But their witness was apparently deep in thought, concentrating on what he'd seen that night. He raised his head and looked at Drayco, then Sarg. "It was *oscuro*—dark. From night and rain. It was light."

Sarg blinked his eyes. "It was dark and light at the same time?"

"No, no, sky dark, rain light."

Sarg smiled. "I see. The car was dark, too, right?"

"Si. *Gris.*"

"I can understand a gray car would blend in with rain at night, Mr. Armas. Where were you at the time you saw this car?"

"In my truck." He nodded at the condo parking lot across the street. "I pulled out. The road was one lane only. This car, it blocked my way. I honked."

"Did it move then, Mr. Armas?"

Armas shook his head. "No. It waved me on."

"The car waved you on?" Sarg looked at Drayco out of the corner of his eye.

"The hand did. The window rolls down half the way, a hand waves me around."

"Was there anything unusual about this hand?"

Armas shook his head again. "I see it was a woman."

Drayco tried to hide his excitement. "How could you tell it was a woman, in the dark?"

"The headlights. The hand was in my headlights. Wearing a shiny watch. Oro and rosa. No man's watch."

Drayco slipped a twenty into Armas's hand, and Drayco and Sarg headed back to their car. Sarg waited until Drayco slid into the driver's seat and all windows and doors were closed until he asked, "Why all the excitement over the watch?"

"You remember when we first talked with Rena Quentin? She was wearing a pink-gold watch." Drayco filled him in on his talk with Lauralee.

"Ah. Well that fills in a few more holes."

"And in the surveillance photos Brisbane sent me, there was a recent one of Rena. If she and Jerold had parted on such awkward terms, why the meeting in person, alone?"

"Didn't she say she went to one of Jerold's concerts recently? Maybe she was just remorseful as she said."

"She would have been one among a crowd there. Meeting him alone that's another matter." Drayco added, "Oddly, the caramels were the kicker."

Sarg raised an eyebrow. "I'm lost."

"By her own admission, Rena is addicted to caramels. You may recall that in Jerold's condo, he had a display of miniature weapons and security gear we thought was a TSA in-joke."

"If not a joke, then what?"

"That little perfect replica of a Nikon camera? It was so unusual, I looked it up. They were prizes found inside Clibo candy. Rena told me at Jerold's funeral she used to irritate him by bringing in Clibo candy she'd fallen in love with on a visit to Japan. If there were such hard feelings between them, thanks to the sexual harassment claims, why did he keep that camera in his condo?"

Sarg nodded. "Makes sense."

"It gets better. In the box of effects Ashley delivered to Jerold the day he was murdered, there was a big box of caramels. Yet, in the list the police made of items in his condo after his death, it was missing. A normal thief would hardly take just candy."

Sarg reached over into the back seat and hauled his briefcase over. He pulled out a folder with a stack of papers. "Here's more reading material for you. Those police files. Wasn't sure why you needed them, but the subjects make a lot more sense now."

Drayco scanned the documents. "I suspected this after making calls to the coroners I told you about. But since the cases happened in different states and were considered accidents, they weren't entered in any violent-crime databases. Certainly not the Bureau's VICAP. And the police never had Rena as a suspect, so they didn't think to track this down. Plus, the first case, Rena's grandmother, happened forty years ago."

Sarg peered over his left shoulder, read what Drayco underlined with his finger, then said, "Sweet Jesus."

"I doubt it's a coincidence."

"Hell no. After Rena's grandmother fell down the stairs, the coroner found a credit card stuck in her throat."

"The theory was she had it in her hand since her purse was found near the body. When she tripped down the stairs, the card somehow got wedged there."

Sarg gave him a skeptical look, and Drayco said, "Yeah, I know. But she was old, she had no enemies, no money, and there were no signs of assault, sexual or otherwise."

Sarg pointed to another report. "And that one says Rena's elderly ex-husband fell down some stairs—his wallet also conveniently located beside his body—and a credit card was found stuck in his throat. But it was after she'd divorced him, wasn't it?"

"That was her pattern, a way to avoid suspicion. It was three years after she left her grandmother's home that the grandmother was killed. Two years after she divorced her husband that he was killed—"

"And only one year after Ophelia and Jerold divorced. Why kill Ophelia though?"

"My guess is she thought Ophelia knew about her scheme with Jerold and was going to turn them in. Rena learned to adapt her methods to suit the occasion."

"This doesn't *prove* Rena killed Jerold."

"The wagons are circling. I'd thought her father might be involved as a partner, but our little trip to see him ruled that out."

"I see most of it. But why the card-in-the-throat thing?"

"Her mother's body was found like that."

"But her father told us he killed her in a drunken rage and doesn't remember doing it. Or exactly why."

"According to that police report in your hand, it was five-year-old Rena who found her mother dead with her mouth open and the card stuck there. It couldn't help but make a huge impression. When she turned to her own homicidal ways, she must have copied what her father did. As to why she killed her grandmother, she told me the woman beat her."

"Hates men too, I take it."

"Or just likes controlling them. Barney Schleissman at the assisted-living home said Rena always likes to be in control. And Jerold liked domineering women. First Ophelia, then Rena."

"The whole sexual harassment thing was just a ruse on Rena's part?"

"Probably had consensual sex, but she turned it around to blackmail Jerold into going along with her plan. Plus, he was in debt, the TSA job didn't pay well, and she probably told him he could make millions. Which he did."

Drayco thrust the paperwork back into its folder. "Sad fact is, she didn't need any of that lottery money after the pot of gold she got in her divorce. Must have been for the thrill of it all."

Sarg tugged on his ear. "Why frame Maura?"

"When she thought Maura was threatening her little scheme, she wanted to make both Maura and Jerold pay for it. It's probably why she stabbed Jerold in the groin."

"She's one clever, sick bitch, you know that?"

Drayco recalled Halabi's account, that even though Ophelia's head was bashed in with a baseball bat, she was still conscious when the ATM card was forced down her throat. Bleeding, in pain, possibly aware enough to be frightened, then the card slowly suffocating her. Poor, innocent Ophelia. Just like her Shakespearean namesake, collateral damage.

He said, "Benny Baskin would say there's wiggle room for reasonable doubt. Though it might make that reference of Jerold's, about going on a trip to Nevada, make more sense."

"You mean he knew Maura wanted to go to Reno, and *Reno* was his way of saying *Rena* was there holding a gun on him? Could be." Sarg grabbed the folder and threw it into the briefcase.

"It's funny, but Rena was every bit as much a con woman as Maura. Maybe more. Pretending to be normal, respectable, even working for the TSA, all the while she was a cold, calculating psychopath."

Sarg said, "We should call Halabi."

Drayco whipped out his phone and dialed Halabi's number.

The detective answered right away. "You must be psychic. I was going to call Agent Sargosian. That key you found in Jerold Zamorra's condo. We finally traced it to a storage facility. Thought he might like to join us."

Drayco told Sarg the address Halabi passed along, and Sarg started whistling the *Peter Gunn* theme as they drove away, down the same road where Armas had seen Rena the night Jerold was murdered.

51

Halabi looked like he wasn't going to let Drayco join in the fun. But then he relented, confirming what Sarg had found out three days ago. "Might as well let you go in with Sargosian, Drayco. The forensic guys say blood they found on the brick outside the back entrance to Jerold's condo was relatively fresh. And definitely his."

He didn't have to say it aloud. If Maura was caught standing over the body with the knife, then someone else—likely the real killer—transferred the blood to the brick as they left. Halabi motioned for Drayco and Sarg to enter the storage unit. It was barely large enough for the three of them and a table and chair, but at least, it was climate controlled with electricity.

Halabi glared at the laptop computer on top of the table, ignoring two of his men who were carting off boxes. "Took longer to trace Jerold's key than I'd hoped because he used an assumed name when he rented this place."

Sarg peeked over the open lid of the computer. "Powered it up yet?"

"We've taken photos, prints, searched the desk—hell, the whole unit, from the corner spider webs down to the snickerdoodle crumbs on the floor. We'll take the laptop back to the office and check it there."

Drayco filled him in on what Vito Armas had told them as well as the info he and Sarg had tracked down. Halabi put his hands on his hips. "Intriguing, I'll grant you. At least as far as Ophelia's murder is concerned. Still doesn't prove Rena was involved with Jerold or that she killed him."

"Prosecutors have built successful cases on far less." Drayco reached into his pocket where he'd stashed a pair of gloves he'd swiped from a box on one of the police cars. He slipped them on and headed to an open box where something had caught his eye.

"Will this help?" He pulled out a voice changer device, the type that plugs into cellphones. He tossed it at Halabi, then maneuvered around the detective and powered up the laptop.

Halabi reached out to stop him, but Drayco batted his hand away. The detective's face flushed a deep red, but he nonetheless moved behind Drayco to watch what he was doing. A password dialog box appeared on the screen, and Drayco typed in LOTTERY. That didn't work, so next he tried CARAMEL. Just as Halabi opened his mouth to protest, Drayco typed CLIBO, and the desktop popped into view.

Aside from the password, Jerold hadn't been particularly careful. It took all of thirty seconds for Drayco to find a spreadsheet with details of Jerold's lottery fraud takings, as well as the address of the D.C. mail drop. It took another thirty seconds for him to find a letter Jerold had typed mentioning Rena's involvement in the scheme, and in case of his death, the police should talk to her first.

Halabi finished reading that bit and scratched his cheek. "He didn't trust her. Or had an inkling of her anger toward him. At any rate, this is enough to haul her in for questioning."

Drayco turned off the laptop and folded down the lid. Halabi promptly gestured to one of his men, who strode in and spirited the computer away. The detective barked at another of his men to button down the place and ushered Drayco and Sarg outside.

Halabi focused on Drayco. "Doesn't mean your mother isn't guilty of something. But, if you add it to the report about the shallow wound on Jerold's body the M.E. now says came after he was dead, well. Gives more of a ring to your mother's crazy story."

Sarg added, "And Zamorra didn't mention Drayco's mother in that letter of his."

"Yeah, there is that." Halabi walked to his car, which turned out to be the one with the box of gloves.

Sarg waited until Halabi was out of earshot. "I take it neither you nor Benny Baskin told him what your mother told you. That she was Jerold's partner?"

"Technically, it's hearsay. If there's no proof of her involvement, they won't be able to convict her. She can admit to it all she wants, but saying you did something isn't the same as proving it. Besides, I have a feeling a certain uncle of mine has already taken care of it."

Sarg looked up at the sky and squinted. "Judging by the angle of the moon, I'd say it's about seven o'clock."

Drayco grinned. "Nice try, but I saw you glance at your watch when I was talking to Halabi."

"Spoilsport."

Drayco watched as Halabi's car sped away. "When this is all over, why don't we drive up to Annapolis for some blue crab."

"If that's your way of saying you owe me, you don't. But Crab Caprese sounds good. Lots of vitamin C. Don't want you getting scurvy."

Realizing he still had the plastic gloves on, Drayco pulled them off and stuffed them into his pockets. He turned back to the storage unit and gave it a hard stare as the last two police officers yanked the door shut.

Sarg said, "Uh oh. You've got that one-plus-two-equals-Q look. You don't think Rena's guilty?"

"Oh, she's guilty all right. There's just something ... I don't know. Put it down to lack of sleep. My brain's turning to mush."

"Let's hope Halabi can charge Rena soon. Then you can sleep for a week." Sarg put a hand on Drayco's shoulder. "What about your mother?"

"Benny's working on it. We should know something tomorrow."

"I don't know if I can get away or not."

"You don't have to."

Sarg gave Drayco a little shove in the direction of the car. "I'd kinda like to meet Maura McCune. Don't have too many friends with mothers who are con artists."

52

Drayco doubted he'd slept more than three hours. Again. Mornings were becoming Drayco's least favorite time of day. Sarg looked better rested, at least.

This time, the comfy chair was front and center in Benny Baskin's office, and Sarg made a beeline for it. Naturally. That left the chair that always made Drayco's butt go numb. Drayco pointed at Sarg's chair. "Benny, where is that thing most of the time?"

"Out for upholstering or something. I'm not a musical-chairs coordinator."

At Drayco's raised eyebrow, he replied, "What?" Then he opened a chiller in the wall unit behind his desk and grabbed a bottle. "Celebratory Scotch," he said.

"Celebratory, sir?" Sarg looked at Drayco.

"After hearing of your new evidence proving Maura was not Jerold Zamorra's killer, I've arranged to get her out on bail. Should be a free woman by this afternoon if all goes well. Tomorrow at the latest."

"We haven't entirely proven Maura wasn't involved, and the PD will need time to make a case against Rena."

"Close enough."

Drayco stared at Benny as he poured glasses of Scotch. "Who's paying the bail?"

"Money was wired into my account for that very purpose. Any guesses on who that might be from?"

Brisbane's little wiretaps were doing their job. Drayco rubbed his eyes and frowned.

Benny frowned back at him. "You don't look as overjoyed about this as I'd expected. I'm going to stop giving you good news."

"Just uneasy, I suppose."

"Don't tell me you think she's not innocent, after all?"

"Innocent of Jerold's murder."

"Well, that other stuff is minor by comparison. As for lottery fraud, we'll handle all that later, as I mentioned yesterday. If it ever happens since there's no evidence."

"That's what worries me. Well, one of the things. This is too neat."

Benny put his hands on his hips. "If you're waiting for the other shoe to drop, I see the two you have on seem nice and tight."

The door opened behind them, and Nelia Tyler popped in. She spied the bottle of Scotch and glasses and poured herself some, then lifted it in Drayco's direction. "Congratulations. Although you don't look too happy, considering the outcome."

Sarg piped up, "Oh, you know junior here. Likes all his dotted-I's and crossed-T's."

Nelia said, "If you mean Rena, it's just a matter of time before she turns up."

Drayco nodded at the Scotch. "Kinda early for that, isn't it?"

She smiled. "I'm taking mass transit."

Benny added, "My wife is picking me up later today," and downed his shot in one gulp. He looked from Drayco to Sarg. "Which of you two drove?"

When Sarg pointed at Drayco, Benny poured Sarg a glass of Scotch and handed it over. "So, Mister Special Agent, how long you think it'll be before Detective Halabi and his minions track down Rena Quentin?"

"Soon, plus or minus. Wouldn't it be a kick if her name is added to the TSA's Do Not Fly list? I still say she's one sick bitch."

Benny poured himself another. "Her attorney will plead insanity. Guaranteed."

Nelia turned to Drayco. "Have you had a chance to talk with your mother about all of this?"

"No, but if Benny works his magic, maybe later today."

"That's good, right?"

Drayco forced a smile. "You three are going to owe me some Scotch later." He didn't miss the look his other three companions exchanged between them. He was happy about all of this, right? His mother was essentially cleared and so was the young Leon Mecko, for that matter. Why did he feel like grabbing that bottle and downing it all at once?

✑ ✑ ✑

The shadows of the morning had long turned to twilight, but Rena was still missing, meaning the police didn't have their suspect in custody. But even so, and despite the fact it took most of the day to accomplish, Benny managed to work his magic and secure Maura's release.

Drayco's mother stood stiffly as the police clerk handed over a small box of TicTacs, ten five-dollar bills, two keys and a paperback-sized beaded purse. She stuffed the items in the purse, then opened it wider and ran her finger along the interior.

Drayco said, "Detective Halabi kept the fake driver's license."

Benny, who was standing on the other side of Maura, chimed in, "You're off the hook for the murder charge, thanks to Drayco."

Maura didn't look at her son but nodded.

After a moment of awkward silence, Benny said, "I knew all along Drayco would get to the bottom of this. He's kept my bacon out of the frying pan more than once. Yep, you should never bet against boy-o, here."

Drayco almost spoke up to remind Benny that when Drayco first approached him, Benny hadn't exactly been encouraging. Even calling Drayco's objectivity into question.

Benny sailed blithely on, "Where ya goin' for your first post-release celebration?"

Maura looked in Drayco's direction. "I think I'd like to go back to my apartment. But I don't have a car."

"I'll drive you." Drayco touched her arm lightly and indicated the hallway to their right. He mouthed "Call you later" to Benny and led the way outside.

They walked in silence under the faint canopy of stars beginning to shine through the gathering darkness until they reached the car. Maura stared at the man leaning against it. "Who are you?"

"Agent Mark Sargosian, at your service, ma'am." He opened the front passenger door to Drayco's car.

"Sargosian? Aren't you Scotty's former partner?"

Sarg and Drayco exchanged a quick look. Drayco hadn't told her about Sarg or why Drayco had left the FBI. She, or maybe Brisbane, had definitely been keeping tabs on his career.

"Yes, ma'am, I am none other."

"But I thought—" She bit her lip, hesitated, then slid into the car. No mention of the former partners' estrangement, but it was clear she knew.

After Sarg closed the door and he and Drayco piled in, Drayco drove down Wilson Boulevard in the direction of his target. When they parked beside Northside Social, Maura frowned.

Drayco said, "Thought you might like some non-prison coffee. And they make a terrific chocolate hazelnut tart."

Drayco and Maura found a table while Sarg stood in line to place the order. Maura looked out the window, and Drayco was beginning to think it was a mistake to bring her here, to try and break the ice a bit.

Without the stress of prison forcing slips of her Scottish accent, she was back to her more measured, American patterns. She said quietly, "I've been there many times, you know, to Casey's grave. Always bring her some yellow calla lilies. Her favorite."

She turned to look him squarely in the eye. "I'm not proud of everything I've done in my life. And I know I'm not the mother you wanted, the mother you deserve. But I won't badmouth my family. It's just who they are and who I am."

"I wouldn't ask you to."

She sighed. "You get addicted to the trickster life. To see what you can get away with. For some people, it's drugs or sex or alcohol, for my family, it's cons. I couldn't tell anyone about them, you can see that, can't you? They'd be tracked down."

Then she reached across the table. "Promise you won't do that, won't say anything to anyone. Forget about them. Leave them be. They're slowly dying off, anyway. And they never killed anyone. You believe that, don't you?"

He reached up to touch the scar on her neck, but she caught his hand and gently rubbed it in hers. He said, "Dugald Iverson was self-defense. And much deserved, it appears. You didn't have to run."

Her eyes widened to mini full moons. "How did you—" Then she shook her head. "My brilliant son. Of course, you'd find out. I was young, scared. Didn't know what else to do. Thought I'd escaped my past here with your father. But a former mate of Dugald's tracked me down and confronted me. Threatened to kidnap you and Casey unless I gave him a lot of money. That's how I knew my past would never stay that way."

Her eyes, bright with unshed tears, pleaded with him so intensely, it shook him to the core how important this was to her—for him to believe, to know, that she wasn't evil. She said, "I have lived my life in so much darkness. Hiding, ducking, running. But all the time, I had you as a light in the darkness, *my* light in the darkness. Through your music, you create peace and beauty. And through your work, you find justice for victims. My real legacy, my only good, true gift to the world is you, Scotty. I will always, always love you and be with you."

Sarg rejoined them, expertly balancing coffees and pastries he served, with a bow. "No tips, please. Although I will accept kudos in lieu thereof." He plopped in his seat, reached for the sugar, but just then seemed to notice Maura's hand clasped in Drayco's. "I'm not interrupting anything, am I?"

She smiled at Sarg and released Drayco's hand. "No, and thank you, Agent Sargosian. For everything."

All of Maura's words took on double meanings. It was as if she was cramming a lifetime of stored-up thoughts into a brief supernova of emotions, as one would who was saying goodbye.

She grabbed her spoon, reached for the salt shaker and poured some into her coffee, as Drayco and Sarg both watched in amazement. She looked amused at their expressions. "What, you've never tried salt in your coffee? You really should. It takes all the bitterness out."

Sarg hid a cough behind his napkin, and Drayco picked up the salt shaker and followed her lead. "You're right. It's quite good."

She tried a bit of the tart, wit.,m h a pleased "Umm," and washed it down with some coffee. "You think Rena Quentin was behind Jerold's murder, but why frame me? Was she that jealous?"

"Rena likes being in control, manipulating actors in her dramas like a Hollywood director. You were horning in on her action. That wasn't in the script."

"I suppose that's true, Scotty, but I didn't even know her. I certainly didn't know she was Jerold's partner." She fingered her coffee cup, then shook her head. "Jerold wouldn't have turned her in, because doing so would out him, too. Seems like she would have killed me, the interloper, instead."

Maura changed the subject to ask about Sarg's wife and kids, and Sarg regaled her with stories from his days with Drayco at the Bureau. When they dropped her off at her apartment an hour later, she hesitated as if wanting to talk some more. But she waved them off with a smile.

When Benny arranged bail, he knew as well as Drayco that Maura was a flight risk, if her past was any guide. Even now, as Drayco and Sarg drove away, Maura stood at her front door looking after them as her smile faded. And Drayco wasn't entirely convinced he would ever see her again.

53

On the way back to Drayco's townhome where Sarg had parked his own car, Drayco pulled into the parking lot of Edwin's pharmacy on a whim. A light rain forced him to use the windshield wipers, but it was easy to see the *Closed* sign on the pharmacy entrance.

"She loves you, you know." Sarg glanced at Drayco. "In her own way."

A parade of missed birthdays, parent-less holidays, and his sister's funeral passed through Drayco's mind. Along the sidelines of that parade were other mothers he'd come across through the years—mothers who'd abused their children, tortured, even killed them. Birth, family, death, the three things you can never escape.

"I've always blamed Brock for pushing her away. But it was never him, not really."

"Like Maura said, she was an interloper. Of sorts."

Drayco drummed his fingers on the steering wheel. "That's why Rena framed Maura, in part. A handy scapegoat. Killing Jerold without that scapegoat might have focused attention on Rena. This way, she could appear all innocent and blameless."

"And since Maura didn't know anything about Rena, she couldn't rat her out."

"But how?"

"What do you mean how?"

"How could Rena be sure Maura didn't know about her? She'd only have Jerold's word unless she was bugging both of them like Alistair did me, which I highly doubt."

"Maybe she extracted that tidbit of info from Jerold when she had him at gunpoint? You know, swear to me blah-blah-blah, or I'll kill you."

The light rain picked up tempo, making larger blobby patterns on the windshield. Patterns. It was always patterns with Rena. Always getting rid of whoever was in her way, even if the reasons were based on little more than a belief. Ophelia *might* have uncovered the lottery scheme. Jerold *might* have cut her off when he partnered with Rena—anything or anyone that bore the tiniest whiff of disturbing her carefully orchestrated masterpiece of deception.

Sarg said, "They'll catch Rena soon. Halabi and his crew are good. And the BOLO should help."

Drayco didn't answer, lost in thought, until Sarg poked him in the ribs. "I said they'll get her, if that's what's eating you."

"Maybe she never left. Maybe she's still in the area."

"Why would she do that? She's probably got tons of money socked away in offshore accounts. And all that TSA experience should make it easier for her to flee the country."

"Eventually, yes. But if there's one thing I've picked up about Rena, she likes everything neat and tidy in an OCD way. She loathes loose ends. And she found out about Maura, probably followed her, knew where she lived."

Sarg sat up straighter. "And now that Maura's out of jail—"

"*Seems like she would have killed me, the interloper, instead.* Those were Maura's exact words, weren't they?"

Sarg took a sharp breath. "You think we should—"

In answer, Drayco threw the car into reverse and peeled out of the parking lot to head back to his mother's apartment.

As they pulled onto the street that led to Maura's place, another car passed them in the other direction going at least twenty miles over the speed limit. Drayco caught a brief glimpse of the driver. From the profile, he was pretty sure it was Rena Quentin.

Drayco tossed his cellphone at Sarg. "Call Halabi. Tell him to send someone to check on Maura's apartment. We'll stick with Rena." It took every ounce of willpower Drayco had not to rush into his mother's apartment right then and there. But they couldn't risk losing their target.

As he turned the wheel and forced the car into a sliding U-turn, he called out, "Hold tight," and tried to keep Rena's car in sight.

Sarg whipped out his cellphone, punched Halabi's speed dial, and barked their location and direction. Halabi must have passed his phone over to someone else because Drayco doubted Halabi would be content to sit by and play stenographer while Sarg kept shouting out the landmarks and streets as they flew by.

Rena's car merged onto I-66, with Drayco and Sarg following at a prudent distance behind, heading in the direction of the District. After they crossed over the Roosevelt Bridge and took the Independence Street exit south of the Tidal Basin toward Ohio Drive, Drayco had a pretty good idea where Rena was heading. But why? He doubted it was for another lesson with her tennis instructor.

In fact, they passed the tennis center as well as East Potomac Golf Course, where Jerold used to play, and curved around Ohio towards Hains Point. Drayco's attention was focused on his quarry, but at the same time, he noted the headlights of a car following theirs. Halabi's men, hopefully.

By now, it was almost completely dark, and Rena's dark car was so hard to see that Drayco almost passed the spot where Rena had parked on the side of the road. He pulled in behind her and hopped out while Sarg took a moment to grab his gun from his shoulder holster.

They were close to the edge of the Potomac, with only a short three-railed fence separating the edge of Potomac Park from the river. Rena struggled with a long, dark object she hoisted over her shoulder.

Drayco started toward her as a voice from behind him shouted, "Rena, no!" It wasn't Sarg's voice. Drayco half-turned to see that the driver of their chase car was none other than Iago Pryce.

Drayco also saw the horrified look on the man's face and turned back just in time to watch as Rena shoved the dark object over the railing and into the water. It was a body bag. Drayco and Iago reached the railing at the same time, ignoring Rena who ran in the opposite direction with Sarg following in pursuit.

As the cold rain continued to fall, Iago looked over the railing and wailed, "I can't swim."

Drayco kicked off his shoes and jacket, took a deep breath and dove into the cold, inky water. He had to get to the bag before hypothermia kicked in and he couldn't feel his arms and legs anymore. It was near impossible to see anything. He fumbled in his pants pocket for his mini-flashlight, praying he didn't drop it.

It was difficult to swim with the flashlight in his hand, but he did the best he could as he conducted a frantic search. Ordinarily, he could hold his breath for five minutes, but the adrenaline and the cold combined to make him feel the increasing pressure on his aching lungs.

His only hope was that there were enough air pockets inside the body bag to help it float gradually down instead of plummeting to the bottom. Parts of the Potomac were close to seventy feet in this area, and he didn't have enough oxygen in reserve for that.

Just as his lungs were telling him he had to surface soon, he glimpsed the edge of an object a few feet to one side. As he grabbed out at it, the smooth, slick texture told him what he needed to know— and then his flashlight fell out of his hand.

Grabbing the bag in the now-pitch-black water, he heaved his body upward with all his might toward the surface. He held on to the bag for dear life with his arms circled around it, kicking his legs hard and fast. Just as he thought his lungs were going to burst, he broke through the surface and took deep, gulping gasps of air.

Where was Sarg? Where was Iago? No signs of either man.

Now that he could breathe again, he positioned his body and the bag as close to the bank as he could and hoisted the bag up over the concrete edge. With one last adrenaline-fueled burst, he pushed the bag onto the grass and dragged himself out of the water.

His fingers trembled as he found the bag's zipper and ripped it open. His mother's face appeared, her eyes closed as if she were sleeping. He bent down with his ear to her mouth and felt for a pulse in her neck. Was it there, a faint blip, or was it his imagination?

He raised up to shout for Sarg to call an ambulance, when he felt two giant hands clasp around his neck squeezing hard. He struggled to breathe as if he were the one drowning. And then Maura's face grew dim as a cold, black veil settled over him and darkness met darkness.

∾ ∾ ∾

When he opened his eyes again, he was flat on his back with Sarg and Detective Halabi bending over him. Sarg's blurry face snapped into focus as he said, "You okay, junior?"

Drayco forced himself into a seated position with a little help from the other two men. At least, the rain had stopped and made it easier for him to look around. "Where's Maura?"

Sarg said, "You got me. When I came back from my hundred-yard dash tryout, you were lying there alone."

Drayco looked around. "But she was there. I got her out of the body bag. I felt her pulse."

"Well, she's not here now. Nor is Iago, for that matter."

"No body bag?"

Halabi replied, "No bag, no body, just you when I got here. And Agent Sargosian dragged Rena in shortly after."

"You saw Rena throw the body bag into the water, didn't you, Sarg?"

"I thought I did, yeah. But as Detective Halabi here says, it was gone when I returned." Sarg held up an object with its trigger guard dangling on Sarg's pen. "We found this on the grass, though."

It was a gun. The one Rena possibly used to threaten Jerold? Had she put in the body bag and it fell out? It hardly mattered now.

Then, with a sudden recall of the hands around his neck, Drayco knew beyond a shadow of a doubt those hands belonged to Iago, Maura's devoted bodyguard. He must have spirited her away. But why did he attack Drayco? And was Maura dead or alive?

A woman laughed, and he whipped his head around. It was Rena, sitting on the ground under the watchful eye of a police sergeant. "You don't have a body. You can't charge me with anything. And I've never seen that gun before in my life. I don't even know how to use a gun."

She added, in a sing-song voice, "Besides, your mother died the day she left you behind."

Drayco stared into her eyes. "Have you never cared about anyone in your life?"

Rena snorted her disdain. "I cared about someone once. He left me when he found out I was pregnant. Caring clouds your judgment, Mr. Drayco."

Halabi and another detective hauled Rena up off the ground, her hands cuffed behind her. Someone grabbed a blanket and threw it over Drayco as he realized his teeth were chattering. The blanket-giver turned out to be Sarg, who stuffed Drayco into the car and turned on the heater full blast.

Sarg's expression wasn't pity, but concern. He started to say something, then stopped and looked over at Drayco, clearly not knowing what to do.

He turned on the satellite radio, tuned to its usual classical station. It was Bach, his mother's favorite. Sarg turned up the volume so they could hear it over the blast of the heater, as they listened to the Shepherd Cantata and its text, "Fly, vanish, flee, o worries."

54

Thursday, March 1

Drayco looked over at the trash can in his kitchen filled with empty bottles of Manhattan Special, an assortment of beer cans, and takeout boxes with congealed food clinging to the containers. They were piled upward into an overflowing trash pyramid like Giza monuments with the mortar cracked and the stones tumbling down the sides.

Rena had been formally charged with Jerold's murder. The police found a key to Jerold's storage unit in her possession, for starters. When they confronted her with the facts—they also found traces of Jerold's blood in the trunk of her car and her fingerprints on the gun that was tracked to Jerold—she seemed eager to talk.

Boasted, more like it. Down to the disposable raincoat, the gloves, and shoe covers she wore. And why she washed the knife clean, to make it look like Maura was destroying evidence when the police showed up. She didn't know Maura was going to pick up the knife, but even better.

Drayco glanced at the box of caramels Halabi had sent to Drayco's townhome. Peace offering or gentle jab, he wasn't quite sure.

He changed the channel on the TV remote but ended up back at C-Span, where it had stayed most of the week. Mind-numbingly boring and no local news, which he'd been trying to ignore. His neglected piano called to him in vain—after starting and stopping the same Chopin sonata ten times, he'd given up.

The phone rang, and he almost didn't answer, thinking it was another meeting with Halabi or the FBI or the TSA or the FTC. He'd talked so much about Maura, Rena, and the Zamorras over and over, he was ready to go MIA.

But it was someone quite unexpected. After hanging up and making a few additional calls, he hopped in his car, made a stop at Ashley's house to pick up his passenger, and drove to the detention facility. Lauralee wanted to meet her mother in person for the first time.

As they waited in the lobby, Drayco asked, "That watch you lifted from the store. Did you take it because you saw Rena wearing one just like it?"

Lauralee's smile was brief and bitter. "Yeah. When I saw her smoking, I took that up, too." She sighed. "All this time, I resented my adoptive parents. I always felt more like a missionary project than a daughter. But at least, they cared and didn't abandon me."

Drayco briefed Lauralee on Rena's traumatic childhood and her mother's murder. "When the police questioned Rena, she said her elderly grandmother told her girls are useless and only boys matter. She said she hated that old woman, and it's not women who don't matter, it's old people with dried-up souls and hearts turned to dust."

"Is that why she married that elderly guy? Just so she could divorce him and kill him later?"

"That's what she says. With the added benefit of his rather large estate."

"But why kill Jerold? I mean, Ashley told me about his gambling and that lottery swindle thing. I don't get the murder part."

"Because he was getting careless—the gambling debts, sending lottery letters to women in his own neighborhood. She confronted him with a gun and forced him to call Maura, who she framed for his death."

He noted the shadows gathering over Lauralee's face. "Are you sure you want to do this? You can still back out."

She straightened her drooping shoulders and smoothed out a wrinkle in her dress. "I want this. I have to do this."

He wasn't sure how much more he'd tell her. At least not right now. Certainly not that he'd found out Rena knew Lauralee was her daughter and never contacted her. Whether it was another symptom of Rena's callous nature or inability to love anyone, it was hard to say.

Drayco asked, "Looks like it could take several more minutes before they take us to see Rena. Need a smoking break?"

She shook her head. "I suppose I should try to quit. It doesn't seem nearly as glamorous as it once did."

He studied her posture—so straight you could raise a flag up her spine. He imagined a flag that read "Free Lauralee." But he liked the new glint of purpose he saw in her eyes, and as the deputy came to escort them, he had a feeling that no matter what happened with Rena, Lauralee would be just fine.

55

Friday, March 2

Nelia Tyler joined Drayco in looking out the window of the car at the Massaponax sandstone gate with its Gothic columns and pointed arch. Beyond, lay a flat expanse of late-winter grass dotted with markers serving as marble and stone flowers.

Nelia said, "We seem to do this too often."

He knew what she was referring to, the ending of the first case they'd worked together and a cemetery like this one. When Nelia called earlier in the day and learned where Drayco was headed, she offered to ride with him. He wasn't sure at first if he should accept, but having her solid, quiet support made him glad he'd said yes. He pushed aside the little nagging voice asking why he hadn't invited Darcie.

His cellphone rang again. This time, he rolled down the window and started to throw the phone out, but Nelia slipped it out of his palm. She checked the incoming number and frowned. "You've labeled this contact as UAB."

Drayco took the phone from her. He pictured the distinguished man with the Greek nose he'd seen from afar twice, as the voice spoke. "I know this is not the most opportune time to call, dear nephew."

"I'm surprised you aren't here."

"Who says I'm not?"

Drayco turned his head sharply, looking all around them. There were a few cars parked several yards away, but they appeared to be empty. "Been trying to get you for two days, Brisbane. All of a sudden, you stopped taking my calls."

"I'm not sure how I could help you."

"You could tell me whether my mother is alive or dead, for starters. And where she and Iago are."

"I'm afraid I don't have that information for you."

"You don't know, or you won't say?"

"I mean that I don't have that information for you."

Drayco rubbed his eyes. "How am I supposed to live with that?"

There was a long pause on the other end. "Some day, Scott, you and I will sit down and have a chat. It's difficult to feel whole when the tapestry of your life is riddled with rips and tears. You deserve a complete picture."

"Why the call now?"

"I wanted you to know I'm setting up a music scholarship at your alma mater, the University of Maryland. It's in honor of you and your mother, but it will be in your name. Hers can't be attached to it, for obvious reasons."

"I'm touched, Brisbane, truly. But I have an even better idea. You reimburse Imogen Layford and all the other victims of Maura's lottery fraud."

After several moments of silence, the other man replied, "That can be arranged." Then he added, "Oh, and don't be surprised if UMD gives you a call to play a recital there as a thank you. I'll be watching."

He hung up and Nelia, who'd overheard part of the conversation, asked, "Watching you play or watching you in general?"

"Probably both. I doubt I've heard the last from Uncle Alistair, one way or the other."

Nelia chewed on her lip. "I've been thinking. Which brother would you say was harming the most people? Jerold scamming elderly women out of money or Edwin watering down their meds?"

"If you go by intent—money—they're even. If you go by results, that will be for the police, the government, and the courts to shake out."

"What about Iago? Won't Brisbane be afraid he gives away sensitive information about his operations?"

"Iago is even more loyal than Greyfriars Bobby, that terrier who spent fourteen years guarding the grave of his dead owner. Iago won't breathe a word about Brisbane."

"But why spirit Maura away, alive or dead?"

"He'd been her bodyguard for so long, it must have been hard to stop. That, and the fact he loved her."

It was Nelia's cellphone that rang next. She looked at the number and thrust the phone back in her pocket. "It's just Tim. He can wait. This is more important."

They watched the figure of a man striding toward the cemetery and through the gate. Nelia reached for Drayco's hand and gave it a squeeze. "I'll be here," she said.

Drayco walked to the man's side, and they both gazed down at the gleaming new tombstone sitting beside a much older marker. A new tombstone for an empty grave. Brock laid some pink roses he'd brought on both grave sites.

Drayco asked, "You know she might still be alive, don't you?"

"Not to me, she isn't. Besides, if and when she is no longer living, we may never know. I think it's important to have this marker here. Casey should be reunited with her mother at last."

"We lost her, found her, then lost her again."

Brock squinted up at the sun. "She was never ours to lose." He looked over at Drayco briefly. "I'm actually sorry I didn't try to see Maura. When she was in jail."

"I thought you hated her."

"Maybe I was still angry. But how could I hate her when she gave me you?"

Drayco pulled two necklaces out of his pocket, the ones with the half-hearts that said *Miz* and *Pah*. Brock looked at them in shock. "Where did you get those?"

"I saved one you threw in the trash years ago. The other I found among Maura's things in her apartment."

"I bought them for us when we got married. I can't believe she kept hers."

Drayco held them up in the air. "You know, Sarg calls me junior and Benny calls me boy-o, but you call me Scott."

"Of course. You're my son."

A strong breeze made the two necklaces dangling in Drayco's hand jingle. He handed them to Brock, who slipped them into his pocket.

Drayco took the lilies tucked under his arm and placed some on the new tombstone, but stopped in front of his sister's grave. "You brought Casey pink roses, right?"

Brock nodded. Drayco laid the remaining lilies on Casey's grave—next to a bouquet of yellow callas already there. Who'd put those there if it wasn't him or his father? Out of the corner of his eye, Drayco caught sight of a dark limousine as the window rolled up and the limo drove slowly away.

He watched it until it disappeared down the road, surprised that he didn't feel an urge to run after it, then turned to his father. "You play any one-on-one hoops lately, Dad?"

The corners of Brock's lips turned up in a rare smile. "Don't think for a minute I'll go easy on you. A foul's a foul, and I call them as I see them."

Brock draped his arm around Drayco's shoulders as they walked away from the graves. This time, there was no little paper message scrawled in a child's hand, no heartfelt cry of loss and abandonment. And maybe if and when he played that concert in Maryland, his father would be front and center, watching.

Printed in Great Britain
by Amazon